STRANGE ATTRACTORS

STRANGE ATTRACTORS

POLESTARS 1

Jaine Fenn

NewCon Press
England

First edition, published in the UK August 2023
by NewCon Press
41 Wheatsheaf Road, Alconbury Weston, Cambs, PE28 4LF, UK

NCP308 (hardback)
NCP309 (softback)

10 9 8 7 6 5 4 3 2 1

ISBN: 978-1-914953-57-6 (hardback)
978-1-914953-58-3 (softback)

Cover Art by Enrique Meseguer; cover design by Ian Whates
Editing and typesetting by Ian Whates

Contents

Path to the Sun	7
Crown of May	23
The Chatterslee Circle	27
Paying for Rain	45
What You Came For	63
Death on Elsewhere Street	69
Fear Not Heaven's Fire	81
High Ground	93
King of Pain	105
Twilight at the Change House	123
Down at the Lake	143
The Sky Weeps	149
Liberty Bird	171
A Dormitory Haunting	189
Sin of Omission	211

The Path to the Sun

Of course it was a hoax. It had to be.

No doubt both the original telegram and the brightly coloured *thing* floating in the cove below were some rustic eccentric's idea of a joke. Dawson was sure he had only been sent on this wild goose chase as revenge for the affair with Alice.

He steadied his bowler hat on his head and leaned forward to speak to the young man who had picked him up from the station. Perhaps the boy could lead him down the cliff to get a closer look at the wretched contraption.

'Sir?'

Dawson turned to meet the intense gaze of a heavily built man with light brown skin, high cheekbones and jet-black hair. He forced his face into a welcoming smile and jumped from the cart. Mud spattered up his trouser leg.

'Mr... Ar... Ahuitzotl, I presume?' Dawson resisted the urge to extend a hand in case the chap took the gesture as some sort of insult. He looked like a U.A.S citizen all right, just as the telegram had claimed. Maybe there was something to this after all. 'I am James Dawson, administrative assistant to Commodore Gordon Cameron, head of the Transportation Research Division in His Majesty's Ministry of War.'

'You are Cameron's secretary?' The visitor sounded faintly incredulous, but that might just have been his accent. 'The Commodore did not come himself, then.'

'Commodore Cameron is an extremely busy man. Your telegram was somewhat, ahem, vague, and he had no way of checking your credentials without risking diplomatic complications. If you had come directly to London, he may well have met you in person.' *And I would not have to stand on this windy cliff-top being insulted by you.*

'If I had come to London I would already be dead, Mr Dawson.' The Aztecan spoke calmly, as though his life were not overly important to him, and Dawson found himself looking along the rugged coastline to avoid the visitor's eyes. 'However, in the same situation, I also would be cautious. But you are the first representative of the British Government I have encountered since my arrival, so it is to you that I must state my plea.'

He paused, then held his hands out in front of him, palms up. He tilted his head towards the sky, closed his eyes, and started to speak, 'I am Ahuitzotl, child of Acamapichtli of the city of Tetzcoco. My Caste is Pochteca, my Clan is Itzconatzin. I have knowledge of the ways of those who were once my enemies, and I have an artifact of those who were once my people. I ask you, James Dawson of London, as a representative of your King, Edward, to grant me sanctuary in this land from now until I die. I offer my fealty and my knowledge, and all material goods which I have brought with me. I renounce citizenship of the Empire of the Sun, which you call the United Aztecan States, in favour of any claims you wish to make on me. On your word, I am reborn.'

In the ensuing silence Dawson was acutely aware of water seeping into his shoe, of the heat of the sun, and of how ill-equipped he was to deal with this situation. Damn Cameron for taking Dawson's interest in his niece as a personal insult! But he was stuck with this mission, so he had better try and placate the foreigner. 'Er, yes. Well, this is rather outside my jurisdiction, I'm afraid. You really need to speak to someone from the Foreign Office.' The Aztecan seemed not to have heard him. He tried speaking up a bit, 'Terribly sorry I can't help you, old chap, but there it is.'

The Aztecan opened his eyes and shrugged. 'I thought you would say something like that.' His tone was casual. 'No matter. You have heard my request, even if you cannot grant it.' He looked past Dawson at the boy on the cart, 'Thomas, please secure the cart and accompany us down to the cove. Shall we go, Mr Dawson?'

'Go where, precisely?'

'To see if I have something worth trading for British citizenship.' The Aztecan smiled, and Dawson noticed laughter lines around the man's eyes. He had assumed Ahuitzotl was younger than him, but it seemed he might be slightly older. 'Please take care. The path is a little slippery in places.'

Dawson followed the Aztecan down the cliff, noting with mild distaste that though the foreigner had adopted European clothes, his hair hung over his collar. 'I must say, er, Ahuitzotl, I really am quite impressed by your grasp of English. I thought your people rarely learnt other languages.' Actually, Whitehall gossip claimed that the U.A.S. ambassador, Nethual… whatsisname, understood English perfectly well, but still used a translator when he spoke to his hosts. Then again, he also turned up at official functions wearing patterned blankets, animal skins and feathers, regardless of the weather or the potential offence to any ladies present.

'Mr Dawson, I speak English well because I am Pochteca.' Ahuitzotl slowed at a switchback in the path. 'I am, or rather was, a merchant. You work for the War Ministry so you understand what that means, I assume.'

'Ah.' Dawson stopped, grabbing a stunted tree for support. 'Of course. I see. A… merchant.' A spy, rather. It was people like this, as much as their fearsome soldiers, which had allowed the U.A.S. to conquer half a continent.

Ahuitzotl looked up at Dawson across the gorse, 'I learnt English, and Spanish, in Sierra, where I lived under a false identity between the ages of twenty-four and twenty-nine. I have travelled extensively in Louisiana, New England and Canada. And it is as you think. In my old life I performed acts of espionage and terrorism. But that is *the past*. You must understand that. I have renounced everything: my home, my culture, my nation. I am not who I was.' He made a small cutting gesture with his hand and strode off down the path.

Dawson glanced back up the cliff, where sparse white clouds raced over the grassy lip, then released his grip on the tree and scrambled after the Aztecan.

Ahuitzotl waited at the base of the path, watching the waves flop and suck across the shingle. He spoke without turning. 'I am sorry, Mr Dawson. If I am to live amongst the English I must do a better job of adopting English ways. I am a little too forward in my speech. Please forgive me.'

'Of course.' Dawson wondered whether this apparent frankness marked the man as a deceiver of consummate skill, or whether he really was the startlingly honest outsider he appeared to be.

Ahuitzotl swept a hand out to indicate the strange device out in the cove. 'Mr Dawson, may I present to you, and your government, the *Cloud Serpent*, the only powered flying craft in the world at this time.' It had a cylindrical body bisected by a flat plank, which presumably formed the wings; some sort of a box on legs squatted over the point where the wings crossed the body. 'Now, if you will follow me, I will prove my claim.'

'I'm not entirely sure I understand your intentions here,' said Dawson, worried that he did.

'I would like you to fly with me to London.'

'Ah, wait a minute, sir. I really don't think I am the man for this. I am no engineer: I would have no way of assessing how well the machine functions.'

'Assessing its function is simple enough. Either it flies, or it does not. The fact that I am here implies that it does.'

'Yes, of course, but I really...' Dawson found himself taking a step backwards. 'Surely you could just take it out for a, well, a fly, while I wait here and watch.'

'I understand your unease, but even if you are convinced, you have already told me that you do not have the authority to grant me asylum without consulting your superiors. That will take time. I do not have time.'

'So you keep saying. What exactly is the problem?'

'If I turn up in London unannounced and unaccompanied the British authorities will assume this is a trick, as you yourself probably do, and turn me over to the U.A.S. embassy, who will torture and execute me for having betrayed the Empire. If I stay here, the Pochteca will soon find me. I know how effective Aztecan foreign agents are. I was one. But if you come with me to London you can intercede for me, if you will.'

'And if I chose not to?'

'Then I will ask Thomas to take you back to Penzance and I will fly to London alone, and face the consequences. But, Mr Dawson, surely this,' he gestured at the craft riding the swell of the bay, 'is one of the greatest adventures of the age. The chance to fly is not something many are offered. Are you not at least curious?'

'Er, well, of course…' Dawson ran his finger under his collar. Actually, he was terrified. But he could imagine Cameron's face if he turned tail and ran now. 'All right, dammit, I'll fly in your infernal machine.'

'Good. Very good.' Ahuitzotl turned and crunched off over the shingle to where Thomas stood by a rowing boat. Dawson glanced up at the seabirds wheeling effortlessly overhead. He had always taken birds for granted.

Dawson addressed the Aztecan's retreating back. 'Just make sure your chap sends my bag back to London. I've left it in his cart.'

By the time he reached the boat the boy had taken his place on the rower's bench and the Aztecan was seated in the prow. 'I'm sorry to presume, Mr Dawson, but would you be so kind as to push the boat off?'

After a brief hesitation, Dawson did as Ahuitzotl asked, even though it left him soaked to the knees. He could always make an expenses claim for a new pair of shoes when he returned to London.

Thomas started rowing with long confident strokes, his cheap jacket pulling taut across his shoulders as he tugged on the oars. On his far side, Ahuitzotl shifted slightly to keep eye contact with Dawson. 'I imagine you have a few questions, Mr Dawson. Please, ask what you will.'

Dawson thought of all the questions he could ask. There was little to be gained from entering any sort of verbal duel with the Aztecan, but neither did he want to miss the chance for information gathering. He needed something harmless to get the man talking. He looked past the foreigner at the brightly painted machine, then said, 'Well, I can't help wondering… why is your craft green? It's a little garish, don't you think?'

'Because green is the colour of beings who fly. What other colour would we paint a flying machine?' At that moment they rowed out of the shadow of the cliff, and Dawson, squinting at the Aztecan, thought he saw a quick smile.

So much for useful information. 'I must say that is precisely the sort of answer I would expect from one of your people! One might almost think you were mocking me, sir.'

'The Azteca are no longer my people. And I am not mocking you. Please allow me to explain. Green is the colour which signifies flight, escape. For the Children of the Sun, colour, place, and time are not matters of chance or whim: they are ciphers, symbols of what we cannot hope to otherwise comprehend. An expression of cosmic order, if you like. I was smiling because I know how strange such ideas must seem to you. If I was mocking anyone, it was myself, for being fool enough to think I could cross the gap between two cultures as easily as crossing an ocean. Yet here I am.' He spread his arms, as though encompassing the sky and the cliffs, then favoured Dawson with a direct stare. 'Do you know who Hernan Cortes was, Mr Dawson?'

'Cortes? Er, no, never heard of him.' The flying machine's growing presence beyond the Aztecan's shoulder was becoming distracting.

'No, I would not expect you to. He was a Spanish criminal who fled to the mainland from the Carib islands to avoid a death sentence. He was the first European to see Tenochitlan, the heart of the Empire. He came with men and horses and guns, and he tried to abuse an ancient prophecy to gain power. Emperor Cuitlahuac saw him for what he was: a lesson from the gods that the outside world would destroy us if it could. I suspect his late brother, Moctezuma, would not have been so wise. It would be heresy for me to say this in the Empire, but if the Azteca not acquired gunpowder and horses from Cortes the Empire would not have lasted four of your decades, let alone four centuries. Technology is power.'

'And what happened to this Cortes chap?' Dawson found his gaze drawn to the *Cloud Serpent*. It looked somewhat flimsy. Wires were strung between every surface, and the only substantial part was the box in the centre, a complicated affair of greasy metal with some sort of wooden bar fixed across the back of it.

'What do *you* think happened to him?'

Dawson tore his gaze away from the flying machine. 'I would prefer not to speculate.'

'All power, Mr Dawson, is in the heart. So Cuitlahuac ate his heart. We have a national holiday to celebrate the event.'

'Charming.' Dawson glanced at Thomas. His neutral expression was a credit to his class.

They were pulling alongside one of the wings; a pontoon on the wingtip dipped down to the water to keep the craft steady and stable. Ahuitzotl reached out and ran his fingertips absently along the edge of the wing. 'Cortes was a European, yet most Europeans have not heard of him. To the Azteca, he is, well, not a hero, but a celebrity. What I am saying is the differences between the two cultures are merely a matter of perspective. What is that quote? "History is written by the victors". We see the world as we are told to see it, because that is the path of least resistance. For the Azteca this occurs to a degree you would find hard to comprehend.' The boat came round to nestle, prow first, in the angle between the wings and the body of the craft. 'It amazes me now that it is quite possible to go almost one's entire life without questioning one's beliefs. I would wish to see you so amazed.'

Thomas had shipped the oars and the boat bobbed gently, not quite in time with the rhythm of the *Cloud Serpent*. Ahuitzotl half stood and grasped one of the legs that supported the box in the centre. 'I will get off first and sit down, then you can follow.'

'Get off onto what, precisely?' The body appeared to be an unbroken cylinder, save for three small fins at one end.

'Let me show you.' Ahuitzotl turned and started to climb onto – no into – the body of the thing, directly below the metallic box. Apparently one sat inside.

Dawson gently poked the material covering the body. It felt disturbingly springy. 'Er, Ahuitzotl, what exactly is this thing made of?'

'The engine, here,' he nodded to indicate the box above his head, 'is a light alloy. The screen at the front is reinforced glass, and the base and frame are wood. The covering, most of what you actually see, is waxed fabric. The trick is getting the right ratio of power to weight.' The Aztecan lowered himself into the body of the craft, setting the boat rocking as his weight was removed.

13

Dawson rather wished he hadn't asked. But there was no going back now. He raised himself from the seat, careful not to tip the balance of the boat. Thomas moved aside to let him step over the rower's bench, and said cheerfully, 'I'll see your bag gets sent back up to London Mr Dawson sir, don't you worry.'

Dawson muttered his thanks and eased himself into the craft. It was not that difficult: the *Cloud Serpent* sat so low in the water that its body rode beneath the rowing boat's prow. Once Dawson was inside Thomas started to move the boat away. As Dawson watched his last safe route to land disappear, the boy smiled and shouted back, 'Good luck, sirs.' Good Grief, was that envy in his eyes?

Ahuitzotl crouched in front of him, 'Please excuse the rather sparse accommodations. Proper seats were a luxury that had to be left out.'

'Actually I'm rather surprised you built it with room for a passenger at all, given what you just said about weight.'

'The space was originally intended for spare fuel and luggage. However the fact that it will accommodate two makes it more valuable from a military point of view. The space could be used to house an observer, or a gunner. And I did not build the *Cloud Serpent*. My son did.' Ahuitzotl knelt up and started fiddling with the engine. Dawson found himself staring at the man's midriff. 'I am afraid I am going to have to presume upon you again, Mr Dawson. I will prime the engine, but then we need to start the propeller. Given how cramped things are with two of us in here, it might be easier if you reach up and do it.'

The propeller? Of course! That was what the wooden thing was. Dawson turned, banging his knee on one of the internal supports, then reached up for the wooden bar across the back of the engine. He wished Alice could see him now: she often got irritated with the restraints and taboos of her upper class world and longed to do something real, something physical. Of course she had, and so had he; and that was why he was here now, performing contortions in a floating box with this mysterious foreigner. Perhaps his life needed a little more unpredictability, just as Alice had said when they spoke for the last time.

A sweet, pungent odour brought him back to the task in hand.

'Sorry about the smell, Mr Dawson. Cane alcohol; engine fuel. Azteca technology has rather taken to the internal combustion engine. Now, when I tell you, please pull the propeller round sharply in a clockwise direction. As soon as it catches you must get your hand out of the way and sit down. That's it. Now.'

Dawson tugged the propeller. After some initial resistance, it spun free. The engine above him coughed, then died. He caught the wooden paddle again.

'It rarely starts first time. We will have to try again in a moment.' Dawson realised that Ahuitzotl's apparent impoliteness in making him push the rowing boat out had been a test. If he balked at getting wet feet there was no way he would be able to deal with this undignified and smelly procedure. 'Now, if you please, Mr Dawson.'

Dawson pulled again, harder, and this time the cough became a roar. He snatched his hand back from the whirring blade and sat down abruptly. The sweet smell became sharper, and pale smoke vented from the sides of the engine. The noise was deafening.

Ahuitzotl was fitting a plank across the space between them for his backrest; he shouted to be heard over the engine, 'You might find it best to sit cross-legged, Mr Dawson.' Dawson adjusted his posture accordingly. He hadn't sat like this since he was a child but he found it surprisingly comfortable.

'Once we start moving things will get a bit breezy. You may wish to remove your hat.'

Dawson realised he was still wearing his bowler. He took it off and placed it on his lap. He shouted back, 'Will it be this loud all the way to London?' He was not sure how he would survive the journey if it was.

'No, it will be much quieter once we take off: the engine position means that most of the noise is swept backwards.'

'I'm glad to hear it. When we get to London, where will you – *we* land.'

'On the Thames somewhere near Greenwich: I would have preferred to come down outside the Houses of Parliament, but there are too many bridges that far up. Are you ready, Mr Dawson?'

No, thought Dawson, but nodded anyway.

Ahuitzotl faced forward again and pulled a lever beside him. The engine note changed and the vibration increased. Dawson grabbed the edge of the craft. He was pressed back against the wooden backrest, gently at first, then more firmly. As the *Cloud Serpent* gained speed Dawson's tailbone was bruised by the craft's tiny collisions with the water beneath them. Then the vibration stopped, and there was a faint lifting sensation in his gut. The noise fell away, as though they were leaving the world of harsh sounds behind.

He was flying.

They climbed quickly. Below them Dawson glimpsed a tiny figure – Thomas – pulling the boat ashore. The high cliffs were a wall which they paralleled and passed effortlessly. He felt, at a visceral level, the lethal distance between his frail body and the cold hard sea. Strangely, the operation of this primitive instinct did not scare him. It thrilled him, as though he were dreaming, and somehow indestructible.

Then they were over the headland, amongst the birds. The wind tugged at Dawson's hair as they dipped slightly and flew into the next bay. The sea sparkled like a mat of diamonds. Some of the birds from the headland followed them out over the sea, curious to see who was invading their world, but soon gave up the chase.

As they swept over the bay Ahuitzotl turned slightly, smiled, and raising his voice to be heard over the drone of the engine, said, 'Do you regret your decision, Mr Dawson? You could be safe on the ground now, heading for the station.'

Dawson found himself smiling back at the Aztecan. 'No, I don't regret it, sir. Not at all. To fly in a craft built by man, to challenge the birds: who would have thought it possible?'

Ahuitzotl laughed, though the wind snatched most of the sound away. 'Not your master, apparently.'

Dawson looked up. Overhead, the sun was pulling itself towards noon, burning off the last of the clouds. Though Dawson knew it must be a fancy, the sun seemed somehow closer. For a moment the fear was back: fly too close to the sun, and your wings will be burnt from you. When he had first heard the legend of Icarus at school he had thought the man must have been a fool. Who would want to risk themselves like that? Better to keep your feet on the ground than attempt to challenge the gods. But a man had built this machine and – dammit – it worked. And even if they did fall, he would not have missed this experience for the world.

To his left the coastline unfurled like a magic lantern show. On the cliffs, a flock of sheep turned and ran from them in perfect unison. What would it be like to fly over people? Would they scatter like sheep?

'I wonder, could we go inland for a while? It would save fuel and time if we cut across the foot of Cornwall.' And I will be the first Englishman to fly over my native soil like a god.

Ahuitzotl hesitated for a moment, then nodded and reached forward. 'Of course.' Dawson felt something shift below him, and the 'Serpent' started to turn in a gentle arc. Dawson began sliding to the right, and braced himself on the sides of the craft, careful not to press the fragile surface too hard. He looked around, trying to locate the piercing hum at the edge of his hearing. The sound was coming from the wires that held the wings in place. His heart-rate quickened for a moment, but he was not really afraid. He realised that he trusted the Aztecan.

As they crossed the coastline the view beneath them jumped into focus, becoming a beguiling patchwork of brown and green and grey. Stone-walled fields lapped at islands of rolling heathland and rocky outcrops. Dawson glimpsed movement and craned his neck back. Their shadow raced across the earth, their only link to the world below.

The land dropped away and they flew over a sheltered valley. On the valley floor a score of whitewashed cottages clustered along a small river. Women sat outside the cottages, spinning yarn and gossiping: their upturned faces were pale smudges. The *Cloud Serpent* was over the settlement in moments, but on the far side a gaggle of children spilled out of the buildings, racing up the side of the valley to keep pace with the apparition in the sky. The children pointed and whooped, though their shouts were muted by distance. Dawson turned in his seat: just before he lost sight of the children he saw one boy stop and wave. He raised his arm to wave back, but the figure was gone, lost in the dip of the land.

If only Alice could see this! If only she could share this with him, then the experience would be complete. Then he would be complete. He still loved her. Now that he had tasted wonder he could, finally, acknowledge that fact. He still loved her, despite the discrepancies of age and social class. But he would never see her again. 'It would have been a boy...' she had written in her final letter.

The wind was making his eyes stream. No, not the wind.

For a while he let tears blur the view. True, he might never get the chance to fly again and should treasure every moment of the journey; but he might never get the chance to cry like this, either.

When his eyes cleared he leaned forward and placed a hand gently on Ahuitzotl's shoulder. 'Thank you,' he said. 'You have created something wonderful.'

For a moment he thought the Aztecan had not heard him. Then Ahuitzotl turned slightly and said, 'When Cozmatzin, my only child, was born, and his horoscope was cast, the priests said this: "He will die young, to chance, but first he will challenge the skies, and his handiwork will change the fate of nations." Do you believe in the power of prophecy, Mr Dawson?'

Up here it was possible to believe anything. 'I don't know. Perhaps.'

'A far better answer than you would have given on the ground!' They were over high moorland now. Occasional farms and abandoned mine workings dotted the heather-bound landscape. 'I do, though there are many things which I once held as truth that I now reject. Prophecies made by Azteca priests do come true more than can be accounted for by mere chance. A month after he finished work on the *Cloud Serpent* Cozmatzin's name was drawn in the spring lottery. One week later he walked the path to the sun. He was twenty-six. Only children and youths die to usher in the spring. The next year his name would not have gone forward. My wife also went to the sun, willingly, ten years ago, as the Azteca always have in times of famine or crisis. I accepted her death. But Cozmatzin was not willing. He should not have had to die. He was so full of life, of potential. I can no longer serve gods who demand that we accept such losses.' Ahuitzotl turned back to his controls.

Dawson said nothing, because there was nothing to say. He was ashamed. In his arrogance, he had not thought to ask the most important question: why Ahuitzotl had risked his life, abandoned his country and his people, and thrown himself on the mercy of his enemies.

Ahead, sunlight glinted on water. They had almost crossed the foot of Cornwall. A cart was pulled up on one side of a muddy track which ran off towards the coast. As they approached, two men jumped from the cart. One pointed up at the flying machine. Dawson raised his hand to wave, then stopped. The other man was hurriedly pulling a tarpaulin off the back of the cart, exposing something Dawson recognised only too well from his years in the War Office.

'My God. Ahuitzotl, they've got –'

'I see it.' The craft banked sharply to the right. Dawson had a last glimpse of the man on the back of the cart bringing the gun to bear, then the whole craft shook as bullets tore into the thin fabric. A triad of holes appeared on the wing, just beyond Dawson's hand. The clatter of the gun was strangely distant; surely it was too far away to be causing the damage magically appearing around him.

Something snapped below him and the *Cloud Serpent* lurched violently. Dawson flailed for a handhold. Splinters pierced his fingertips, but he managed to get a grip on the internal struts.

Ahuitzotl had been thrown forward: he pushed himself back into his seat and grabbed for the controls. He was calling out something in a language Dawson did not recognise. It sounded like a curse, or maybe a prayer. The craft twitched and veered for a few seconds, then came round to fly straight again. Dawson could no longer hear gunfire. He started to settle back into a more comfortable position.

The engine cut out.

The *Cloud Serpent* stalled as though snagged by a giant hand. The front end dipped sharply and Dawson's fingers tore into fabric as he scrabbled for purchase. He piled into Ahuitzotl's backrest. The view ahead, once full of sky, was now terrifyingly full of earth. The only sound was the rush of the wind and the thrumming of the wires.

Ahuitzotl started pulling levers. The *Cloud Serpent* shuddered and jumped, and their descent slowed almost at once. They were no longer heading straight for the ground. But they were still losing height rapidly.

The sea seemed an impossible goal. They would not reach the water before they came down.

Dawson found himself less concerned about the probability of dying than the certainty that the flight would end. Such a short taste of freedom. And they had not even been struck down by the gods; it had been men, with their stupid politics, who had broken their wings. He shimmied back and pressed himself as far as he could into the body of the craft, pulling his legs to his chest and wrapping his arms around them. He closed his eyes. He would prefer not to see the moment of impact.

Yet despite the lack of power, the *Cloud Serpent* flew remarkably well. Their path began to even out into a shallow glide. Perhaps they could reach the relative safety of the water before they crashed. He might even live through this.

Dawson opened his eyes and raised his head. 'Ahuitzotl?'

The Aztecan did not reply; presumably he was still intent on the controls before him.

'I'm sorry. This is my fault: if I hadn't asked you to fly inland they wouldn't have seen us.'

Ahuitzotl shook his head, 'No apology needed.' His voice sounded strained above the eerie whistling of the wind. 'If the Pochteca had not stolen the gun from your government, they would not have shot us with it. Do not curse fate. Wonder at it.'

The open land below gave way to sand dunes. Dawson caught his breath: their grass covered tops seemed close enough to touch.

Then they were over water.

The sea rushed up to meet them.

At the last moment Ahuitzotl pulled the front of the craft up, and they belly-flopped into the waves. As it hit there was a loud crack, and the craft slewed violently to the left. Dawson was thrown upwards: his head hit something, but for some reason the pain was in his hand. Then he was flying again, no need of a machine to help him now.

Everything crashed down. He was under water, mouth and nose full of brine. He kicked out and his foot hit something solid. He kicked again. Sand. He realised he was still clasping his legs, and forced himself to uncurl and stand up. The water came up to his chest. His left hand hurt abominably, and he lifted it out of the water to examine it. The back of his hand was a bloody mess. He put it back in the water so he didn't have to look at it.

He looked around. To his left, perhaps thirty yards away, was a beach. Ahead, the *Cloud Serpent* rode the gentle swell. The pontoon had been torn from the shoreward wingtip and the craft was listing badly, but did not appear to be sinking.

He started to wade towards it, passing a tattered shape of black felt which might once have been a bowler hat. The only sound was the swoosh-sloosh of his own progress. Coming up from behind it was difficult to see inside the craft, and he called out Ahuitzotl's name. There was no answer.

Once he was past the wing he could see the Aztecan slumped across the broken screen. He called again and Ahuitzotl stirred and pulled himself upright. He shook his head, then, ignoring Dawson, reached forward.

Dawson came up to stand beside the craft. The *Cloud Serpent* had tipped towards him, and his head was level with the Aztecan's chest. Ahuitzotl pulled himself upright, then turned and offered a large map case of waxed leather over the edge of the craft.

'Take this.' There were dark stains on the leather.

'You're hurt, sir.' Dawson could smell the sickly fuel, and something else fainter, metallic.

'Yes. That does not matter. These matter, now. The plans, for the *Cloud Serpent*. For the others not yet built: all Cozmatzin's dreams. Please, take it.' Ahuitzotl closed his eyes as Dawson took the map case.

'Let me get help. A doctor –'

Ahuitzotl waved the suggestion away, then put his hand on the edge of the craft to steady himself. 'I am not important. What is important is history: "the fate of nations".'

'I'm sorry?'

Ahuitzotl opened his eyes and looked down at Dawson. His gaze was still intense, but it seemed to be dimming, as though the light were leaking out from behind his eyes. 'You have to hear this. The priests know. The Empire will fall. Europe is the new power. Your sun is rising. But first you must suffer... the worst war in history. Power over the air... will win that war. Win it quickly. Save more pointless deaths. That power is yours now. Use it well.'

'I... of course. Now let me help you –'

'No. I have played my part.' Ahuitzotl drew back his hand, leaving a red smear on the vivid green of the bodywork. 'All I ask is... a small favour... if you please.'

'Anything within my power.'

'I had matches. They... got damp. Do you have a light? Perhaps one of those, ah, excellent petroleum lighters which work when wet?'

'Yes, yes I do,' Dawson put the map case under his left arm and fumbled in his jacket for his lighter. 'Can I ask what you intend to do?'

'Damn myself to the lowest circle of hell... if the priests are right. The Pochteca must have seen us crash. If they get here and the plans are gone... they will hunt you down. Cane alcohol burns hot, fast. No traces –'

'Good god, you can't be serious.'

'You know I am. Give me the lighter. Then go.'

Dawson handed the lighter to the Aztecan, then took a step back. 'Sir. It has been an honour.'

'For me also,' Ahuitzotl's voice was a whisper. 'May you ever travel with the Earth below you and the Sun above, and never walk in shadow.'

Dawson turned and waded ashore. Standing dripping on the sand, he took a last look at the marvellous craft. Ahuitzotl stared back across the water at him for a moment, then raised his hands. Dawson was too far away to see the flame until he dropped it. Then, for a moment, the *Cloud Serpent* shone brighter than the sun.

This was my first professionally published short story, and it's one I'm still pretty proud of. It's also the first time I exercised my long-term obsession with the lost worlds of pre-Columbian America, in this case through an alt history where the Europeans arriving in central America got their arses kicked by the locals, giving the world a rather difference balance of power.

Crown of May

Am I really damned? Will the gods strike me down before dawn for my sin?

I think not: the sky is already beginning to grey and the birds have started their mindless twittering. Yet I am still very much alive.

The other villagers have been up for some while already, preparing for the ceremony. They are trying not to disturb us, but the occasional whisper or quiet footstep gives them away.

Megan and mother are still asleep beyond the curtain. I have not slept; I have been making my sister's crown.

Megan and I gathered the May branches last night. We walked upriver beyond the falls, to the old grove. Where the path was wide enough we went side by side; when it narrowed, Megan led, glancing back at me often. She was trying not to cry, for my sake. I wanted to cry, for hers, but no tears came.

At the grove we worked without speaking. I tried to lose myself in our task. I listened to the chatter of the water, the swish of the leaves, the rasp of the knife on the branches; and thought about nothing at all. But then Megan startled a blackbird and it exploded into the twilight, shrieking its alarm. Megan let go of her branch, and it whipped back, showering us both in blossom. She raised her face to the pure, brief rain of flowers, and smiled, though I saw her cheeks were wet. 'I don't want to remember the sorrow,' she whispered, still looking up, 'I want to take joy with me, when I go.' I said nothing, but went and put my arms round her and let her cry. After a while she started to talk of the past: memories of our childhood games, our favourite places, our friends, our shared secrets. I joined her in memory, but part of me felt unclean, dishonest. For the first time in my life I have a secret I cannot share with my sister.

And now I'm making her bridal crown. Weaving the May stems together by lamplight is hard work: the wood is tough, the thorns are sharp, and it is too easy to dislodge the petals. And I hate the smell. The stifling, sickly sweetness reminds me of rotting flesh.

Megan's dress hangs on a wooden frame by the lamp. It is lamb's wool, white as the May blossom. A beautiful thing, soft and clinging. How I would turn heads if I wore it. It gives me pleasure, to be adored like that, and I do not see that as a sin. Neither does Megan, though she would shrug and say that such things are merely a matter of appearance, and appearances do not matter. I disagree: appearance is all we have. Even if there are gods around us, as Prydion says, then we cannot see them, cannot know their will. We should believe our eyes, I say.

It is strange, but people assume that because we look alike we must be alike in all things, my sister and I.

Ah, teeth of hell! I've pricked my finger again. The blood looks like a big black bead. And now the bead breaks. The blood drips on the floor of the hut and – look! – it's gone. Thirsty, thirsty earth. More than happy to take our blood.

I asked Prydion how we will know if the ritual had worked. He said we must have faith. Prydion seems to have no trouble believing in things he cannot see. Perhaps that is true of all priests, perhaps that is what makes them what they are. Or maybe they are just good liars, so convincing that they believe their own lies. Whatever else, I suppose we'll have saved ourselves two mouths to feed.

If the blight comes again this year we'll all be dead by next spring. Maybe Megan is the lucky one. Her end will be quick. That would be a cruel joke: I damn my own sister, just to starve to death with the rest of the village.

Who's that? Ah, Owen's younger brother. Being shushed by his mother again. And Owen is a strange boy; he likes to stare at nothing, as though he can see wonder beyond the mud and famine and sorrow. When we were younger I used to tease him about never looking where he was going, and sometimes I would trip him up, and laugh when he fell. But perhaps being able to see beyond the world is a good thing for the Winter King. Yet he is so young, younger even than Megan and me. What if he cannot perform his duty? He is the only virgin lad in the village, just as we are the only virgin maids. The Summer Queen and Winter King must be pure, or what is meant to bring fertility will bring disaster.

Or so Prydion says.

I am nearly as tall as Prydion. He is the priest, the only voice the elders always heed, and I had thought he would always be taller than me. But he is getting old; his breath grumbles in his throat, and his hands shake when he is nervous.

I hate myself, but what is done cannot be undone.

There, the crown is finished. I have tried to trim off all the thorns, to make it as comfortable as possible. I must keep it safe until sunrise comes, when I will dress my sister and follow her out to meet her fate.

At least I will not have to witness the final blow. When Prydion has spoken the words of joining over Owen and Megan, and they go into the grove together, I shall return to the village. The others will wait outside the grove, and when Prydion gives the word, they will follow him inside and watch him wield the knife. I wonder, will they really let him strike the blow? And will Megan and Owen just lie there, oblivious as lambs, when the knife descends. I suppose I must hope so, if the ritual is to work and appease the gods. Assuming the gods are watching.

This would be so much easier if I still had faith. But then I would be damned, would I not?

Ah, Megan is stirring behind the curtain. A murmur, a gasp. Will she gasp at the touch of the Winter King? Will his desire be her pleasure, or just her duty? Will desire, or duty, be enough to blind them both to their deaths?

Prydion was the one who told me I could stay away when the other villagers witness the sacrifice. Prydion was the one who told the elders that it was Megan, not me, who should be the Summer Queen. Prydion decides who lives and who dies.

I had felt his eyes on me for some time. I was thrilled to gain the attention of the most important man in the village. Then, just after the last new moon, he stopped me as I was carrying water from the river, and asked after my health, and Megan's. He said, very gravely, that he had been discussing the Spring Rite with the elders, and did I know what it meant to be the Summer Queen? I said I did. He looked at his feet and asked, did I know that the Summer Queen must be a virgin? I said I knew this also. He put his hand on my arm. There was so much being said without words. I had not planned anything like this – how could I? – but I told him to come to the grove above the falls that night. And so he did.

I could have lied to him, said I was not pure. I could have lied for Megan, though that would have been more difficult for him to believe. But I did not. Instead I gave myself to him, let his cold hands run over my body, his rasping breath grate in my ears. I was appalled at how weak he was, how human. I cannot believe the gods would choose such a pathetic creature to be their instrument. And I was appalled at myself. But I was surprised too, at how easy it was to control him, how my whispers could turn his will. Are all men that weak, I wonder?

I will never forgive myself for making Megan take my place. But I have seen power, I know something of it now. It is nothing to do with the gods – it comes from us. We control our world. And if my sister dies in vain, and the blight comes again in autumn, I will not submit, I will not give up. I will leave the village, and walk out of the valley, beyond our fields and forests. I will find my own place, where the lessons I have learnt here can bring me power and luxury. The other villagers are too weak to contemplate such rebellion.

No, I am not damned: I am free.

I think of this early story as my schedefreude story. I attended the Winchester Writers Conference for several years, and whilst I learnt some of the craft there it was quite pricey and I got sick of the way other newbie-writers edged away with wan smiles when I told them I wrote SFF. I also entered some Conference competitions, though I never made the shortlists. On the last year I bothered to go I thought this piece might stand a chance in the 'short short story' category' but couldn't find it listed so decided not to pay through the nose to attend the prize dinner. It won anyway, even if I wasn't there to claim my prize.

The Chatterslee Circle

'Run!' shouted Phil, but Astral was already sprinting towards the edge of the field, scrawny legs pumping and blond dreadlocks flying.

The dogs rounded the corner of the barn. There looked to be at least a dozen of them. Phil decided not to wait around and check. Ahead, Astral was halfway to the fence. Despite his habitual lethargy and toast-rack physique, the boy could really run when it mattered. Must have had plenty of practice escaping irate farmers in his time as a New Age traveller.

For Phil, being chased off private land by dogs was a new experience, but terror gave him that extra burst of energy. He was carrying enough weight to make him an easier catch, and a tastier snack, than his companion.

Ahead, Astral vaulted the stile without breaking stride. Phil thought the sounds of pursuit were dying away. Or perhaps he was just getting faint due to the unaccustomed exertion. He forced himself to keep running. Still expecting to feel teeth ripping into his jeans at any moment, he hauled himself over the stile and collapsed onto the verge. Looking back through the fence he saw two mangy collies ambling up to the edge of the field. A third dog had given up the chase and was slinking back to the farmhouse. Well, they had sounded vicious enough.

'Shit. Astral,' Phil panted, 'The next... the next time I say "Right, we'll be off then" to a man holding a shotgun, we just leave: no questions, no hesitation, no wandering off. Okay?'

Astral stood and looked around with his usual air of placid bewilderment. 'Sure, mate. I'd have gone and checked it by myself, you know.'

The last dog padded up to the fence, gave a desultory growl then, duty done, sloped off.

Phil sat on the grass, wincing and massaging his side. 'Yes, I know you would. In fact you did. I was most of the way down the drive before I spotted you.'

Astral waved his hands around with vague enthusiasm. 'But it was the field, see? The actual field!'

Phil pulled himself upright on the stile. The pain was going away. That meant it was just stitch, not kidney damage. He glanced at the digital camera slung round Astral's neck. Other than some grass stains on the bottom of the case, it looked fine. Though Astral had few talents which would be appreciated in modern society, he was a surprisingly good photographer, even if he had no concept of the cost and fragility of photographic equipment. Phil sighed, 'Yes. It was a field. A field with a barbed wire fence and a sign saying 'Trespassers will be Dealt With'.'

'No, not just a field. *The* Field.'

Phil took Astral's elbow and steered him away from the fence. They were still in full view of the Georgian farmhouse, with its Victorian owner and his Edwardian shotgun. 'The field where the Circle was? Yes, I know. If you remember I specifically said we shouldn't mention the Circle to Farmer Psycho. I'm sure he enjoyed the extra cash from the admission he charged last summer, but he made his attitude to the Unexplained clear enough in the papers. And the Chatterslee Circle was the best documented crop circle hoax in history. Even you've got to admit that. I mean, the blokes who did it took a reporter from the Daily Star out to another field and showed her how they'd done it!'

'Like we believe the media,' said Astral petulantly, shrugging free of Phil's hold.

'Astral, old mate. I hate to break it to you, but we are the media.'

Phil started down the road back towards the village. As the roads round here were not wide enough for a Volvo estate to pass a muck splattered tractor – a fact he knew from recent bitter experience – Phil had parked his newly dented car in the car park of the village church, next to the sign saying *St Michael's church. Historic fourteenth century nave. Teas on the lawn on Bank Holidays. Please give generously to maintain this Historic Building.* Though he was in no position to give generously, he'd slipped fifty pence into the wooden collection box in case the locals were watching.

Astral ambled after him, 'No, no, we're not like the Establishment media. Not at all. We're redressing the balance.'

Phil decided not to point out that the main difference between them and the woman from the *Star* was that she got paid every month. 'In theory, yes. But as far as the respectable villagers of the charming village of Chatterslee are concerned, we're here to listen to whatever they want to tell us. We're not here to convince them that they live in "Weird Shit on the Wold".' Though Astral approached paranormal investigation with all the rational caution of a Teletubby on speed, Phil took care to maintain a professional objectivity. Obviously not all unexplained phenomena – or U.P.s as Phil preferred to call them – were symptoms of things beyond mankind's ken, so if he was ever going to find a genuine mystery amongst the superstition, misunderstandings and hoaxes, he needed to start from a sceptical viewpoint, and work towards belief. 'We ask about the documented instances, and let them bring up anything else they want to tell us. Saying "Mind if we just check out the alien landing site?" is not going to work. We're dealing with closed minds here.'

'Sure, mate. I know that. I just got carried away.' Astral thrust his hands into the pockets of his frayed cargo pants and walked on in silence. Around them the English summer was at its fecund yet civilised height; the trees were as full and plump as children's drawings, purple and yellow flower heads swayed in waist high grass and the air was thick with the scent of cut grass, pollen and environmentally dubious agro-chemicals.

Despite himself, Phil felt guilty. Astral was one of nature's innocents, a person who, through a combination of natural inclination, unusual up-bringing and chemical self-enhancement, had concluded that the world was a wonderful, magical place. Phil hated disillusioning him, especially as Astral was one of his oldest friends. They'd been playmates on the north London estate where Phil had grown up until Astral's gently barmy mother had decided to take her offspring with her to join the Peace Convoy. When they'd met up again at Stratford University on the media studies course five years ago, Phil had felt like he was discovering the long-lost little brother he'd never had. Or perhaps the long-lost little brother who had been replaced with an almost perfect copy by the faeries or aliens, because Astral's naïve enthusiasm was truly otherworldly at times.

Despite, or perhaps because of, their differing worldviews, they had renewed their friendship. Astral promised never to slip mind-altering substances into Phil's food or try and convince him to spend eight hours in a room full of pounding noise and flashing lights, and in return Phil never discussed computers, wargaming or his various failed relationships with the opposite sex. And though they approached the world of the Unexplained from opposite directions, they worked well together. Not well enough to make a living, but Phil still took the occasional contract as a games designer to top up his finances. He preferred not to speculate on how Astral got by.

'Tell you what. We'll check out the "beast" sighting then pop in the local hostelry for a pint before we follow up any more reports.'

Astral's sulk evaporated instantly at the mention of a chance for intoxication. 'Yeah. Great idea.'

Phil often envied Astral's lack of attention span. Words like 'angst', 'mortgage' and 'deadline' simply didn't register with him.

After about fifty yards Astral paused, un-slung the camera, and started taking shots of the village nestled in its low valley, surrounded by cornfields ranging in colour from lush green to heavy gold. Phil leant against an ivy-covered stone wall and wondered if he'd ever be able to afford to live in a place like this. Of course, he'd probably have to get married and find a job involving the pointless movement of large sums of money, not to mention shaving off his beard and pretending he wasn't a socialist, but he could dream. His reverie was broken by a glimpse of a dark shape moving amongst the flint cottages.

'Astral,' he whispered, 'Check that out, just coming up to the church.'

Astral pointed his camera, and Phil strained to get a closer look. He realised as soon as he had spoken that it was only a car, but the sleek black shape looked out of place in this rural idyll.

Astral, with the uncharacteristic concentration he sometimes displayed when behind a camera, carried on recording the strange

30

car's progress until it disappeared into the maze of thatched roofs. Then he turned and walked back to Phil. 'How about that, eh? MiBs.'

Phil frowned, 'Well, I don't know about Men in Black. But it was odd, yes.' Actually, anything out of the ordinary was a bonus. They had come here on the strength of a few reports of bizarre events and unexplained sightings collected from local newspapers by a friend who lived in Swindon and kept up an interest in the Unexplained to offset the tedium of living in one of the most boring towns in England. Up till now they had seen nothing remotely unusual.

They entered the village proper and set out across the central green. Curtains twitched in the surrounding cottages, but there was no sign of the mysterious black car. 'What do you reckon, Astral? I'd say the pictures in the Salisbury Echo were taken from over there, by the church.'

Astral shrugged. While Phil gave all areas of investigation equal weight, Astral was biased towards the more off-the-wall U.P.s. Sightings of animals outside their natural habitat did not fill him with the enthusiasm that he showed for reports of alien abduction, spoon bending or disappearing genitalia.

Three cottages stood in a scenic huddle along one edge of the green. The middle one had honeysuckle climbing the arch over the porch. Phil set his face into a friendly smile and picked his way up the gravel path to the first cottage. Astral, canny enough to know how unwelcome his type was likely to be, hung back and tried to look inoffensive.

Phil's smart rap on the wrought iron knocker was answered with suspicious speed by a heavily made-up woman in her late twenties.

Phil held up his press card and went into what he thought of as 'polite official mode', 'Good afternoon. We're sorry to disturb you, but we're investigating some unusual occurrences in the area and we wondered if you might have seen anything.'

She squinted at the card. 'Such as?'

'Well, specifically, we wondered if you might have seen a large tawny coloured cat.'

She looked dubious. 'A cat? We've got a ginger tom. But… are you selling something?'

'No, not at all. A large cat – much larger than any domestic breed – was sighted just over there.' Phil pointed across the green towards the church. 'The first sighting was about eighteen months ago. It made the local papers.' Phil put the fact that the reports hadn't made the Nationals down to the lack of a suitably colourful name. The 'Wiltshire Wildcat' just didn't have the shock value of the 'Beast of Bodmin' or the 'Surrey Puma'.

'No. We only moved in last spring. Are you sure you're not selling something?'

He knew he was on to a loser. Resisting the temptation to say 'No, ma'am, we're journalists,' he stepped back and said. 'No. Well, thank you for your time.'

There was no answer at the honeysuckle cottage.

At the next one, whose name plate announced it to be 'Ye Old Forge', the door was opened by a wizened old woman reeking of gin and lavender. Her glance shuttled between him and Astral as he introduced himself. She waited until he'd finished speaking then said, 'Go away, you filthy hippies,' in a cut-glass BBC accent, and slammed the door.

Phil suggested that now might be a good time to hit the pub.

The car park of the Queen's Head held a couple of mud-splattered land rovers, half a dozen third-hand Jaguars and Rovers, a well maintained green MG sports car and one immaculate black BMW. Astral elbowed him in the ribs and nodded at the BMW. He had to agree that it might well have been the vehicle they'd seen earlier.

Inside, the small bar sported the obligatory low wooden beams and agricultural equipment impaled on the walls plus a chalk board menu offering such traditional English fare as Thai Green Chicken with Sautéed Lemon Noodles or Terrene of Mediterranean Vegetables with Chick Pea and Garlic Couscous. Three tweed clad old codgers looked up from their dominos to scowl in unison as Phil and Astral walked in, but the majority of lunchtime punters were office workers out from Swindon for an extended Friday lunch or dubious tryst with a co-worker. The largest table was occupied by a group of individuals of military bearing wearing improbably smart suits. It seemed safe to assume that they were the people with the black BMW.

Phil ordered a half of bitter and an overpriced ham sandwich. Astral, for whom food was an occasional vice, said he was 'fine with the cider'. Phil had to agree that it looked like a meal in itself.

They settled down at a scrubbed wooden table under prints of unrealistically proportioned racehorses. By mutual consent they chose a spot with a good view of the Men in Suits, who were just finishing their lunch.

'Whoa,' said Astral a little too loudly, 'These MiBs aren't all Men!'

Phil had noticed. What was the correct term? Woman in Black? Didn't sound quite right. But whatever the jargon might be, she was seriously cute.

Helen pushed her plate away, took a sip of orange juice and resisted the temptation to look at her watch. Down the far end of the table Barry Vickers was recounting an oh-so-hilarious tale of rain at the eighteenth hole to Nigel and James while Mike Frost and Andy Belcher discussed United's chances this Saturday. Hey guys, anyone remembered why you're here? Of course they had. They were here to 'see her off'. And weren't they all glad to see the back of the token woman.

Nigel, for whom golf and football took a distant second to more horizontal entertainments, was looking the most relieved. He was even laughing at old Vickers' jokes. Bastard. She should have told his wife. Then again, she doubted it would have made any difference. Helen's impression of the old cow from the Christmas do was that she was perfectly willing to overlook her husband's frequent infidelities in return for the social status and financial security of being married to a high-ranking officer in British Intelligence.

Helen decided her mother might have been right last month when, with uncharacteristic insight brought on by too much sherry, she'd said that Helen's problem was that the last part of a man she looked at was his conscience. Still, she would probably have left anyway, even without having joined the ranks of Nigel's discarded conquests. She'd had enough of dealing with men who never looked higher than her chest when assessing her assets.

She glanced round the lounge bar where, as usual, the locals and office workers were politely ignoring the 'boys from the bunker'. Except those two. They weren't the usual clientele. The skinny one looked like the sort you saw being arrested on anti-Globalisation demos on TV. The other one... the word 'geek' would have perhaps been accurate, but cruel. He wasn't her type, but then again her normal type invariably turned out to be lying, callous bastards. And he had a lovely smile, open and self-effacing. He looked away quickly, his cheeks colouring, and rummaged in the large document bag on the seat next to him. His friend seemed to be trying to attract his attention back to Helen and her colleagues, but he got out a large map and, after fighting with it for a few seconds, laid it flat on the table. He and his mate were soon absorbed.

'Though I'm not the pro you are Barry, I usually manage to make a birdie, don't I, Helen?'

She looked over to see Nigel smirking at her from the far end of the table. Sex and golf, both games of conquest for him, and in both cases he wasn't half as good as he thought he was. Before her brain had caught up she heard herself respond, 'Shame you can't extend your form to a regular hole in one!' Amazed at having managed to find the response Nigel deserved, Helen stood and excused herself. As she passed the table with the two alternative types, the scrawny one made an unconvincing attempt to watch her whilst seeming to check out the bar décor. His friend glanced at him, looked exasperated, then flashed Helen a small apologetic smile. Here was a man whose conscience was probably as clean as Nigel's shirts.

When she emerged from the ladies they'd gone back to their map. As she crossed the room there was a lull in the background conversations and she heard the nice one telling his friend, with an earnest patience. 'No, here. The fish fall was here.'

Aha. So that was why they were here. Hmm. Helen smiled to herself. Yes. Why not? It wasn't like she had anything to lose. In a few hours she'd be free of that chauvinistic, bureaucratic, cynical purgatory.

Her unexpected show of independence seemed to have put a damper on her colleagues' lunchtime jolly, and no one made a move to get the next round on her return. With much hmmphing and comments about noses back to grindstones, they reached for their jackets. Helen hung back, hoping that her increasing sense of euphoric mischief didn't show on her face. Unlikely – as usual, they were ignoring her. In the car park, she muttered something about forgetting her purse and darted back into the bar. Before she had the chance to lose her nerve she walked up to the visitors' table, looked the sweet geeky one in the eye and said, 'The B345, lay-by opposite the turning to Wilmslow Chase. Eight p.m. tonight. Right?'

Her last sight of them before the door swung shut was a picture of open-mouthed astonishment.

'That was fantastic,' breathed Astral as they left the pub.

Phil had to agree. She wasn't pretty as such, but she had the loveliest dark brown eyes…

'We've got a genuine lead from a MiB! I mean WiB. Fantastic.'

'Er, yes.'

Astral stopped, looked his friend in the eye and said with rare insight, 'You fancy her, don't you?'

'Well, no. I mean yes. She could be very helpful in our investigations.'

Astral clapped him on the shoulder. 'Go for it, my man. Go for it. Just make sure you get the full brain dump on what's going on while you're at it.'

Phil sighed. 'That's what makes working with you such a pleasure Astral. Your professionalism. Right, let's check out the rest of the reports.' His intellectual desire for the Truth was currently taking a back seat to simpler yearnings, but if they weren't thorough they'd only miss something. Besides, he needed to keep Astral out of trouble till this evening.

They started by checking out the two remaining reports of crop circles.

The first farm, an ugly modern building whose yard contained more cow shit than Phil had ever seen in one place, appeared deserted. Phil, trying to breathe through his mouth to avoid the

35

smell, managed to restrain Astral from 'having a poke round the back'.

At the second farm, a smaller, older building about half a mile out of the village, the door was answered by a gaunt-looking youth who, whilst he didn't seem overly friendly, was at least unarmed. From the corner of his eye Phil saw Astral's nostrils flare; yep, he could smell it too. Probably grew his own. Where better than on a farm?

The youth took them out to the field where the circle had occurred, giving a laconic commentary as they walked up the track. Yeah, there were loads of circles around the village; yeah, he'd seen strange lights in the sky; yeah, loads of weird stuff happened round here – did they know about the herring? Phil assured him that they were going to investigate the herring. He was torn between relief that they'd finally found someone who came from the same planet as him and a growing certainty that crop-circle hoaxing was just the kind of thing this stoner would do to while away the long summer evenings. Astral, encouraged by finding what he would call 'a cool person', got out his dowsing rods. Phil let him wander round for a while – dowsing, like ghosts and crypto-zoology, were something that Phil placed in the category of 'might be something to this' – but when Astral started to steer the conversation towards the best fertiliser to use on your homegrown Phil suggested it was time to move on.

The walk back to the village was uncomfortable in the late afternoon heat, and they looked longingly at the locked doors of the pub before heading into the relative coolness of the village shop, where Phil browsed the notice board and bought a copy of the parish magazine while Astral went through the chilled drinks cabinet in a vain search for a drink without artificial additives. A flick through the magazine showed a complete lack of reports of strange disappearances and cattle mutilations.

It was time to move on to the most well documented U.P. after the Chatterslee circle itself: the rain of fish. 'Herring Terrace' as the Salisbury Echo had dubbed it, was a row of brick and flint cottages with red tiled roofs and long narrow gardens.

There was no answer at the first cottage. Cottage number two was occupied by a stressed-out looking woman with half a dozen pre-school kids running riot in the low-beamed living room behind her. Though she heard them out Phil got the impression she wasn't really listening, and only kept the door open as something to lean on. She seemed to think that they had come to view the house. When Phil looked baffled she pointed to the 'For Sale' sign hidden in a rose bush. Phil explained that they were not here to buy a house; she rolled her eyes, and closed the door.

Her immediate neighbour was a gentleman who was old enough to wear his flat cap indoors. He welcomed them into his home, which appeared to have been unchanged since the end of the Second World War, and offered them tea. He knew about the fish, yes, but he'd been visiting his daughter when the incident occurred. Would they like to see a picture of his daughter? Phil, carefully polite, made the mistake of saying he would. It took them the best part of an hour to escape from Mr Flat Cap. The only extra information they managed to glean were a couple of improbable and unoriginal ghost stories, but Phil consoled himself that he had livened up a lonely old man's life for a while.

The occupants of the next two cottages were out, for which Phil was guiltily grateful: time was getting on, and he didn't want to be late for the meeting with the Woman in Black.

The door on the final cottage was opened by a woman in her sixties. From her expression Phil expected a reception similar to the senior citizen on the green; when Phil introduced himself she narrowed her eyes and asked suspiciously, 'Which paper did you say you were from?'

Astral, who had remained dutifully silent throughout Phil's pitch, said chirpily, 'The Daily Mail.'

Phil tried not to stare at his companion. Astral never ceased to amaze him.

Mrs Suspicious, presumably believing that no one could lie about something so sacred, smiled and invited them in. Though she didn't know anything about the lights in the sky, and was firmly convinced that all crop circles were the result of Young Farmers on Drugs, she had actually been sitting in her garden on the day that several hundred herring had fallen from a clear sky over the terrace. Most unusual, she said. Made a real mess of her husband's dahlias. And the smell! But, she had decided to keep a couple, in case they were needed for 'evidence'. For or against what she didn't say. She led them down to a huge chest freezer in her cellar, and from under the prime joints of British beef she produced a small bundle wrapped, unsurprisingly, in a copy of the Daily Mail.

Inside were two small silver fish, one intact, the other with an unpleasantly mashed head and missing tail. She offered to let them have the fish, for a small consideration, but Phil declined, though he got Astral to snap a picture of the beasties with a promise that she'd get a mention in their article. Not exactly a lie; he just didn't mention where the article was likely to appear.

As they left Mrs Daily Mail's immaculate house the sun was just touching down on the edge of the hills, and Phil, distracted by thoughts of short tight skirts and dark brown eyes, was considering calling it a day and making their way to the rendezvous. But he made a point of following all leads, no matter how unsavoury or ridiculous, so they made their way across the village the Old Rectory.

The building was a Victorian edifice with an immaculate garden, and Phil's heart sank when the door was opened by a middle-aged gentleman who looked to be the rector himself. Phil gave his speech, extra polite. The man looked perplexed, and said he hadn't witnessed any strange lights, or animals, or unusual rains. Astral, emboldened by his success at the last house, again ignored Phil's standing order to let him do the talking and said, sotto voice, 'Ask him about the bras.' The clergyman blushed, muttered something inaudible and retreated into the house. His wife, with generous bosom and floral apron, appeared from a door down the hall a couple of moments later and inquired politely, 'Yes?'

Phil realised he had backed himself into corner, 'We were, erm, investigating unusual occurrences and we, ahem, understand there was an… underwear related incident here.'

To Phil's surprise she smiled and said in a broad Wiltshire accent. 'Oh, you mean the bras!' and proceeded to recount, with an entirely straight face, how for three consecutive mornings last month she had noticed women's brassieres draped over the back hedge. She seemed happy to answer questions, and Astral, obviously enjoying himself, took the opportunity to ask such useful questions as 'How Many?' 'What Size?' and 'Frilly or plain?'. Phil let him get on with it for a while, but pointedly glanced at his watch when Astral, his face on the verge of breaking into a full smirk, asked if there had been any matching panties.

By the time they'd escaped the clergyman's wife and walked back to the car it was quarter to eight. Phil reminded himself that she might not turn up, and Astral, ever prone to paranoia, mused that she might be an official representative of The Authorities. But there was no question of not getting to the rendezvous as fast as possible, even if that meant breaking the local speed limit. They tore up the side of the valley towards a dark skyline broken by intermittent patches of woodland on the edge of Salisbury Plain.

They arrived with two minutes to spare. The lay-by was in a stretch of road running between open fields overhung with occasional trees. They waited five minutes, and then got out for a look around. The darkness was complete now, and the fields beyond the trees had faded into the gloom. Phil was just about to suggest they call it a night when he spotted a pair of headlights approaching. They turned out to belong to the green MG they'd seen in the pub car park earlier. The sole occupant was their Woman in Black. She parked up behind Phil's Volvo and lowered her window. Phil and Astral went over.

The woman was still wearing her suit, and looked uncomfortable, but one corner of her mouth twitched into a half smile as Phil leaned in to speak to her.

'Hi,' said Phil, a little lamely.

'Hullo.' She looked ahead, then frowned and turned to meet his eyes. 'You're not recording this, are you? I'm sure you understand that I'm talking off the record.'

'Er, yes.'

'Is that "yes" as in you're taping this conversation?'

'No, I mean it's 'Yes I understand'. I'm not recording this. I don't record stuff without asking.'

'Good. I thought you looked too nice to work for a tabloid.'

'Er, thanks.'

'Well. Believe it or not – and I don't necessarily expect you will – you've stumbled onto a genuine conspiracy.'

'Fantastic,' breathed Astral.

'As I'm sure you know, a lot of the land round here is Ministry of Defence. A few years ago some grunts on exercise shot a small mountain lion. It probably escaped from a zoo or circus. The officer that followed it up never found out the full story. But he did find out that there had been sightings of a big cat from the vicinity of Chatterslee village. And yet the locals, even those who had apparently made the original reports, seemed to be in denial. He was in psy-ops – that's military psychology to you – and realising how easily the villagers dismissed what turned out to be a genuine incident gave him an idea. Just how much could you challenge the average insular Brit's view of reality before they cracked? He sold it to his CO, also mentioning the opportunity to test new technology, and they went for it. Project Oblivious has been in place for two years now. And, rather depressingly, not one of the residents of Chatterslee has tried to investigate why so many odd things happen around their village. No one has, really. Until you two came along.'

'Wait a minute. Are you telling us that your lot, the military, did all the weird stuff?'

She was starting to sound more relaxed. 'Well, not all. Like I said, we aren't sure where the mountain lion came from. And the Chatterslee circle was a hoax, of course. Actually that was a godsend, as it convinced the locals that anything odd must be explainable. Which was true, of course, but we wanted to see how far we could push them before they started to question their assumptions.'

'What about the other circles?' Astral asked. Crop circles featured high in his Weird Shit Top Ten.

'Hoaxes too. Not that we witnessed them all, but they were generally a lot simpler than the one that got a centre page spread on the Daily Star, and there's not much else to do around here, is there?'

Astral, his voice shaky, continued, 'And the UFOs?'

'The lights in the sky? A couple of test flights for classified aircraft kitted out with nonstandard lights, and some laser technology. Sorry.' She flashed Astral a sympathetic grin over Phil's shoulder.

'Oh.'

'Presumably you had nothing to do with the local ghost tales?' Phil asked.

She laughed. 'Find me a village that doesn't have a ghost story!'

She had a lovely laugh. If he'd met her under other circumstances... No, he must be professional. He might never get another chance like this. 'And the herring?'

'The boys had a high-altitude precision guidance system which needed testing. Given that the fall was isolated to an area of less than four hundred square feet, they considered the test a success.'

'Okay,' Phil hesitated, but he needed to be thorough. 'How about the bras?'

'Ah yes, the bras. One of the other divisions wanted to test their new stealth suits, and they wanted an observable way of recording the success of the, well, penetration. A signal or sign.' She sighed. 'You'd be amazed at how juvenile the average military male is.'

No, thought Phil, I wouldn't be amazed. Just vindicated. 'Um, I'm probably going to regret asking, why are you telling us all this?'

'Because I've recently found myself to have a stubborn streak of morality, and I'm sick of deception. You might not think that's a particularly good reason, but it's the truth.'

'It's a great reason.' He believed her. 'But won't you get in trouble? I mean, I assume you're involved in this Project Oblivious.'

She sighed. 'Not any more. I've left. Besides, I'm afraid no one is likely to believe you. Project Oblivious only succeeded in proving that people believe what they want to believe, regardless of evidence. But thank you for your concern.'

That didn't sound like sarcasm. That sounded more like an invitation. 'Er. Listen, can I, erm, ask you something?'

'Sure.'

What was the worst that could happen? She could roll up the window and drive off over his foot. An acceptable risk, Phil decided. 'Would you be willing to give me a way of contacting you? I mean, assuming you're no longer in the military, and you'd be willing to discuss your experiences further. Perhaps we could meet up again, somewhere a little less open.'

She frowned, and Phil braced himself. Then she said, 'Okay.' She rummaged in the handbag on the seat next to her, got out a pen and paper and wrote down a number. 'My mobile number. Good point about this being open. I don't want to fuel your paranoia, but my ex-colleagues did notice you this afternoon, so it might be an idea if you didn't hang around longer than you need to.'

'Er, yes. Sure. Can I, um, give you my number.'

'Why not?'

She waited while he tore off the bottom of her note, scrabbled around for a pen, and wrote his mobile number down. She was definitely smiling at him.

She took the paper and slipped it into her handbag. 'Well, it's been… cathartic talking to you. Thanks.'

Phil stepped back, 'Be seeing you.'

'Quite possibly.'

Phil led a downcast Astral back to the car. 'Well, you've got to admit that this was real conspiracy,' he said as he started the engine.

Astral grunted. 'Yeah, a conspiracy to prove that people are idiots. Already knew that.' He smiled wanly, 'Still, she was a babe. And she definitely liked you.'

'You reckon?' Phil still didn't want to get his hopes up.

'Oh yes. I could feel the vibes. You two are going to make it, I'm sure.'

'Thanks Astral.' Even when he was on the rebound from having his view of the Fundamental Strangeness of Reality challenged Astral was a good mate. He hoped he was right about their attractive informant. Getting to the bottom of the mystery was satisfying in its way, but he could understand Astral's disappointment at discovering such a mundane and deniable explanation. Still, it hadn't been a complete waste of time. He wondered what her name was. Well, give it a couple of days and maybe he'd phone the number on the piece of paper in his pocket, and find out.

Helen watched the Volvo's single working tail-light recede down the lane. Nothing would come of it, of course. The story lacked the sex and corruption angle the mainstream media craved. But she'd done the right thing in telling them. She felt better about herself than she had for months. And it didn't do any harm that she'd also got the phone number of a not-entirely-unattractive man with half a brain and a whole soul.

She turned the key. Nothing happened. The engine was dead. Bugger. And the evening had been going so well.

Movement out of the corner of her eye. She turned to look over her shoulder. There was someone in the field next to the lay-by. A light. Someone with a torch? Her heart rate quickened. Her ex-colleagues? No, they'd bring a car. And besides, they had no idea what she'd done, and probably wouldn't care anyway, despite her warnings to the investigators. Must be a farmer. Two farmers. There were two lights now.

But no people. The field was empty.

Two small silvery lights, hovering low over the field. There was no obvious source; the lights just hung there. A third light blinked into existence. Helen watched, more fascinated than afraid, as the first light started to move. It began to sweep around the field in a low lazy arc. In its wake the stalks of corn bent low to sit in a perfect ninety degree angle. The movement was sedate, like a dance. The second light joined it. Then the third, weaving and shimmering through the still night air.

She reached for her phone.

I had an interest in 'Fortean' matters, long before I knew what that meant. This early story – which hasn't dated very well – was sort-of meant to be the start of something bigger, though somehow I never did get round to writing the Great British Fortean Novel. In the two decades since this little tale was published such fringe interests have become more mainstream, and whether or not you think that's a good thing, it's produced some great stories by others that I've enjoyed reading.

Paying for Rain

'He says: Rules don't hold on the mountain.'

'Fine. Whatever.' Jamieson shaded his eyes and gazed out across the valley. 'So is this a money thing, an offerings thing, or a respect thing?' He dropped his hand and turned back to his two companions, flashing his best appease-the-locals smile at the aged Aymara native before addressing the man who had spoken, 'No, don't translate that, Francisco. It's just that we've been following Angelo here over hill and dale for three days now without any clear idea when I'm going to be "allowed" up the mountain – or even which mountain – and I'm getting a bit tired of being led round by the nose. So can you just ask him nicely whether he could please explain exactly what it is he needs now.'

Francisco nodded, his face expressionless as ever, and started to speak rapid phrases in the Aymara language to their guide.

Jamieson had first met Francisco a decade ago, when he'd been covering South American hiking holidays for the *Western Cultural Traveler*, a publication he still thought of as *National Geographic Lite*. Fresh out of college, he had thought he'd pulled a peach but it turned out to be a thoroughly unpleasant assignment. Basic accommodation, gritty food, surly locals. Well, except for Francisco. And his lovely sister, of course. Presumably she'd never mentioned what had happened that night during the thunderstorm to her brother, or Francisco might not have been so eager to renew his friendship with Jamieson when he'd turned up in La Paz last month looking for a guide. But now Jamieson was freelance, on his own timetable, and on a more lavish budget. He just hoped the rewards were worth the effort.

While the two Bolivians spoke, Jamieson turned back to the view. They were on the Cordillera Real, easternmost of the monumental ridges that form the Andes. The only signs of life in the valley below were the dirt road he and Francisco had driven up on, a few clusters of simple stone houses, and some half-hearted terracing along the lower slopes. Further up, the brown-grey crags were relieved only by drab patches of scrub and occasional wisps of low cloud coiling round the valley walls. To the west, Lake Titicaca shone ethereal and distant.

'Senor Jamieson?'

Jamieson turned back to the two men. Angelo was favouring him with his impressive grin; when Jamieson had first been introduced to their guide he'd expected the gap-toothed smile of a man brought up in a culture which had no word for 'dentist', but Angelo had a full set of perfect – presumably false – teeth.

'Senor, Angelo says he only warns you of this as his duty, though since you mention offerings, more alcohol would be good. But, he says, a gringo like you will have enough trouble carrying what we have all the way up the mountain.' Francisco gave a slight shrug, distancing himself from his countryman's insult. 'So, if more is needed, money will have to do.'

Jamieson tried not to grimace as he held Angelo's moist-eyed but steady gaze. 'Sure. Tell him we'll manage with what I've got. It should be enough.'

Money would usually do, for the fabulously poor peasants of the Bolivian highlands. And more was usually what was needed.

I am so cold. I would have thought, being nearer the Sun, that it would be warmer up here, but that was just another of the Sun-Priest's lies.

On the way up I saw the whole of our Valley from above, as though I were a Condor. The fields and terraces looked like a patterned shawl draped over the land. Even when we were too high to make out the houses any more, I could see the way they pulled on the pattern of fields, like a thread catching in cloth. I saw right across the Lake of the Cat and into the mountains beyond. Everything I have ever known, and places I had only heard of, all laid out below me.

So beautiful. So small.

Will they miss me, my mother, my father, my brothers? They will say I am with the gods now, in the arms of Father Illumani. But when visitors come and ask, they will have to be careful and say instead that I am with the Sun.

'Can we take a break?'

Francisco turned at Jamieson's request, inspected him for a moment, then shouted ahead to their companion. Jamieson liked to think of himself as pretty fit, and he hadn't wanted to give in, especially as it looked as if this mountain might finally be the one. But then again, he wasn't used to exerting himself in air so thin his blood felt like it was evaporating from his veins.

Angelo and Francisco came back down, Francisco at his usual measured pace, Angelo bounding over rocks with an agility that belied his advanced years and heavy backpack. Jamieson eased his own rucksack off with a sigh and sat on a rock spattered with yellow lichen. Angelo said something to him in Aymara, his dark eyes twinkling in his leathery face. It sounded like a question. Francisco translated, 'He asks, are you maybe having trouble with the height here?'

'As a matter of fact, yes I am.' This was something new. Insofar as he acknowledged his existence at all, Angelo seemed to regard his patron as a fount of money and a source of amusement. Sympathy was an unexpected development.

'Then we rest,' said Francisco, and sat down. Angelo accepted Francisco's decision, though he did not sit, and instead looked out over the valley, whistling tunelessly. Jamieson was glad that Angelo seemed so happy to go along with Francisco. The ex-policeman and amateur archaeologist seemed to know everyone in the region, and even claimed that he was distantly related to Angelo, though Jamieson found it hard to see any resemblance between the tall translator in his immaculate light-weight suit and panama hat and the wrinkled semi-alcoholic local in his ragged poncho and hand-knitted cap.

Angelo stopped whistling and turned back to his charges. He said something, another question by the sound of it.

Francisco translated. 'He asks whether you are really a storyteller?'

'Not exactly. I'm a reporter, as you know.' Not that Angelo would know what a reporter was. He probably couldn't even read. 'But for the sake of this conversation you can tell Angelo that yes, I am a storyteller.'

Angelo and Francisco had a short conversation – possibly an argument, though it was difficult to tell with the weird cadences of the Aymara language – and then Francisco said shortly, 'Angelo says that he must now tell you a story.' Angelo had already sat down cross-legged on the rough ground and started to speak. Francisco translated:

'This is not the first time that the Sun and Rain have been out of balance. It has been so many times before. Once, in such a time, the chief of this Valley had a son who was both wise and beautiful. Some say he was the fairest child ever born in the Valley. He was so perfect that the King of the Sun heard of his beauty, and asked that he be sent to his Court. But the people of the Valley did not yet acknowledge the King of the Sun, and they refused to send the child.'

Angelo stopped talking and addressed Francisco directly. Francisco shook his head, and Angelo reached into his poncho for an unmarked glass bottle, no doubt containing *chicha*, the local cure for sobriety and a functioning liver. Angelo extracted the cork with his teeth, took a mouthful, then spat it out, spraying the foul liquor over Jamieson's feet and the surrounding countryside. The first time Jamieson had seen him do that he'd laughed: *chicha* was made of rotted corn and human spittle, so he could understand the reaction. But this was just Angelo's drinking ritual, and after messily offering the booze to the local vicinity, he proceeded to take a long swig.

Jamieson took the opportunity to check his watch: just gone three o'clock. He hadn't realised it was so late. He had been hoping to get up and down again before they lost the light, but at this rate it looked like they would be camping on the mountain tonight. He started to get up, but Angelo waved a warning hand, and Francisco said, 'The story is not finished yet.'

Jamieson's heart sank. He didn't have time for this. Carol had been the one for stories; she'd happily spend hours crouching in a smoke-filled hut listening to some unwashed shaman droning on about how the world was created from a corn stalk and a lump of goat poo. Right now, she was no doubt collecting or collating the meaningless tales of some primitive culture, though since the divorce she'd probably have to settle for driving her beaten-up car to the local Indian reservation. Hey, it wasn't his fault that she was a snob who saw anthropology as an entirely academic pursuit and refused to acknowledge the increasing popular appeal of the subject. He'd take fame and fortune over poverty and elitism any day. And he had always made it clear that he wanted children, so if she chose a badly paying career over family, she'd just have to live with the consequences. Of course he was grateful to her for kindling his interest in mythology and ritual, even if she had been unable to see the commercial potential. Treasure and murder: that's what sells books and gets documentary tie-in deals. Jamieson knew he'd be lucky to find much treasure, but he'd settle for a little murder.

Angelo had started up again, his voice slightly slurred. Francisco translated, his expression looking as close to disapproval as Jamieson had ever seen it.

'The King of the Sun was angry, and he threatened to send soldiers. But the boy said to his father, 'Father, there is drought here: the Mountains are angry with us, the old gods are angry with us, and the Lake will not give water to the sky unless we feed the earth. Tell them that though I will not go to the City of the Four Quarters, they may send a priest, and we will do as he says and make obeisance to the Sun. To the eyes of their priest, we are obeying them. But the sacrifice we make will be the one we have always made: to the Mountains, not to the Sun.' And so the boy's father sent word to the King of the Sun, and he sent his priest. After the preparations had been made the priest and the boy went into the mountains. The priest, thinking that the Aymara were scared primitives who would not dare disobey the King of the Sun, did not stay on the Mountain long. Believing that the child gone to be with the Sun, he left the people of the valley in peace. But the boy had fooled everyone: left alone at the last, he had not let the Sun burn and whither him; instead he had fed the earth to make the rain, as it always has been. And so the drought was broken.'

Jamieson smiled at Angelo. 'Nice story.' He turned to Francisco. 'What exactly does he mean by 'fed the earth' Francisco? Are we talking human sacrifice?'

Francisco said curtly, 'These tales are not literally true.'

'Well no, it's just that this kind of stuff might be useful for my book. Obviously artifacts are the main priority, but if I can tie a story to the place, that's a bonus.'

Francisco waved dismissively, 'It is a story I have heard before. If you like I will re-tell it for your tape recorder when we come down off the mountain.'

'Yeah, that'd be great.' Jamieson started to get up. 'But time's getting on and we really need to – whoa.' Jamieson staggered for a moment as dizziness washed over him. Though they were on relatively flat ground, he felt as though he was being pulled off the mountain by the vertiginous drop to the valley below.

Francisco took his arm. 'Senor Jamieson? Are you all right?'

'Yes, it's just the altitude. I'll be okay.'

Angelo thrust a bunch of greenery into Jamieson's swimming vision.

'He says, this will help.'

'What? Coca. That's coca isn't it? No thanks. Already met this one's descendants. I don't do that shit anymore.'

Francisco let go of his arm. 'It is not 'shit' Senor. Not at all.'

'Okay. Whatever. But I don't do drugs, right?'

'Not drugs. Coca. This will help, with the altitude. It is not the same as the white powder.'

'I'd rather not.'

'Angelo says you must.' Jamieson hadn't heard Angelo speak over the roaring in his ears. 'If you do not chew the leaves, you will not be well enough to climb the peak today.' Francisco dropped his voice to a conspiratorial whisper. 'And as you said yourself, Senor, there is a good chance that Angelo may change his mind again, if we do not carry on now.'

'Good point. So, I just chew them?'

'Yes, chew and swallow as much as you can of the juice.'

It felt like chewing string dipped in weed killer, but within a couple of minutes the trembling in his limbs gave way to a kind of enervated thrumming and the pounding in his head subsided to a manageable level. For the first time since they had climbed above 12,000 feet, he felt that he could draw breath and actually get the full benefit of the oxygen in his lungs.

'Let's go.'

They will hold a feast tonight. Father killed his best llama. The Priest smiled smugly at the sacrifice, though he frowned a little when Father poured blood from the bowl onto the earth. It was a sleek, healthy animal, and when the Priest has had his share there will still be plenty of meat for everyone.

I wish I could stop thinking about food; it is terribly distracting. But I am so hungry. I have not eaten for two days, as part of the purification; another practicality disguised as mystery, leaving my body empty and receptive to the final, bitter cup.

I am not angry with them. There is no fury in me. I know them better than they know themselves. My father is a good man, but he worries like a woman. And my brothers are not fools, for all that they have been content to live in my shadow until now. My family will manage without me. The Valley will manage without me.

It is not a blessing to see into men's hearts and know that the truths we live by are merely our own inventions. I would have been happier to live in quiet ignorance. But we have done the right thing, all of us, according to our beliefs and needs. There is no room for anger when you are true to yourself.

Ah, the poison is rising. I cannot...

'What the hell is that?'

'What Senor?'

'There, down that ravine. It looks like a cola bottle!'

'Yes, it could be.'

'What do you mean, 'It could be'? I thought this was an unclimbed mountain.' The coca had left a bitter taste in his mouth but had suffused him with energy. It lacked the compulsive certainty of cocaine but it still had the anger in it, the old anger he knew so well.

'Unclimbed by any gringo, yes. And rarely climbed by others. The Aymara do not climb for sport, Senor.'

Further up the slope Angelo stopped to watch them, his head tipped to one side.

'How about grave-robbing? Do they climb for profit, if not for fun?'

'What do you mean Senor?'

'I mean, how do we know that none of the Aymara have thought to rob out the tomb? It's not like they couldn't use the money.'

'We cannot be sure. But the tomb is not generally known about. I believe it is not even visible unless you know exactly where to look.'

'And Angelo does know, does he?'

'So he says.'

'Well, I guess that will have to do.'

I must smell terrible. I tried to keep my retching quiet, in case the Priest was still on the Mountain, though I doubt he would have heard me through these walls of stone. And now I am covered in the remains of the 'sacred drink' he gave me. Foul stuff, intended to steal my will and wits and leave me waiting meekly for a slow death.

While I wait shivering in my cold stone box, I try to preserve the memories of my loved ones, or to focus on Arhua, on what she is doing for me; but the face I saw as I vomited over my robes was that wretched Sun-Priest. He is not much older than me, but he yearns for power, and he will do anything to get it, even travel through inhospitable mountains to minister to savages like us. The people were so reverent, so careful to appease him. But behind his words of acceptance and grace he despises us. We are foreigners, not true subjects of the Empire. He is right, of course. The Sun-King is mighty, and he has the power to bring peace. We are just peasants, living in our little Valley, farming the land, revering the Mountains and the Lake. They are clever, the Inca: they claim their lineage comes from our Lake, from a Mother and Father born from our sacred waters. We think we are special to them, because we live in a place they hold sacred. So, we will obey them, and send them tribute of wool and maize and children. Father does not dare disobey them, even though he loved me too much to send me to them when I was an innocent child.

And so, I must die.

Though there was hardly any wind, the cold was all-pervasive, and Jamieson decided to put on his Gore-Tex coat. The procedure was more complicated than he remembered. His two companions stopped when they noticed him struggling with his pack, Francisco looking away politely, Angelo grinning at him and taking the opportunity to fortify himself with more *chicha*.

When they set off again Francisco nodded up to the thin blade of the ridge before them. 'This one, Senor, I think it is nearly the last.'

'The last… You mean the last before the summit.'

Francisco nodded, and Jamieson, his spirits lifted by the prospect of achieving his goal, strode off ahead. When he drew level with Angelo the guide offered him a drink but Jamieson waved the bottle away.

It wasn't the final ridge, but it did mark the start of the steepest part of the ascent. Soon they were scrambling up the narrow spur on all fours. This was raw, jagged terrain and Jamieson forced himself to move slowly and carefully, focusing on each movement as a separate painstaking process, ignoring his physical discomfort and never thinking about the sheer cliffs on either side. Hurrying would only get him killed. Angelo, apparently ignorant of the correct way to climb a mountain, virtually capered up the rocky slope. Francisco brought up the rear, taking as much care, and, Jamieson liked to think, at least as out of breath as him.

He was so intent on what was directly in front of his eyes that he didn't realise he had reached the summit at first. A thin whistling sound and a change in the gradient under his hands alerted him that something had changed, and he glanced up, blinking sweat out of his eyes. They'd come out onto a gently rising rocky plateau about fifty feet across, the higher southern end of it carpeted in snow. The whistling was the wind, thin and chilling.

Angelo was meandering towards something this side of the snow patch; it looked like a brightly coloured bush. Jamieson started to ask what he was doing, but his mouth was so dry he could only croak. He took a few steps onto the summit, shrugged off his pack, and pulled his canteen from his belt. The water tasted wonderful, and he closed his eyes, lost in the sensation of earth below him, sun and air above him, and life-giving water going into him. Suddenly

53

the canteen was knocked from his hand. He opened his eyes to see Angelo backing off rapidly. For a moment, Jamieson was too bemused to react, and he found himself staring at the water spilling out of the canteen and seeping into the parched soil. He tore his gaze from the strangely hypnotic sight.

'Why'd he do that Francisco?'

Francisco dropped his gaze. 'I am sorry. A misunderstanding,' he said, then stalked off after Angelo. Jamieson frowned. Francisco was normally so reasonable; this surliness was something he'd never seen before. No, he had once, a long time ago. When he had offered to help clear up after the storm, the night after he and Rosa... no, his imagination was running away. Damned altitude.

Jamieson felt a flash of anger. 'Wait up.' Francisco didn't seem to have heard him. Perhaps he should remind him who was paying for this expedition. Jamieson strode across the plateau to where Angelo and Francisco stood by a waist-high wooden crucifix adorned in ribbons, strings of beads, plastic necklaces and paper flowers. At the base of the cross was more junk: empty bottles, model cars, half burnt sticks of wood, shapeless lumps of candy and a handful of tiny seashells.

Francisco looked up at his approach and moved to intercept him, his expression contrite. 'Senor, now is the time for the Misa.' Jamieson, confused by Francisco's change of demeanour, nodded. 'Yeah, the Misa. Right.' The locals never went up into the mountains without doing their own weird version of the Catholic mass, which they called the Misa. Francisco gestured towards Jamieson's pack. 'Shall I fetch your offerings?'

'Yeah, sure. Thanks.' Jamieson wasn't sure if it was the coca, the altitude, or the surreal experience of finding sea-shells and Tonka toys on top of a fifteen thousand foot mountain, but he was beginning to feel a little disconnected from reality.

He looked around, trying to ground himself in his surroundings. Lake Titicaca shone like a jewel in a fold of the mountains, turquoise and serene in the evening sun. The valley below was in shadow, mist rolling up the flanks of the mountains from the cooling land.

'Here, Senor.' Francisco handed him two bottles and a woven string bag containing sweets, ribbons, a small rust-blotted mirror and several badly pressed metal trinkets. 'You must give the offerings for the Misa to Angelo, as we are here for you.'

The Aymara elder was muttering to himself in a mixture of Latin, Spanish and Aymara. Jamieson caught the Spanish words *padre* – father – and *lluvia* – rain. As Jamieson approached, Angelo stopped and gestured for him to put the offerings on the ground by the cross, then rubbed his thumb and two middle fingers together and looked at Jamieson questioningly. Jamieson sighed and dug into his money belt, producing a handful of small denomination notes. Angelo took the money and nodded in dismissal. Jamieson headed back to stand next to Francisco.

'Will this take long? We need to find somewhere sheltered to camp, preferably off the summit, and I'd rather get to the tomb tonight, in case Angelo changes his mind tomorrow.'

Francisco shrugged. 'The Misa cannot be hurried, Senor.'

'Yeah, I thought not. Well, I suppose we'll just have to wait then.'

The sun had all but disappeared behind the mountains by the time Angelo finished. Jamieson passed the time by wandering round the summit, stamping his feet to keep warm and taking pictures of Angelo at his ritual. He assumed Angelo wouldn't mind: the Aymara didn't buy into that old cliché about the camera stealing your soul, though they did tend to hold their hands out for cash once you'd finished taking pictures. At one point he looked up from his viewfinder to see Francisco, who had stood impassive throughout, crossing himself in unison with the old native. Well, that was Catholicism for you. He also photographed the surrounding peaks; the tip of snow-covered Mount Illumani in the distance would make a particularly nice shot, especially with Angelo in the foreground. It was a shame the light was going, as they were high enough, and far enough east, that he might have been able to glimpse the edge of the Amazon basin if everything in that direction hadn't been in darkness.

Angelo stood, crossed himself a final time, and walked over. Then in a startlingly familiar gesture, he took Jamieson by the elbow and started to lead him up the snow-covered southern edge of the plateau.

'Now he will show you where the tomb is, Senor Jamieson,' said Francisco, striding across the summit to join them. Despite having nothing more on his feet than a pair of sandals soled with old truck tires, Angelo ploughed into the thin covering of snow, dragging Jamieson with him. He stopped just short of the southernmost edge. The mountain fell away for fifty feet to a flat-bottomed gully which ran diagonally away from the peak. Mount Illumani dominated the horizon.

During the course of the Misa, Angelo had disposed of the alcohol they had lugged up here, either onto the rocky ground or down his throat, but now he produced a small green-tinted bottle from under his poncho, and made another attempt to get Jamieson to drink, waving the bottle and gabbling incomprehensibly. Jamieson looked at the old man, at the bottle, and at the frightening descent. 'Francisco?'

'Yes, Senor?'

'Please don't tell me that this crazy old man wants me to drink that rotgut, and then try and climb down this precipice.'

'I am afraid, Senor, that this is exactly what he wants.'

'Okay. That's it. I'm cold, I'm tired, my head feels like it's full of Japanese drummers and my credulity has been stretched to breaking point. Tell him "No".'

Francisco came up to stand beside him and pointed downwards. 'Follow my finger Senor.'

Jamieson focused where the translator was pointing. There, almost directly below them, on a small flat space at the edge of the gully, was a square box built of rocks, roofed with a flat stone slab.

'Yes! Okay, we're going down. But without the booze, right?'

Francisco said something and Angelo shook his head. 'Senor, he insists. He says that there is only one safe way down, which he will only show you if you take *chicha*.'

'For God's sake... Oh screw it.' Jamieson, elated that his goal was finally in sight, grabbed the bottle off the old man and poured the contents down his throat. It tasted just as vile as he expected and hit his gut like lava. He handed the empty bottle back to Angelo, who smiled, nodded, then dashed the bottle on a rock and started down the escarpment.

It was not as hard as it looked. The slope was rough and steep but there were plenty of handholds, and no loose rocks. Jamieson could feel the corn-liquor burning into his stomach lining. It combined with the coca and the excitement of being within reach of his goal to make him feel sickly ecstatic. Get there, find the tomb, then he could vomit, shout, pitch camp, pay these people off, whatever. He distracted himself by running internal pictures of the few previous finds of intact Inca mummies: the faces of sleeping children nestling among perfectly preserved fabrics, feather cloaks, ornate idols and, if he was really really lucky – and didn't he deserve it, after all the trouble he'd been to? – golden ornaments.

As soon as they reached the bottom of the rock face he stumbled towards the stone box. His vision was blurred by the alcohol and the descent from sunlight into shade but the tomb almost seemed to glow in the semi-darkness. It was definitely man-made. It was the right size, just large enough to hold a young adult if they sat with their knees drawn to their chest. Yep, this was the real thing all right. He felt round the stone lid. It rocked slightly: it was balanced expertly, as only the Inca knew how, and one good shove should shift it. He bent down and put his shoulder to it. The lid moved a little, then stuck. He heaved again. There was a grating noise and the lid slid into the gully with a resounding crash.

I hope I can learn to love Arhua. She is none too clever, and her love for me makes her more foolish still, but she is pure and true and she has given up everything for me. When I asked her to fetch herbs from the wise-woman's hut the night before the Sun-Priest came she believed that I had accepted my fate and asked for the purgatives only to purify my body before I drank the Priest's drug. The full truth scared her – she fears all and every god, even those that are not of our people – but still she did not question.

The men built my tomb very well, though I doubt Arhua could have moved the stone lid by herself had I not been helping her from inside. She was weak with cold by then; although the Priest brought me up here for dawn and didn't stay longer than he had to, Arhua waited until the sun was high in the sky before she dared come out of her hiding place and free me. The fear in her eyes was not just for herself – though she can no more go back to the Valley than can I – but fear of disobeying the gods. As we put the lid back (we want any future visitors from the Sun-King to think we obeyed him, after all) I tried to explain that I was condemned by politics, not by the heavens, but she just looked away. She is happier now, as we have let each other's blood, made the offering as my father would have had it made. Not too much blood though: we will need all our strength if we are to survive the journey through the mountains to the land of the tall trees.

Jamieson looked up from the waist-high stone box. 'Francisco! This is an Inca tomb, right? And the Inca buried their children with all that ceremonial shit and treasure, and you told me, you specifically told me, this one had definitely *not* been robbed out. And it's fucking empty. Not even a goddamn feather.'

'Nothing, Senor?' The translator watched Jamieson blandly from the other side of the tomb.

'See for yourself.'

Francisco made no attempt to look inside. 'I have not lied to you, Senor Jamieson.'

'What are you talking about?'

'This tomb was built by the Inca, as I said. And it has not been robbed out, as I said. But it was never used. This is Aymara land, never really part of the Inca empire. The Aymara have their own ways.'

'Inca, Aymara, bloody Egyptians, I don't care who built it, what matters is that it's empty!' Jamieson felt the bile rising in his throat. 'Ugh. Oh, I see. That little story Angelo told us. Meant to be some sort of clue. Very funny. So the joke's on the gringo now, eh?' He glanced around but he couldn't see the old man, and turning his head made him feel dizzy.

Francisco favoured Jamieson with a small self-depreciating shrug. 'He insisted on telling you the history of this place, despite my misgivings. It was a test to see how much attention you were really paying. Not much it seems.'

'So you knew? You knew the tomb was empty and you still let Angelo drag us up here?' He had trusted Francisco. He had paid him a generous advance.

'I did not know for sure. But Angelo told me, and I trust his word.'

'What exactly are you saying here?' Anger was giving way to fear. 'What's your game, Francisco? Wait a minute. No one knows I'm up here. Just the two of you... Jesus. You're going to rob me. Shit. Now listen. I don't have any more money on me. We used it all. In the Misa, see? But back at the hotel – take me back to the La Paz and I can get more money. Lots more money. I'm rich now, much richer than last time. If that's what this is all about, then money is not a problem.' He gulped back the taste of vomit.

'It is not about money, Senor. It is about blood, and honour. If it were simply matter of money then I would have gone to the American Embassy to try and trace you ten years ago.'

'What? What the fuck are you talking about now?' Darkness was eating at the corners of his vision; he gripped the edge of the tomb for support.

'You did not leave us a contact address, but the Embassy might have been able to help. As it was, Rosa would not have it. And after she died bringing your son into the world I adopted him as my own, so your money would not have been welcome.'

'My... son?' He couldn't hold back the nausea any longer. He sank to his knees and heaved up his guts onto the stones. Francisco's words whirled round his head. Rosa had fallen pregnant. It simply hadn't occurred to him. He kept his head down for ten seconds or so after the worst had passed, pressing it against the stone of the tomb, trying to think what he should say. Finally he raised his head and straightened his back. Francisco was still standing on the far side of the tomb, his expression neutral. 'Listen – and you have got to believe me here – the whole thing with your sister was a misunderstanding. I really, genuinely thought she wanted... I misread things badly, at the time. But if I'd had any idea, any idea at all she was... Jesus, I've got a son. That's amazing. Where is he?'

'In my house. As I said, he is part of my family now. He knows of you and, amazingly, does not hate you. You will not meet him, though.'

'Whatever, and I mean whatever, I can do –'

'You can do nothing, Senor.' Francisco almost sounded sorry.

Jamieson heard muttering behind him and started get up. Something heavy dropped onto the back of his calves, pinning his legs to the ground. 'Jesus shit! What the fuck!' There was a blast of foul breath and Angelo's face swum briefly into view. The old man was muttering something under his breath. Jamieson looked up through the tears of pain to Francisco, who had stepped round the tomb.

Francisco said quietly, 'I am sorry about the discomfort. There is a rock on your legs, to keep you still.'

Jamieson just stared at him, taking short hard breaths.

'For whatever reason – global warming or the displeasure of the gods – there has been no rain here for three years. In desperate time we 'primitives' will tend to look for desperate solutions. You are a powerful rich man from a powerful rich nation. You are also, through unhappy accident, part of my family. This makes you perfect.'

'Perfect for what?' panted Jamieson. Then he saw what Francisco was getting out of the pocket of his well-pressed suit. 'Oh shit. You have got to be fucking kidding!'

Francisco handed the razor to Angelo. 'It will be quick, I promise. Angelo is very skilled.'

Over the sound of the old man's chanting Jamieson heard the snick of the razor being opened.

Francisco stepped up to stand beside him. 'Understand that we do not take such steps lightly. Blood alone is normally enough. But in your case there would be questions. And there is the matter of Rosa's honour.'

'For fuck's sake!' Jamieson's voice broke, along with his bladder control. 'You can't perform Inca sacrifices in the twenty first century.'

Francisco laughed mirthlessly then bent down and whispered in Jamieson's ear, 'You haven't listened, have you, Senor? We are not the Inca. The Inca are long gone. We are the Aymara. We have always been here. Our ways endure.'

Angelo laid the blade against his neck. Jamieson screamed, oblivious to the piss running down his leg, reduced to an animal by fear.

The blade was sharp: he hardly felt the cut. Then the blood flowed, and his scream was swallowed up by the mountains.

This story is not, technically, SFF, but it is another example of my interest in pre-Columbian American cultures. Selling it to a prestigious market funded my first trip to the Milford SF Workshop. A couple of years later I actually went to Lake Titicaca and took the (short) guided trip up the mountain where an Aymara shaman performed the Misa for us tourists, most of whom were a little bemused, both by the ritual itself and by this one English woman's unexpected enthusiasm at witnessing it.

What You Came For

The house is halfway up the hill, cantilevered out from the fierce slope on a rotting wooden platform. Since the last legal resident left just after the millennium the garden has rioted through the small plot, shrouding the building in weeds and creepers, nudging at the boundaries separating the house from its respectable neighbours and sending leafy emissaries onto the cracked concrete pavement.

As is your custom, you pause before crossing the threshold. Above, the sky is refreshingly blue. The surrounding hills, clearly visible from this high vantage point, are pleasantly green. The air is pure if a little chill. Despite its fame ('Baldwin Street – the World's Steepest Street') the street is deserted. Perhaps there are more visitors at the weekend.

You step from the pavement onto the short path of naked earth that leads up to the house. Small creatures patter away into the undergrowth at the unexpected intrusion. You pause again, at the three steps on the end of the veranda. To your right, downhill, the tangle of the abandoned garden is all but impenetrable. Though once boarded over, the space below the cantilever will have been made accessible by decay, scavengers, and human curiosity. It will be a dark, fetid place and that makes it a likely location. But you would have to fight your way through the rampant foliage to get to it, so you decide to try the house first.

You step up onto the veranda. The middle step creaks and sags beneath your foot.

Here is the first possibility. Rachel Levinson came to New Zealand with her husband in 1949. They barely survived the Nazi bigotry of World War 2 Europe, and after the war ended they were finally uprooted by a house fire that killed their surviving child. The Levinsons chose to come here, to a new country, as a way of escaping the past. Rachel was far from happy to move to a house made of wood – a combustible, dangerous house – but she deferred to her husband, as ever. Within six months he was dead of tuberculosis, and she was alone. She lived on in the house by herself for thirteen years, quietly looking for someone to blame. She died on this verandah, rocking in her chair, still searching the far side of the valley for reasons, long before the now-wild garden sealed off the view. She did not die happy, but she did die quietly. Not her, then.

You move on. A pair of empty wooden window frames flank the doorway. The front door has been missing for some years, giving free passage into a hallway that stretches through the length of the house, ending in a damp-stained door. You step into the primal reek of decomposing wood. Beneath it are other, fainter, smells: Smoke, rotten food, urine.

You take the first door on the right, an arbitrary choice, and find yourself in the main bedroom.

Now here is someone unexpected. A middle-aged man by the name of Frank Harris. He was, in his own opinion at least, a painter. He had money and ego enough that his inability to make a living by painting did not particularly concern him. He was also a transvestite, back before such things were considered an acceptable lifestyle choice. There, against that wall where the wallpaper now hangs down in mouldy strips, he had his special wardrobe. He kept it locked, even though he rarely had visitors. Frank Harris inhabited a quiet, secret world, spending hours at his dresser, just out of sight of the window, making himself glorious. He had dozens of 'correspondence lovers' as he called them, men he encountered through advertisements in certain magazines. But whenever he left the house he always wore a respectable suit. And he never invited his lovers here, in case reality disappointed him, and shattered his private fantasies. He lived in the house between 1962 and 1973. He did not die here.

Across the hall is the living room, the largest room in the house. The smell of smoke is stronger here and a few charred lumps of wood lie in the cast iron grate. The wallpaper has peeled away from three walls, but on the back wall it is still possible to make out the pattern of flowers, nature pinned flat and bound between vertical lines. The mantle shelf is gone now, but once it held a gold carriage clock, the prize possession of George Marchant and his wife Beth. George and Beth spent their final years in the house. They moved in after Frank Harris left, and, a quarter century later, they died here. Beth went first, to a stroke, bent over a bed of pansies in the garden. She hung on in the cold white hospital for several weeks. George's suffering during those weeks, though short lived, still marks this room. He faded within a year, was ushered into the arms of the state by concerned neighbours, and died in his sleep in another town, in a home that was no home to him. George and Beth were uniquely common. They believed the government, communicated just enough to get along, did their part when required. They expected, and got, small rewards for their simple loyalty. They were the last of a breed now gone from the world. Their suffering was simple, clean and stoical.

You are not here for them.

At the back of the house it is darker and danker, and fungus scabs the walls. There are three doorways, two still with doors in them. You choose the one without a door.

Light seeps through boards covering the window of a small bare room. A nest of woodlice has turned the skirting board into a mush of pulp and splinters. This used to be the dining room, but in 1999 Tom Lawson converted it to a second bedroom. Tom and his wife Elaine, a quiet god-fearing couple, were awaiting the birth of their second child. Their first, James, had died in his sleep in their old house the year before. A blameless accident. One of those things. You move on. The Lawsons moved here, and tried to forget. But when their newborn daughter Mary proved to be a problem child, sleeping no more than two hours at a stretch, the secret thoughts and buried regrets came to the surface, and the love that bound the Lawsons soured. They blamed each other. They blamed their God. They blamed the screaming infant who would not settle, would not stop crying. And one day Mrs Lawson walked out and left the child to cry alone, until her father had her taken into care, and moved away himself, leaving the empty unloved house to decay on its steep hillside.

Jaine Fenn

You leave the dining room and open the door opposite. It creaks and wobbles on its hinges. From the jutting pipes and tiled walls it looks like this used to be the kitchen. A few algae-etched shards of glass hang in the window frame. The room faces upslope, and the foliage, starved of light, has not invaded beyond the sill. Rustlings and occasional bird calls sound from the back garden.

And here is the builder. Or rather, here is the woman he built this house for. A young man called Lawrence Cutler, one of the émigrés who came to New Zealand between the two World Wars, hoping to build a new life for himself. And he did, claiming this less-than-desirable plot of land, building this house with his own hands, and waiting, patiently, to be noticed by a woman who might have him for a husband. In the summer of 1941, he met and married a local girl called Hilda. In the autumn of 1941, he kissed her goodbye, and went to do his duty in the war. And in the spring of 1942, he died in the deserts of North Africa, converted from person to unidentified meat by a misfired mortar from his own side. Hilda, knowing only that he was missing in action, did not give up hope. She waited, keeping the house he had built spotless, keeping his memory alive, until one day she woke up and realised she could wait all her life. She put the house up for sale, moved to Australia, re-married, had children, and died without ever knowing what had happened to her first husband.

Such small, everyday hurts are not your concern. You are after rarer prey.

Only one room left, behind the stained door at the end of the hallway. The door is stiff, half off its hinges, and fungal blooms ooze at the edges of the wood.

This was the bathroom. There is still frosted glass in the window, though pallid tendrils of foliage have crept through the cracks and gaps at the corners. The toilet and sink are gone, but the heavy zinc and enamel bath still sits beside the side wall. The floor is crusted with stained lino, through which rotting planks show like patches of raw skin.

Ah, here he is. Michael Fortune, the last resident of the house, living here illegally for a couple of months after his parents threw him out. He was nineteen. He still lives in town, in a scruffy studio

66

apartment, and he works as a mechanic at the cut-price garage whose roof is just visible from the road outside.

His family was average, his childhood uneventful. He had no excuse. He did have a fertile imagination, an unruly ego and an unquenchable sexual deviancy. Magic, the sort that promises to grant your every wish if you are strong enough to force your will on reality, holds a natural appeal for Michael Fortune.

Her name was Hene O'Hara. She could have been anyone; he didn't know her, though they might have passed each other once on some other street in this small town. She was eleven years old. She loved her parents, hated her appearance, and put up with school. Like most people, she had problems of her own, and she huffed her way to the top of the World's Steepest Street one blustery autumn afternoon to look out over the town and the hills and get a sense of perspective on a life overfilled with homework and parental disputes.

There was no one else on the street that day, either.

He saw her go up the street from the verandah where he sat. This is a dead end street, so he knew she would be back.

Michael Fortune was intoxicated with the possibility of combining pleasure and power. He wasn't smart, but he was clever. So when Hene O'Hara ambled back down the street he called her over – *Hey, wanna see something really cool?* – and when she wandered up the bare earth path he grabbed her and dragged her into the house. He pulled her into the bathroom, this room, where the big zinc bath was still plumbed in. He bound her with cable ties to stop her struggling, and gagged her with masking tape to stop her screaming, and then he did everything he'd ever dreamed of doing. Afterwards, he let the blood drain down the plughole, and used a woodsaw to section the body before burying the pieces in the wild garden.

She took some hours to die: the room stinks of her agony. You imagine that even a human being entering this room would feel the corruption here.

Hene O'Hara's disappearance remains a mystery to most people in this town. There have been no others yet, but even now Michael Fortune is wondering if he should try again. After all, what does he have to lose? He got away with it before. And maybe this time he'll get it right, and after he has indulged his desires he'll get a high that's better than sex, better than chemicals, better than fear: the ecstasy of magic. Last time, he waited all night to feel the rush. But this is not his land; he does not understand how magic works here. The power he craved never came to him.

Instead, a year and a day later, you came.

In a few short breaths you change. You are smaller now, your skin darker, your disobedient black hair pulled back into the ponytail. You wear a grey school pinafore and sensible shoes.

You have what you came for. Now you will act.

You leave the way you came in. The sky is still cloudless blue, the air still clear and chill. The street is still deserted. No one sees you. If anyone did, they might think you looked a bit like that poor girl – what was her name? – who disappeared a year or so back. Mrs O'Hara would know you for her daughter. And Michael Fortune will certainly recognise you.

Briefly.

When people ask writers the inevitable question 'Where do you get your ideas from?' the answer, for me, is often 'from places I visit'. The (main claimant to) the world's steepest street is indeed in New Zealand, and is indeed very steep (I walked all the way to the top) and does indeed have a derelict house halfway up it (or it least it did in 2005, when I visited). This story is also a rare foray into horror, which I'm not massively into, but despite this I think of it as a feelgood tale because just desserts get dealt to someone who deserves it, which so rarely happens in real life.

Death on Elsewhere Street

'You, girl. Stop. Wait there.'

No chance: I'm off. I'm not hanging around to get jacked or beaten on by some topside girl gang. A leap against the tug of gravity, and I'm running for the Street, heading for the safety of the crowds.

Take a sharp left down the next alley. Can't hear anyone behind me – can't hear anything 'cept my own breathing. My legs are starting to burn – won't be able to run for long up here.

One more turn and I'm on Chow Street. Open space, people everywhere, smells of spiced meat and burnt sugar. I was gonna eat here on my way to Elsewhere Street. Change of plan.

I dart through the crowd, cursing and flailing my arms. Get outa the way! Coming round the end of a queue at a sweet-meat bar, I run into a citizen with his face in a bowl of noodles. The impact nearly floors me. His dinner goes flying. As I spin away he shouts after me, 'Bloody downsiders!'

Ahead, a pedicab, stopped. I dash behind it, crouch down and peer back. Plenty of people looking this way, but no one coming after me.

The pedicab starts moving. *City's sake!* There goes my cover. A pair of rollers stare across from their seat on the 'cab as it pulls away, looking at me like I'm gonna to explode or something. I give them a quick grin then turn and slip back into the crowd, hunching low, trying to ignore the pain in my legs. Need to keep topside short, move nice and slow, blend in.

I let the crowd carry me up to the next alley then peel off from the flow into the sidestreets, straightening as soon as I'm out of the light. No food tonight, but at least I'll be early. Jacard'll be late. He's not a bad sort, better than some I've screwed for pleasure or favour, but reliable he ain't.

Someone shouts behind me. Might be nothing to do with me but there's no point taking chances. I break into a run, risking a glance over my shoulder.

Big mistake. My feet go from under me and – splat! – I'm on my back staring up at the big orange sky. Good job the stinky garbage I slipped on gave me a nice soft landing or that would have really hurt. Soon as I can breathe again, I roll over, slowly lever myself up onto all fours, and raise my head.

Before me stands an apparition in black and scarlet.

Aw, fuck. It's an Angel.

'Have you no respect, girl?' Her voice is soft but her gaze is hard.

Shit and Blood, I ran from an Angel. She's gonna kill me. 'I didn't realise... thought you were some smoky cove... tryin' to jack me.' I scrabble to sit up. If I'm gonna die, I'm not doing it on my knees.

'You know your mistake now.' She's pureblood downsider, like me. Tall, slim, large pale eyes and fine white hair. Unlike me she's clean and well-fed, and while I'm decked out in cast-offs she wears a shiny red bodice over a skintight black bodysuit. 'I need you to come with me. To be my witness.' She offers me her hand. Too stunned to argue, I reach up and take it. I've never touched an Angel before. Her palm is cold and hard.

She pulls me to my feet then strides off at a fierce pace. Topside gravity is no problem for her, blessed amongst downsiders, sacred instrument of the will of the people, yadda yadda yadda. As she turns, I notice the narrow black case on a strap over her shoulder. She's on City business. That's what she meant about me being her witness. She needs witnesses to make a removal legal; I don't really follow the Concord, so I couldn't say how many, but it looks like I'm one of them. Great.

When I came topside tonight I'd been thinking how my luck'd finally changed for the better. Jacard was my ticket to a better life. He's got plenty of cred, loads of contacts, and he likes me. Says he's fixed with his new boss for a topside apartment and though we can't live there full time I've always dreamed of having a place to stay up here. A chance to sleep somewhere with a door that can be locked and neighbours who don't want to eat me would be top prime. Jacard was going to meet me in The Vision Tree and take me to see the place. If I don't show he might decide I'm not worth the effort. He'll never believe I got commandeered by an Angel.

After a few steps the Angel stops and looks back at me. Her eyes glitter like she's upset, stoned, crazy, maybe all three. Scared, I freeze, but then she makes a small noise of irritation, turns and carries on. All right, Lady, I'm coming, keep your spurs on. We don't all have City juju in our bones to help us deal with the gravity up here.

After that she slows her pace, and I just about manage to keep up, stumbling along at her shoulder while she leads me through the backstreets. She's heading for Elsewhere Street, which suits me fine, but it's not what I expected; I thought we'd be off to the State Quarter. Still, I'm sure some politicos like to hang out in the Leisure Quarter, and I don't think there's anything in the Concord about where they have to be killed. I'd ask her about the hit but she doesn't look to be in the mood for talking. At least no one's going to mug me now, not when I'm with an Angel.

By the time we reach Elsewhere Street I've got used to the ache in my legs. I heard somewhere that we downsiders came from topside stock, back before my ancestors took to living in the vanes and nets under the City. Given the way some of us make a living there's probably a bit of topside blood in all of us. Whatever the reason, once I get into my stride the pain eases off a bit.

There's a glow at the end of the alley. We're almost at Elsewhere Street. It's a quiet Street, but bright as any in the Leisure Quarter.

The Angel stops at an intersection where another sidestreet runs off our alley. We're still ten meters from the Street. 'You know this area, girl?'

I nod. It's here then.

'So do I.'

I hear the threat: I'm not stupid.

'Go round the corner into the Street. Cross over, walk along a ways, then come back to this side. Go into the next alley up and come back down this sidestreet. You understand?'

'Aye, Lady. Er, what am I looking for?'

She smiles tightly. 'Anything you think should concern me.'

I've never seen a removal, but I thought they were pretty formal affairs; failed politicians getting their just reward from an Angel while the coves and rollers politely applaud and bet on exactly how the poor bastard will take the fall. This seems too casual. Messy even. But I do as she says.

The alleyway running up to the Street is clear. No windows overlooking it and no one there. I saunter out into the holograms and crowds of Elsewhere Street. You get a better class of punter here than on some Streets; there are still a few burn-outs who've decided to sink into their own version of reality near the source, but they're just human litter, they don't bother anyone.

I'm a fair way out from The Vision Tree: I can barely make out their logo above the crowds. They have a tree that looks just like the real ones in the Gardens, with weird shaped fruits on it. The fruits are flatscreens, showing the fun to be had within.

I take care crossing the Street; lots of pedicabs here. This ain't a sightseers' Street, not like Soft or Groove. Here the pleasure to be had is in your head, and you just take the quickest route to get to there. The most popular parlours and bars have queues.

One of the net-heads against the wall looks up and mumbles something as I pass, but when I stop and reach for my blades he holds his hands out, smiling and drooling. No idea what Street his mind is on.

Wish I knew what's making the Angel so jumpy. Anything that worries an Angel should sure as shit be worrying me.

I cross back. I'm dodging against the main flow of the crowd now, but most people get out of my way. Citizens think we're scum; they live here, and they know how we envy them their nice safe topside world. For the rollers – tourists here for the fun and danger – the lethal romance of the Angels reflects on all downsiders. Same result either way – no one hassles me.

The alleyway feels too narrow and dark after the glare of Elsewhere Street. My mouth goes dry: paranoia must be catching. This is where she wants me to go, so go I do. Halfway down, a sudden movement makes me jump. Just a rat. Still, I'm glad to reach the other end of the alley.

The Angel is leaning against the wall. She watches me approach. 'Well?'

'It's not that crowded. I didn't see anything odd.'

She looks annoyed. What did she expect? It's not like I know what I'm meant to be looking for.

She steps forward, puts her hands under my arms and suddenly we're shooting upwards. I gawk at her chin and swallow my words.

She kicks, we go sideways, and she drops me. I claw the air, but I'm only half a meter above a solid surface. My legs fold, and I sprawl onto a flat roof. She touches down and looks around while I gulp my guts back down my throat.

I'd like to stay where I am but she gestures for me to stand. 'Watch the back and sides of the building. When I'm set I'll not be able to pay attention there. When you pass the front stay away from the parapet.'

I stare dumbly at her. My body hasn't recovered from being flown up here yet.

'Do you understand?' Her eyes look huge.

I pull myself upright. 'Aye, Lady.'

Ignoring me again, she sits back on her heels, swings the case round onto her lap, and opens it. I decide to take a walk. The people in the Street look weird from up here, just heads and feet. Most of the holo ads play below the level of the roof, and whole sections of the crowd are lit up in colour. There's a holo generator up here, and other stuff I don't recognise. No obvious way down, though.

'What are you called, girl?'

I look back at her. She has her gun assembled now. 'My name? You want to know my name?' Telling her my name makes things too real, too personal.

'Aye, child. Your name.' She picks up the gun and stands. Every Angel customises her gun. This one has a heavy-looking barrel, though the stock is a silver framework, decorated and fancy. The finger-pads are marked in silver.

'My name is Geal, Lady.'

'Geal.' She says my name as though it seals a bargain. 'I want you to remember this, Geal. Remember what you see today.'

I nod. Doubt I'll be able to forget it.

'I am the Angel Thiera. I am thirty years old. As an agent of the Concord, I have taken sixteen lives, never once knowing why they must die or who they really were.' She grimaces and glances down at her gun. 'I'm worshipped for that.'

Not by me she's not. Angels are the chosen – enhanced, privileged and respected – but I've always been happy to avoid them.

She walks to the front of the roof and kneels down, holding the gun casually under one arm. Fascinated despite myself, I move over to stand behind her. She's focused on her task and doesn't notice. She lays the gun across her folded legs and bows her head briefly, then lifts the weapon and kneels up, slipping the barrel onto the parapet. She focuses down the sight. I follow her gaze.

On the far side of Elsewhere Street, near the net-heads, something is going down. Two groups, about half a dozen in each group, are approaching each other purposefully. The figures are distorted by the holos, but one group look like rollers – taller than citizens and dressed weird but smart. The other lot are coves in sharp suits, a second walking half a pace behind the main man, flanked by a pair of downsider guards. I recognise one of the guards. It's Jacard.

This is no faceless politician. This is someone I know. She can't kill someone I know.

I throw myself at the Angel. Her shoulders are tense, fingers already over the firing pads. At the last moment she sees me and pulls to one side. Her hands leave the firing pads.

That's all it takes.

There's no sound: Angels' guns are silent. They fire invisible light, light that burns. The first sign that she has fired is a screech from below.

I stagger past her. She stands. She's looking in shock and fury. The gun is still pointed down into the Street.

There's a popping noise and something above us explodes in a shower of sparks. She ducks and returns fire. Her gun is an assassin's weapon, not designed for a stand-up fight. She presses her fingers to the firing pads and releases, sweeping the gun across in front of her in a slow arc.

More screams. No more shots.

I'm frozen, stunned. Will she just keep firing until the screaming stops, till everyone is dead?

She steps back from the parapet and holds the gun out at arm's length. She looks at it in disgust, like it did the killing, not her. Then she drops it. The gun falls with a clatter. She turns to face me.

'Look what you made me do.' Her expression is twisted, but her voice is small and quiet.

I scramble to my feet and fumble for the knives at my wrist.

She laughs, a low, hollow sound, and takes a step back, delicate as a dancer. Then she flicks her wrists forward.

From the front of her wrists blades protrude: thin, gleaming, metallic, nearly as long as her forearm. My blades are no more than a child's pathetic copy of her weapons.

I'm gonna die now.

'Enough.'

The voice comes from behind her. We both freeze. Her eyes don't leave my face but the laugh becomes a snarl.

'I said, "Enough".' The speaker floats above the back of the roof. Another Angel. She's shorter than Thiera, a dark-haired half-breed, dressed in a one piece black suit with a pattern of scarlet lines at neck and wrist. I recognise her; she used to live near me. Her name is Nual; she has a perfect record – over a dozen clean kills – and a reputation for knowing stuff without being told.

Thiera gives me a look of cold contempt. Without turning she says, 'I thought it was you following me. I'd have to do more than take to the Streets to shake you.' She sounds calmer than she looks.

Nual says softly, 'You've killed a lot of people today, Thiera.'

'Aye,' she moves her head slightly to indicate me, 'Thanks to this stupid bitch. All I wanted was to make a difference. To kill one who deserved it, for once.'

'I'll not deny that. But he was still a citizen, an important one. And you killed without orders. That makes you rogue.'

'So it does.' She inclines her head and turns slowly, spurs still out. The other Angel says nothing, as though she knows words won't help any more. Below us, someone is shouting for help.

'You're going to call feud on me then?'

Nual nods reluctantly. 'I have no choice.'

'So be it.' There is triumph in Thiera's voice. Without waiting for a response, she leaps for Nual's throat.

Nual throws her arms up to deflect Thiera's attack. The impact spins them round and flings them off the roof. They hurtle across the alleyway and hit the far wall in a tangle of limbs. Thiera kicks back off the wall, trying for the distance to swing her blades again.

Nual bounces after her, but Thiera gets her knee free and kicks Nual into the wall.

Nual must be stunned: she still doesn't have her spurs out.

It looks like Thiera has her cold, but then Nual drops out of sight. Thiera follows her. I run up to the parapet to see them clash again, one storey below.

Thiera fights wildly, fiercely, trying to get space to stab or slash her opponent. Nual stays close, concentrating on parrying the other Angel's blades; her own weapons are still not out. Unmodified, her hands would have been cut to ribbons by now.

The alley's too narrow, and they bounce off walls, spinning and flailing, falling steadily, too busy fighting to concentrate on flying.

Thiera punches her knee into Nual's stomach and throws herself backwards. She kicks off the far wall as she touches it, heading back across the alley while Nual gasps for air. Thiera comes straight at her, arms out. As she hurtles forward, she sweeps her arms back. Nual raises her hands as though to catch her. There is a flash of metal. Thiera hits her full on, and they slam into the far wall.

I expect movement but they just hang there, unmoving, faces close enough for a kiss. Then Thiera's head droops to one side. Nual glances up at me and closes her eyes. They start to fall, slowly.

When they reach the ground Thiera sags in Nual's arms. Nual follows her down, lowering the other woman to the ground. As she stands I see the darker stain over the red of Thiera's bodice, catch the quick motion as Nual flicks her blade back into her arm. She bends down to close Thiera's eyes before kicking upwards.

I shrink back from the parapet, but Nual steps onto the edge and holds out a hand in invitation. The other hand, by her side, drips red.

I can't go near her. I hold my own hands out in a futile gesture of innocence. 'I... I never wanted to hurt anyone. Please.' There are noises from the Street below, bad noises, death noises. She should kill me for interfering, for causing this. But I have to try and explain myself first. 'I thought she was trying to kill... someone I know. I couldn't allow that. I made her shoot wild. Then she shot again. As if it didn't matter any more. I'm sorry.' Pitiful excuse. My whole body is shaking: I feel like I could fall apart at any moment.

'You were trying to save your lover.' She states it as bald fact.

'Aye, Lady. But...' I force myself to walk over to the parapet. I have to know. If she won't punish me then I have to do it myself. She doesn't stop me. I look down. Most of those who can still walk are gone, though a few are helping others get clear of the carnage, crouching low, looking around fearfully. They have no idea where death came from, no way of knowing if it will come again. At least two dozen are dead or beyond help. Some have obvious wounds, some have parts missing, some are apparently intact. There isn't as much blood as I'd expected.

Jacard is lying face up near the middle of the Street, one hand outstretched, eyes open. The only sign of the wound that killed him is a thin burn across the front of his shirt. I feel desolate, mourning not just for Jacard, but for the whole gross stupidity of it.

'It is done. It cannot be undone. Come here.'

I look at her sharply, in case this is the death I deserve, but she's just offering me a way down. I go to her, and she puts an arm around my waist and lifts me from the roof. Where my hand brushes her clothes it comes away red. For a moment I think I'm gonna puke, but we drop quickly, and she lets me go as soon as my feet touch the ground.

She crouches down beside Thiera, laying one hand on the bloody breast. I gesture at the body. 'W-Why...?' I stutter, not sure what I'm asking.

Nual looks up at me and says, 'For some Angels there comes a time when the killing becomes repugnant, or worse, necessary. And we all need ways to evade the ghosts of our victims. Thiera had been flirting with chemical oblivion for some time. When the drugs got the better of her, she tried to break the addiction. She failed. So, she chose to cut the problem off at the source. To save herself, and maybe others. She wanted you here to witness her attempt at redemption, knowing that was all the memorial she would get.'

For the first time in my life, I see Angels as people. Not as minions of the City, not as goddesses, but people who had to live with what they did. As I'd have to live with what I had done. Thiera had done the right thing, in the end. Assuming she'd succeeded. 'The dealer, is he dead?' I whisper.

'No.' Her eyes, darker than any I've ever looked into, hold my gaze for a moment. Then she looks away, puts her hands under Thiera's body and lifts the dead Angel carefully. Thiera's head rests on her shoulder, like a sleeping child.

Somehow it doesn't seem right that the one person who *should* have died today is still breathing.

I walk past her, into the aftermath. The Street is deserted; even the surviving net-heads have gone. I smell burnt flesh, but at least the screams have stopped. Eventually the baton-boys will arrive and clear up the mess. I'll be long gone by then.

I'm not shaking any more. I am filled with purpose.

The dealer is easy to spot, by his clothes, by the way the dead cluster around him. He's leaning up against the wall, hunched over an arm burnt to the bone, moaning softly to himself. No need to hurry; he ain't going nowhere.

I stop beside Jacard's body.

I didn't love Jacard. Love is dangerous, and I'll live longer if I avoid it. But I liked him. I almost trusted him. I certainly didn't wish him dead.

When I bend down to close my lover's eyes the skin is already cold. All that life, all that possibility: nothing but meat.

There's something wrong with my eyes. I look up, blinking to clear my vision.

The dealer's noticed me. He looks up and calls out, 'Hey you! Come here. That's right. Over here.'

I straighten, and without speaking, without looking back at Jacard's body, I go across to him. His gaze says he thinks I'm simple, or maybe in shock. I squat next to him. He doesn't notice what my hands are doing.

One of his thugs died inconveniently, pinning his legs. He pushes at the body with his undamaged arm, a mime I'm meant to pick up on. 'That's it, help me shift this thing. If you get me to a medic there'll be a reward for you, girl.' He's not paying attention to me. He's in pain, and I'm just some downsider joygirl. When I don't follow his instructions, he glances up. His eyes track sudden movement, and he opens his mouth to cry out.

Then my knife is in his eye. Someone told me that once: on an incapacitated foe, go for the eye. A sure killer with a thin blade, and less messy than the throat.

He makes a noise between a hiss and a snort and raises his good hand, flailing weakly. I move back a little, to keep out of the way. After a few moments his mouth gapes and he stops moving.

I pull the blade from his eye; blood and nasty clear stuff comes with it. He's meat too now. The good and the bad, all meat in the end.

I've never killed before today – always preferred to talk or fuck my way out of trouble – but I had to finish the job Thiera started, to make her death mean something. This scumbag won't be bringing any more of his shit into my City. I wipe my blade on the arm of his suit, then stand.

The Angel Nual is watching me from the mouth of the alley, her dead sister cradled in her arms. I nod to her and re-sheaf my knife. As I turn to go she gives a small, sad smile, and takes to the air.

In some ways this is the oldest story in this collection. I started exploring the idea of the place that become Khesh City, a democracy by assassination where the law is enforced by flying cybered assassins, off the back of my cyberpunk obsession while in my early twenties. This was one of the first stories I wrote set in what became the Hidden Empire universe, though the first version garnered a sufficiently scathing rejection from Interzone that I gave up trying to write fiction for several years as a result. I came back to this story after having actually learnt how to write, and made a better job of it, and it's since sold and been reprinted multiple times.

Fear Not Heaven's Fire

Despite my good intentions, I have sinned, Lord. I have spoken to a man.

It was this morning, soon after Prime. I had run out of wool, and the other sisters were in the fields, taking advantage of the early spring to sow corn and beans. They would not have known if I had just let the distaff drop and sat idle in the sun, but I try to be good, truly I do. So I went to fetch more wool. I felt my way along the stones of the church, out of the cloister then crossed the outer court to the granary. The sounds around me told me the wind was shifting: the trees were restless, and I could no longer hear the sheep on the hill.

As I edged back down the granary steps I heard something. I thought it must be a stray goat or sheep, broken through the fence into the outer court, so I stopped at the bottom of the steps and waited for it to give itself away. After the initial rustle, there was silence, and I walked on. Then I heard a small sound of pain, quickly stifled. It came from under the granary. I turned and went back to stand by the steps. I could feel the chill on my legs where the wind blew through the open space under the granary floor.

'Is someone there?'

No answer. Perhaps only an animal, then. But I was not sure.

Remembering how one with sight would react, I twisted the unspun wool into a tight knot within my skirts, then bent down to put my head below the level of the raised floor. The breeze blew the smell of damp earth and rotting corn into my face. Someone shifted in response to my movement, and now that I had my ear at their level I could locate the person by sound. They were in the corner, against the hurdling that protects the space below our food store from the worst of the rough weather that blows in from the north and west.

'I will not hurt you.' I did not think as I spoke how little threat a blind nun might be.

'Please, I need water.' The voice was weak, but male. Somehow I had not thought it would a man. Yet this man had the sweetest voice I have ever heard. Even parched and in pain, it was a voice better suited to singing than talking. The sound of it made me dizzy, and I reached up with my free hand to steady myself against the steps.

'It...' I tried to remember myself, to stay calm. 'It is our duty to help all God's creatures.' He made a sound then, something like a snort, but I carried on. 'Please, come out and I will try and find the almoner. She will give you food and water.

'No. I can't come out... into the light.' He sounded afraid.

'You are hurt?'

'Yes. No. I am... resting. Hiding.'

From the law? We had offered sanctuary to fugitives before, though the Thane's men were apt to disregard the sanctity of hallowed ground when it suited them. 'You will be safe here. Let us tend your ills...'

'I am not badly hurt. But... can you bring something to drink?'

'Of course. But will you not come out?'

'I cannot.'

I straightened and turned. I knew I should go and tell the others about our guest. But they were in the fields; they would be back soon enough, I could tell them then. So I went to the refectory, filled a pitcher with small beer, and carried it back to the granary.

When I returned I leant down and balanced the pitcher against one of the stone columns that support the granary floor. I could hear nothing of our visitor, though I was sure he was still there.

'How did you lose your sight?'

The loudness of his voice startled me; he had moved forward to the front of his shelter.

I started and sat back on my heels. 'A foolish accident.' I was not used to hearing compassion from the lips of men. It disconcerted me.

82

'Ah.' He saw the lie, his voice said it. But he did not pursue the matter. I heard him reach out, heard the scrape of pottery against stone as he took the jug. For a moment I felt a strange warmth, and smelt something other than damp and rot, something like honey or blossom.

'Will you come to the almoner now?' I asked over the sounds of him slaking his thirst.

He made a sound of appreciation, somewhere between a sigh and a smacking of the lips, and when he spoke his voice was stronger. 'No. It would not be… appropriate.'

'But men are forbidden here, other than those being given healing or charity. If you are in need of either we can provide them. But I cannot leave you here alone in the dark. '

'I am cursed.' For the first time his voice faltered. 'I-if you could see me you would run from me.'

I thought of the rare times when strangers had come to us, and how I had heard in their voices, and felt in their movements, the disgust at the ugly ruin of my face. There had been no such sign from him. 'I understand. But…' I let my voice trail away: I was not sure what I should do.

'I do not want to cause you trouble. If you would bring food and ale for a day or so, until I am stronger, then I will move on.' He sounded desolate, as though he had nowhere to go, no aim or goal or hope.

I wanted to comfort him, yet I stayed where I was. I know my vows well enough. 'Yes. It would be un-Christian to do otherwise.'

I heard him move back into the depths under the floor. 'And I am sure you are a good Christian.'

Was that mockery in his voice? Sometimes I imagine too much. 'We are a house of God here.'

'And what is your name, little sister of God?'

'Elfleda.' As I spoke, the chapel bell rang, summoning me to Terce.

I heard him turn away. 'Go to your prayers, Elfleda.'

I have not told them yet. You have heard the words formed as I sat in Terce. You know my heart, Lord. I could not concentrate on my devotions, but I have formed my confession. I will tell my sisters later, when the time is right. They are busy now.

After the others returned to the fields I took bread to him. It was my food: I am permitted a greater share of the priory's meagre wealth, on account of my infirmity, but I rarely take it. Food is a base thing, a sign of weakness. If I were truly pure I would not need it at all; I could live on the word of God, and the light of the sun. But of course I am not truly pure.

He asked me to stay while he ate, and though I should not have, I sat on the earth under the granary with him. He kept his distance, and I felt no threat from him. I could smell his sweet scent over the dark smells of the earth. He asked about life in the cloister, and about my devotion to God. He seemed to find such devotion strange, and I asked him if he was not a Christian. He certainly had a strange accent, and if he were – God forbid – a northman, he might also be a Pagan.

'I lost my faith.' His reply shocked me, and allowed for no further discussion.

Other than this admission he showed no desire to talk about himself or how he came to be here. When I asked his name he said I could call him John, if I wished, as though he did not much care what I called him. I admit, Lord, that I found a certain pleasure in speaking to him, in holding his interest. I do not know what category of Sin that might fall into, but as you who see all must know, I defended my faith, and my calling, and made no improper remarks or gestures. But when I told him of the priory's holdings, of our small parcel of land, he said, 'So fertile ground is precious, no?'

'Of course. We praise the miracle of life and food coming from the soil.'

'What of this soil, then?' I heard him thump the ground, and felt the fine vibrations of his touch on the earth.

'I do not understand.'

'This soil, through no fault of its own, is hidden. The sun never reaches it. It never brings forth fruit. Is that not a terrible waste?'

Again that tone of mockery. This time I knew what he mocked. Anger rose up in me. 'Do you think we are fools for denying our flesh?'

'I did not say that.'

'But it is what you meant. If you have lapsed in your faith, that is not my fault. My faith is strong.'

'Your faith in a virgin, and a God you cannot touch? What of your faith in people, Elfleda?' I heard him shift.

'People are fallible. They sin.'

'And did you ever forgive those who sinned against you?'

I recoiled slightly, not only from his words but from his hand, which he had raised to my face. I felt his heat, as though I had walked into an unexpected shaft of sunlight. 'I remember them in my prayers.'

'That is not what I asked.'

'You cannot know...' The nearness of his touch burned me, took away words and reason.

'Then tell me. They were men, yes? More than one?'

'Yes. I do not wish to speak of it.' Now, feeling his warmth go through me, I most certainly did not want to speak of it.

'I am sorry Elfleda. I did not mean to cause you pain. You should go.'

'Yes.' As I sat back I felt the boards of the granary floor above me brush my head through my veil. How I had loved such places as a child. At that moment I remembered something I had not recalled for many years; once, when I was perhaps five or six, I had lain on the earth alone in my den in the woods, and wriggling out of my clothes had spread mud on myself like an animal. Deciding not to put mud in one particular place I had, instead, explored it with my fingers, feeling my own warm moisture and a thrilling pleasure, a whole new world of simple joy.

I felt my face grow hot, and turned to leave. 'I will return this evening.'

I have been dozing in the sun at the south side of the cloister, out of sight of the others. When I have spun enough to earn my keep, I sometimes allow myself this luxury.

But while I slept my body betrayed me. Of course we sometimes wake in the night, full of foul desires. It is a temptation all flesh must bear. But to have them visit me here, in the light! He makes a fool of me. I must tell the prioress about our visitor. I will tell her tonight. I must. And tomorrow when we confess our sins, I will ask formal forgiveness, Lord, for letting my base nature take its course, for not holding back the hand that snaked by itself into my clothes, and felt my secret places, for not stopping its foul beating until I gasped out loud. And for seeing light as I did it, seeing the light that I know comes from the man beneath the granary.

I will confess, do penance, and be absolved.

I went back that evening. I did wonder, as I walked to the granary as though drawn by an invisible cord, whether he had bewitched me. I decided to confront him with my fears before the heat of his presence stole my will.

I put down the pitcher and plate, then asked quickly, before my nerve failed me, 'Are you a demon?'

He laughed, and his laughter was like falling water. There was no offence in it. How could I have such wicked thoughts of one who had such an innocent laugh? 'Not at all! And I will not trouble you for much longer, if you do not want me to.'

'Perhaps that would be best.' I sat down and shuffled into the shade with him. I was very aware of my women's parts, the small stickiness there. Perhaps he could smell the sin I had committed alone in the sunlight. Perhaps I wanted him to.

'Is it a good life, here?' He conversed as though we were friends at a social gathering, not a woman sworn to chastity and a strange man hiding under a building.

'It is easy enough, compared to those who must make their way in the outside world. And I have my faith.'

'Which I envy you.' Such talk made me uncomfortable. I shifted backwards a little, to be out of his heat. 'I am sorry, little sister. I am just curious and unused to your ways.'

'I should get back...'

'I would like to repay your kindness, Elfleda.'

'Charity is a virtue. I try to be virtuous.'

'Still, I would like to help you.'

'I have everything I need.'

'You know that is not true. Firstly, you do not have your sight. That was taken from you, wasn't it?'

'Yes.' I prayed he would not ask me how. I would have to tell him, if he asked.

His voice dropped to a whisper, yet it was loud in my ears. 'And you are not... complete. I cannot see how it is right to abstain from pleasures which God gave us the capacity to feel. That was my error. To question the virtue of denial.'

I thought I must have misheard him. 'What do you mean?'

'Is denial of pleasure such a good thing? Must you be sorry for doing what feels natural to you, and harms none?'

O Lord, I forget that others have sight! Had he crept out and watched while I abused myself? Had he seen my evil hand at its work?

Of course not. He would have had to leave his sanctuary and risk being seen by the others. 'Some pleasures are God's gift. Others are the Evil One's temptations. I know the difference well enough.' I felt shame at the superior tone of my voice.

His voice had that mocking note again. 'Of course you do.' Then he sighed. 'Are you afraid of me, Elfleda?'

An odd thing to ask, though I was glad of the change of subject. 'No, I am not.' And it was true. He held no fear for me, only fascination. Sinful fascination.

'Would you let me help you, then?'

'I am not sure what you are asking of me.'

'Let me give you what you lack.' He had come closer again. I should move away, I knew it, but I could not. His hand startled me, but he just rested his fingertips lightly on my forehead, nothing more. I felt his warmth, and smelt flowers and musk. 'Men betrayed you. I am... a man. I would like to undo some of the harm done. Think of it as a last act of kindness from one entering damnation.'

His words made no sense, but all I cared about was his presence. I stretched my neck to him like a cat, leaning into his touch. My stomach fluttered and I felt the arm supporting me start to give way.

'No –' I murmured, and shook my head.

'The choice is yours, child.' His touch withdrew. 'This time, the choice is yours.' I heard him move back into his dark sanctuary.

I fled.

I knew then that I could not tell the prioress, could not tell another living person about the visitor; for my face would betray me, and they would see the longing I tried without success to hide.

Night is the time of temptations, the bridegroom's hour. Once I had a real bridegroom. I was promised to a man of flesh and blood. I had seen how he looked at me, how my passing stopped his words. The Thane's son, looking at a girl of low status. I was sure Alfric loved me, and the difference in status would not matter. I was such a fool. I took his gifts, flirted with him, held the image of him behind my eyes when I pleasured myself. I would have given him joy, and sons, and even obeyed him, mostly. But no, he could not wait. Rather than let me give freely he had to take for himself.

They came at night, four of them, Alfric and three of his friends. They made no noise, and they stopped my mouth. But they did not cover my eyes. I had always seen well in the dark, and I knew them. As they held me down I saw their profiles, and I knew them. One of his friends must have seen the look on my face as he leant back after sating himself; he whispered, 'She can see us!'. Alfric gave a low laugh and murmured, 'Then we'll be the last thing the bitch sees', and reached back for something. Such pain, such white burning pain, as the lime burnt into me! Shame and pain, that was all there was for a while.

The raiders from the north are such monsters, said the villagers. To come among us in the night and deflower a virgin child, then blind her. Of course, no one would believe my version of the night's events. Not even my mother believed me, and she sent me here to the priory for my own safety, in the end.

So what should have been pleasure became pain. If I remember that night at all I recall fear and betrayal. I try not to recall the worst of it: that if they had not thrown the lime in my face I would not have told anyone what they did. I would have let them have me, because to fight would make them harm me more, and to comply would make them think they had power over me. But really I would have power over them. Despite their inexpert fumbling and grunting they did not really hurt me. They were rough, certainly, but I already knew how to take pleasure where I found it, and the thrill of making them into undignified fools before my womanhood was a wicked joy to me. If only they had not seen me watching them, seen the recognition in my eyes. I knew them for what they were, animals at the mercy of their lust. They saw that, and they could not stand to be looked at in that way.

I open my eyes. I feel the lids part, and see the pre-dawn sky out of the dormer window.

I am dreaming. I have my sight again, therefore this must be a dream.

I sit up, my head swimming, then stand, seeing the faint grey outlines of the world around me. Yes, a dream. If it is a dream then I cannot help my actions. We are blameless in our dreams.

I pull my cloak on and walk between the beds of my sleeping sisters. The wooden floor feels real enough beneath my bare feet. After two steps I am afraid; I can see them, so they will see me. I close my eyes. Now I am in a familiar place. But as I reach the door and the chill of the pre-dawn air seeps into me it all becomes too real, and I must open my eyes again, and return to the dream.

From here, I can see two buildings. Ahead, the granary. To the left, along the cloister, the chapel. Their dark shapes loom like choices. Well, I still have my faith. Even in dreams, I am the bride of Christ, though he is a cold and distant lover. For that thought alone I might be damned, if I were not dreaming.

Mud oozes beneath my toes, and I trail my hand along the outside cloister wall as I pass. It would be easier if I closed my eyes. I know where I am without my sight. But that would shatter the dream. The chapel door is heavy, and it creaks. I walk up the altar, barely lit by the vigil flame. I cross myself and kneel to wait for the grace of God, but it is not my heart or soul that is filled with the love of Christ. It is a lower part, a baser part. The longer I kneel, the stronger the warmth becomes and the less I can concentrate. I pray with my eyes open, fearful of losing the dream. Then I realise that I am not alone. Movement out of the corner of my eye. I ignore it for a while, but the burning will not abate, so I stand and turn.

There is a pale figure in the aisle behind me. He wears rags, though once his robes were white as heaven's grace. I see paleness behind him, and I know the truth.

Now is the final choice. I can dismiss him, and wake myself up. I can lock my womanhood away forever. If I close my eyes I will not see him, and he must go.

But it is no choice, really. I know myself truly now, in this dream. I go to him. Everything is silent, as though I had traded my blindness for deafness. The air is cold but his touch is the fire of the sun, flaring through every part of me. His arms enfold me and his wings re-furl themselves to hide us. How can this be wrong?

For a while he lets me bask in his touch. But I want more of him. I must complete his fall. No longer God's virgin, now I am God's harlot. I take his hand and pull it to my sex. He smiles and closes his eyes. I am giving pleasure to an angel!

We sink to the floor, kneeling at first, his hand still on me. Such fire, probing me! Waking what has slept for too long. I lean back, knowing I cannot fall. He lowers me to the flagstones. As he leans down to kiss me the feathers of one wing dip and brush my arm. This I have renounced? This I have given myself to God for? I am a fool, when God's own messenger can come to me now, like this!

We are told that angels are beyond the flesh, neither male nor female, but through his tattered robe I see that this creature is certainly a man.

I remember the boys' rough hands and their ungainly little pricks. They were nothing: this is how it is meant to be. I lift my shift and guide him into me. At once I am filled with light, his light. Now, at last, I close my eyes, to contain the light within me. I would cry out but for fear of waking myself.

There is a time of light, of desperate joy, and my only thought is how like beasts we are, and how this is a good thing, as God made the animals too. And it appears that even angels are animals. No grunt and fuss from this celestial creature though. He is intense, and, it seems, a little surprised to discover that pleasure is so simple to achieve.

I would not stop until I have completely had my fill of him, but finally he pulls free of me, and I feel the stone floor and the chill night air again. 'Don't go yet,' I say, the first words I have spoken in my dream.

He takes no notice, just stands up and murmurs, 'My fall is complete.' Then he turns and leaves without a backward glance. He moves painfully, slowly, like a wounded beast. He will not get far. I fall back and rest a while, but the stone floor is cold and rough, so I get up. My thighs are damp with the unctions of an angel. I turn back to the altar, where the vigil flame and the cross look down on me. I feel a sense of elation, and release, and no shame at all.

I wait, eyes on the cross, for God's wrath, but it does not come. So, then, this is Your will. My gaze leaves the cross, drawn to the vigil light, and I know what I must do.

He gave me what I needed. Now I must give him what he needs.

I wake to fuss and shouting. One of the other sisters tells me to be still. There has been a fire, she says, but the church is safe. We take the first office of the day as though nothing has happened. The smell of burning fills my nose.

We have confession. The priest talks to the prioress in whispers; we strain to hear as we kneel and wait our turn. I have little to confess, other than a brief night temptation. What cannot happen did not happen.

But as I stand and leave, I see brightness in the centre of my vision, and when I walk into the sunlight the space behind my eyes pulses red where the shadow of the cloister falls across my face. I pull my veil closer, and keep my gaze down.

While I sit and spin, the darkness and light resolve themselves, and after a while I can see the outline of the spindle. I run out of wool just after Sext, and walk to the granary to get more wool, half expecting it still to be standing. It is not, of course.

At the ruins of the building I squint at the broken, charred timbers. My sight is almost perfect now: his promise was not idle. He did indeed restore me to what I was. He gave me my vision back, and, for a while, he made me a whole woman again. Though it was at the cost of the last of his grace, poor fallen creature. He was not happy here, in the purgatory of our world. He was neither pure enough for heaven nor base enough for hell.

Seeing brightness in the ruins I bend down to pick up a feather. It is blackened and scorched along one side, but where the fire has not touched it, it is perfect white.

My sisters have already moved the body and will bury it tomorrow, in hallowed ground. They know nothing of their poor dead visitor, which is as it should be. Just an unlucky trespasser, they will say. They would not be strong enough to comprehend the truth, because they, unlike me, have not known what it is to be complete. And they, unlike me, have not been permitted to sit in judgement on an angel.

I release the feather; the wind catches it for a moment before dropping it back into the mud.

I did right, Lord, did I not?

Perhaps unfairly, I think of this as 'the wanking nun story', a profane bit of levity meant to dilute the uneasy taste it can leave. Leaving aside the twisted sexual stuff, this story comes from an old obsession with the interaction of the human and the divine – especially with angels in the traditional sense – and a prurient interest in the strange excesses that can occur in cloistered communities.

High Ground

On the second day they brought me food, and I wondered if I might live.

When they had first captured me, they'd taken me to an interrogator. He wore a good suit and rested his elbows on the edge of a scratched wooden table. He asked my name and rank, which I provided. He did not react to finding a noble serving as a common soldier. He moved onto questions I could not answer about orders, troop movements, plans, intentions. Occasionally he looked away from my face to catch the eye of one of the guards behind me.

Though I had resolved to be brave, fear beat at my temples. I recalled barracks-room tales of pulled nails, bruised bodies, peeled skin. Soon he would summon a guard or reach down for the black case containing the instruments of his trade.

Except, nothing happened. He just paused after asking each question, giving me time to answer. I began to relax and notice details: how my interrogator usually looked at the right-hand guard; the way the shadows wavered as the light above us moved in the breeze; how the scratches on the table all went one way, reminding me of fingernails dragged over the wood. I found myself impressed that my interrogator remembered so many questions without referring to notes. Eventually my stomach began to rumble; I had not eaten since the previous afternoon when my unit set off for its ill-fated mission.

When he reached the end of the questions the guards marched me to a cell. Here, I fell into a trance, becoming a numb speck in a stone box. I drank from the jug and relieved myself in the bucket but I felt nothing. As good as dead. Sometimes I thought dully of how my death would be received: my mother's tears, my father's fury. My beautiful Angia, elegant in her mourning robes, accepting condolences from strangers.

Eventually I drifted into uneasy sleep. I woke with the panic of a recollected nightmare, yet on discovering my dream was true, slid back into numbness. I accepted my fate. Our unit had failed in its mission. I should embrace my inevitable death with courage and dignity. Still, it irritated me that I must endure stomach cramps for what remained of my life.

When the door opened I assumed the guards had come to take me to my execution and was confused when they moved to flank the door. A man entered with an empty bucket to replace my full one. Another man followed him and put down a tray in the centre of the room. On the tray I saw a jug of water, a rough piece of dark bread and a bowl of something pale, lumpy and steaming. I wondered how something that looked so unappetising could smell so good. I was still wondering when the door slammed. Then I threw myself at the food.

Only after I had eaten did it occur to me that if they were feeding me they must want to keep me alive.

My first thought was that they thought I did know the answers to the questions I had failed to answer the day before. The food turned to ash in my mouth as I imagined an interrogator who was not be so pleasant as the gentleman with the good memory.

Time passed. The fear faded. The door remained closed. Perhaps they thought that making me wait would break my resolve. I determined to prove them wrong.

Determination faded. Boredom set in. I realised they would not interrogate me again. We interrogated all prisoners on capture and there was no reason to think the enemy did otherwise. Only if I'd shown any sign of possessing useful information would they waste time on further questioning. I had never been so grateful to be ignorant.

So why keep me alive? I wondered if they had recognised me and were loath to kill a poet, then decided that I credited them with too much taste. Perhaps my nobility held the key. For generations the conflict that shaped all our lives had included the taking and ransoming of hostages. I remembered the lines from "The Dream of Five Princes":

To the land's only hill
Where no blood can be shed
The enemy came

Beneath snapping pennants
The Princes made truce
For sons thought lost

Did such practices still have a place in this age of machines? Could that be why I was being kept alive?

Speculation was pointless. However, recalling the poem gave me an idea. I would exercise my memory in honour of my patient interrogator. My literature tutor had made me learn the whole of "The Dream of Five Princes" for Harvest-tide. I had hated the poem, thinking it a stark, colorless piece full of heavy-handed moral warnings. I wondered how much I could remember. Ah, yes...

In the Season of War
The son of a noble house
Went forth to seek glory

Though my attempts at recall were imperfect and frustrating, my efforts passed a few hours. By the time darkness fell hunger had returned. I attempted to meditate, without success.

Sleep came slowly and brought dreams. In the only one I could recall, I stood on a barren, wasted plain. The clouds above me flickered and rumbled. Somehow I knew that only my presence held back the storm. I raised my hands and shouted at the sky.

I awoke excited and elated, only to have the grey reality of my cell dispel my elation. Already this place was familiar enough not to surprise me, though it depressed me beyond words.

I waited while the door opened and the morning procession entered. This time I left half the bread for later, soaking it in the slops left in the bowl to soften it.

I decided to catalogue my prison. After my release, when I wrote about my ordeal, I would need to be able to recall details and, as yesterday's exercise had proven, my memory had become flabby with disuse.

Though I'd been brought here blindfolded I guessed the room was part of a partially buried bunker. The bottom half was hewn from rock, the top built from well-matched stone blocks. Sunlight came from a high, barred slit, no doubt designed for poking a weapon out of. The bunker faced west, so it had been one of ours originally; I must still be near the front. The fact that it was behind their lines at all was testament to how much ground we had lost this decade.

I shared the room with a lumpy mattress, a rough blanket sporting stains I chose not to examine, a tray, and a slops bucket. Hardly the accommodation I was used to. The young man who had joined up so eagerly six months ago would be appalled, but the army had toughened me. I had the necessities. I would make do.

I decided to complete my meal when the rectangle of daylight reached the point where the wall went from rock to stone. I would need such routines. I must organise myself to fight boredom and fear. It was my duty.

I recalled more of "The Dream of Five Princes", getting the lines straight in my head before reciting them. As a reward I let myself think about Angia. If hostilities had been resumed she would have gone with my mother and sisters to the hill outside the city, the high ground where the truce always held.

By then the golden bar on the far wall had reached the position I had designated as second meal, so I ate. The bread was not improved by its soaking.

After my meal I exercised, combining elements of the army fitness regime with gentler stretches my personal tutors had taught me. Just as I must not let my mind fall into despair, so I must not neglect my body.

That night I slept easily, hardly noticing the lumps in my bed. I did not dream.

The next morning the same four people came in but they seemed more tense than before. Part of me was glad to see my foes discomforted, though I would have given half my family's fortune to know why. Another part felt regret; I had harboured hopes of striking up a conversation. One of my narrative poems dealt with a gaoler and doomed convict who become friends. Though this was different, I longed for human contact, even with the enemy.

Such irony. When I had enlisted my father had called me a naïve fool, saying I was so sure of my own worth that I sold myself short of it. He didn't understand. In this new age, with its airships and guns and moving pictures, we nobles must set a good example. We can no longer trade on our past. I spent my time in the army trying not to be treated differently for my heritage and talent, enduring mockery and jokes in the barracks. But now I wanted to be seen as more than an ordinary soldier. I yearned for some acknowledgement that I was special, not just an anonymous victim of war.

After my morning visitors left I warded off boredom by completing the assessment of my prison. I paced the walls toe to heel and discovered that my cell was not, as it had appeared, perfectly square. The walls themselves held little of interest. The gaps where they met the floor had an infestation of green-brown slime currently dried to a crust. In the rains this place would be most unpleasant. I spotted a tiny pallid beetle crawling across the film of dried algae. I was trying to coax it out with a crumb from my loaf when I remembered that today Angia would go for her first scan. I felt sure it would confirm what I had hoped for. Today she would find out that she carried our firstborn. A son, I was certain. Whatever happened to me here, I would have a son and he would carry on the family name and avenge me. I shouted 'You can't kill us all', and then, when the door remained closed, the sky unclouded and the beetle unimpressed, started singing some of the cruder soldiers' songs, the ones about the personal habits and parentage of our foes.

After a while it occurred to me that this was not the behaviour of a hero staying sane for the sake of his country, his wife and his unborn son.

I spent the rest of the afternoon exercising. In the evening I recited the "The Dream of Five Princes" in its entirety. One triplet kept coming back to me:

Weep, mothers and wives
For the men you have lost
Yet smile for their sacrifice

Had I made such a sacrifice? I had set out to make a difference but in the end I had not behaved nobly.

In the night I heard thunder in the distance and woke to see distant flashes on my cell wall.

The next morning I decided to ask my gaolers if I might have a pen and paper. I suspected the answer would be no, a pen being a possible weapon, but perhaps the act of asking would break the ice. They were only doing their jobs, after all.

I didn't get the chance. When they came in they refused to look at me. Instead they exchanged gazes of chilling complicity, until one of the guards crossed the room in three quick strides, said 'This is for my sister,' and brought the butt of his rifle down on my groin.

The blow condensed my world to an instant of agony. I sprung closed around the pain, part of me terrified more blows might come, part of me incredulous this one had.

He did not hit me again and by the time I could see straight they had gone. I considered what he could mean. I had never hurt or dishonoured this man's sister, nor any man's. Had they mistaken me for someone else in my unit? Possibly: my unit had contained a couple of seasoned soldiers who had told tales of conduct they found amusing and I found disturbing. But everyone else in my unit was dead.

As should I be.

We had crossed into land currently claimed by the enemy, a daring and foolish move by my commanding officer in a time of truce. I remembered the last time I saw him, half his face gone, the rest looking faintly affronted. As a common soldier I had not been party to the reasons for the incursion. That was why I had surrendered while the others fought on and died. I had told myself that I would not die without knowing the reason. I was too important to be expended in a futile act.

"The Dream of Five Princes" has much to say on the subject of honour.

Is your pride so great
That you hold your small life
Above honour and trust?

I had done just that. My tears of pain turned to tears of shame.

My father says only fools and cowards cry. I now knew myself to be both. A fool for retaining that secret joy at being above my fellows, for thinking of my service as a way to experience the extremes of life in order that I could later turn them into art. And a coward for not dying when honour demanded it.

When the tears were spent I crawled over to the tray, which they had left in its usual place. My left testicle still ached and I felt weak and nauseous but I forced myself to eat and to complete my exercise regime.

Only when my limbs quivered and the sweat ran into my eyes did I stop. I tried to console myself with thoughts of Angia but though I wanted to recall her laugh, her mannerisms, I could only think of the pale silk of her body. In my frustration I punched the wall. The pain brought me back to my senses and I sat on the cold floor nursing bleeding knuckles.

I slept uneasily and was already half awake when they came for me.

At first I thought I was dreaming the dark shapes who swarmed into my cell. Then they pulled me from my bed and forced a hood over my head. The heavy fabric smelt of vomit and mould.

I bit down on my desire to cry out, letting them cuff my hands behind me and march me from the cell. I heard shouts, dull booms, the sound of distant machinery, all muffled by the hood.

The voices fell away and the other noises grew louder. I felt chill air, smelled smoke and rotten meat. Someone murmured in my ear, 'This is all for you, poet. How does that make you feel?' Before I could work out what he meant my toe hit something solid. A gun prodded my back and I stepped up onto a surface that shifted under my weight. I was half pushed, half thrown onto a seat. A door slammed and we started to move. A lorry, I was in a lorry. Something screamed overhead and I heard a dull concussion away to the left. The hood amplified the change in pressure, making my ears ring, while at the same time partially cutting me off from the horror I should have been feeling.

Having no idea about the incoming rocket, I did not tense up like the others. This saved my life.

Someone shouted, we swerved, then an explosion threw me into the air. I landed like a sack of grain, too confused to react. When I smelled fuel and flame I panicked. My arm hit something warm and damp that groaned. I flailed away. My legs hit metal. I tried to make sense of the world, to be calm and think, and not to lose control of my guts.

The truck was on its side. The metal I'd hit was the tailgate.

I pulled my legs up and rolled again. My ankle hit something, then I was free. I rolled out onto a hard dusty surface. The ground sloped down and the roll became a tumble. Something close by made a noise like a stick whacking a table. Pain exploded in my left knee. Dust had gotten into my hood, into my mouth. Attempting to breathe resulted in a mouthful of vomit and dust-laden cloth. I found that I had failed in my resolve not to shit myself.

Then everything went bright and loud, just for a moment.

They do not allow news in the ward. I remember my father saying last year that the ministers had decided that when the conflict next erupted into open war hospitals, schools and other vulnerable places should not be permitted access to sources of news. For the sake of morale, they said. The staff project brittle cheerfulness but will not talk about the outside world. If I ask a direct question they look away. From the bustle that passes the door and the exhaustion in the nurses' eyes, I suspect the hospital is overfull. However, I have my own room, brighter and larger than my old cell. They have not allowed me knowledge of the outside world, but they have allowed me paper and pen, which is an improvement on my last prison.

Yesterday, three days after I regained consciousness, and the day after I wrote up my imprisonment, my father came to see me.

He swept in with a gaggle of journalists. Poses were struck, cameras whirred, quiet statements made. Sedatives must have been included in my morning medication, as the whole scene felt unreal. I lay on my bed like a prize pig at a country show.

When the journalists left, he stayed. A nurse brought a wheelchair and lifted me into it. By now I had broken free of my daze enough to speak. 'What is it? Are we at war again?'

He regarded me with pity and something else I couldn't identify but which scared me. He did not answer my question. Instead he muttered something to the nurse, who pushed the chair from the room. My cell had smelled of shit over disinfectant. The corridor smelled of disinfectant over shit.

Those who passed us gave small bows of respect. I recalled the chain of office round my father's neck, heavier and more ornate than the one he had worn as a member of the Lords' Chambers. More like those worn by the Inner Cabal.

We reached the lift and he dismissed the nurse. When we were alone he said, 'Yes, we are at war.' He spoke with the same calm, toneless certainty he had used with the reporters. 'Our requests for your release went unanswered, so we retaliated.'

'You mean the truce was broken because of me?' I felt appalled, honoured, unworthy, proud. Whatever drugs they had used to keep me calm for the cameras had worn off.

The lift lurched and my father grabbed my wheelchair. 'Do not flatter yourself. You could have been anyone. What mattered is that they had captured one of our soldiers, stopped him from taking the honourable path of suicide and –'

'– that's not how I –'

He hit me. A quick slap across my hand, as though I was a child. More shocking than painful. I knew what he was saying with the gesture: this is the truth because I say it is, and you *will* accept that.

The lift doors opened. We came out into the hospital's roof garden. A red-brick path led between a twin row of glossy-leaved clove trees, their hot scent dispelling the hospital stink. Though the sky was grey I felt my heart leap at being outside again. But I also felt the continuing sting of my father's blow.

As he pushed the chair down the path he said, 'You once tried to convince me that we lived in a new age where the old rules no longer held – where a man's worth would be judged not by how high he was born but by how far he could rise. It seems you were correct. The age of noble hostages is over. These days we value all our soldiers enough to fight for them.'

Unsure what my father wanted me to say, I said nothing.

We turned a corner. Tubs had been planted here, shrubs and ground cover. A jewel-green lizard darted across a cushion of pink flowers. I thought I caught the faint trill of birdsong, though as we approached the edge of the building I heard only the sounds of the city below, the thrum of motor-carts and the cries of the street-sellers. The scent of the flowers mingled with the dust and exhaust fumes. As he pushed me towards the sturdy fence running along the edge of the roof, my father said, 'We were morally justified in our retaliatory mortar attack. We could not know that the Raja and his family were visiting the border town we hit.'

I opened my mouth to say that this was an unfortunate accident but he ignored me and continued.

'In response, they loaded up their largest airship with bombs and flew a suicide mission deep into our territory. We had assumed they meant to hit the city. We were wrong.' He stopped the chair in front of the fence. 'Do you see, now, how wrong?' For the first time he came into my eye-line, bending down to point over the roofs to where the farmland outside the city sloped up to a lone hill. The high ground, location of the country homes of the nobility. A place of truce throughout history. At this distance I could see only that the colour was wrong: brown and grey instead of green and gold. Then I saw the thin tendrils of smoke running up from the ruins into the leaden sky.

Finally I spoke. 'Is Angia all right?'

'No. The summer house took a direct hit. Your wife, your mother, your sisters, they're all dead.' Finally my father's voice showed some emotion: the weariness of a man who has gone beyond grief.

'But the high ground, they can't –'

'They did,' he spat. 'Afterwards, the enemy realised they'd gone too far. Within twelve hours they had offered to return you.'

The numbness that had eaten at me in my cell began to creep back. Dead. All dead. I tried to concentrate on the miracle of my own life. 'So that's where the lorry was going. That's how I got out. But someone shot at the lorry. I was lucky to survive.'

'Very. We intended to destroy the lorry and everyone on it.'

'What? You mean you – we – shot at me?'

'Since the enemy bombed the high ground our forces have been infused with righteous energy. We have taken back territory lost before you were born. To have our hostage returned would give the moral initiative back to them. An artillery unit was told that the convoy contained enemy commandos and must be destroyed. Somehow you escaped. When you were found, shit-stained in a ditch, you were recognised as the son of a newly promoted minister and evacuated. As you say, you were lucky.'

'You would have had me killed? Why? Because I'm a coward? Because of what happened to the family?' I looked up at him as he stared blankly at the smoking ruins of our home.

He shook his head but did not look at me. 'Selfish as ever. As it turns out your survival serves just us as well. Our country needs heroes. What better figurehead than a noble who resisted his captors and then escaped?'

My father's thought processes were as alien to me as the enemy's: I had never once thought about trying to escape my cell. And surviving a prison is not the same as escaping it.

Finally he looked at me and said, 'What, my son, has the poet no words?'

I held his gaze, despite the contempt I saw there and said, 'I'm… sorry. For everything.'

'We are all sorry. When you leave hospital the press will want your story. I am sure you can satisfy them.' He jerked the chair round and began pushing me back along the path. 'I will return you to your bed now, to rest.'

He was right. I would find the words they wanted. It was my duty, after all.

Jaine Fenn

Making moral points through fiction can be tricky and is often unwise; it's all too easy to be heavy-handed. But one of the 'places I get my ideas from' is news in the real world, and I find that writing about something that evokes strong negative feelings – fear, fury, disgust, horror, whatever – is a good way to deal with those feelings. This particular story was inspired by an absurd and depressing incident in the ongoing conflict between Israel and Palestine, a war with very little moral high ground, and no clear resolution. It needed to be written with an unsympathetic protagonist and an unhappy outcome. It did nothing to change events in the real world. But I felt better for doing it. Writing is therapy.

King of Pain

Queen Iralae surveyed the crowd from the cover of the portico. Courtiers and dignitaries packed the windows and balconies around the square, and farmers, merchants, bureaucrats and soldiers jostled for the best position on the mosaic pavements. The king's bodyguards had already fanned out along the grand terrace, and Requarn, Lord Stargazer and Speaker of Destiny, had just tottered to a halt in his appointed place.

Iralae took a deep breath and stepped out onto the terrace, surreptitiously kicking the hem of her gold and crimson brocade robe to avoid tripping over it. Though she enjoyed most customs and beliefs of her adopted nation, she hated Naralakti formal dress.

The normally garrulous citizens of Naralakt waited quietly, witnesses to the workings of Fate, a force they revered with a passion Iralae found disconcerting. In the expectant silence she heard waves breaking on the lakeshore and the distant twittering of birds settling for the night on the roofs of the city.

Her husband, King Arzachel, passed her with a rustle of fabric, masked head held high. Below, some of the crowd averted their eyes in piety. Others looked to the far end of the square where Lake Naralakt lapped at the stone quay. The queen spotted the approaching boat, a small craft such as a lone fisherman might use, or a noble couple might hire for a day's sport amongst the coves and inlets. As the boat approached the landing stage people pressed forward, cutting off Iralae's view. Whether through respect or due to the efforts of the city guard, the crowd parted again a few moments later. A man in a white robe began to make his way through the corridor of free space forming along the centre of the square.

At first, Iralae saw no resemblance between her husband and the approaching figure. From his long unkempt hair and weather-beaten face she would have said that the stranger was past his prime years, though he was younger than Arzachel.

At the bottom of the steps to the terrace the guards crossed their pikes. The stranger stopped and bowed his head, and the guards uncrossed their weapons. Iralae sensed hesitation beyond the ritual challenge, and the king's personal bodyguard kept their hands near their swords.

As the stranger mounted the steps Iralae saw the similarities between the two men; the quick intelligence around the eyes, the nose a little longer than average and the expressive mouth, inclined to sudden laughter or judgment. Though he strode onto the terrace boldly, he looked tired and a little apprehensive. She rarely witnessed such unguarded expressions in the stiff formality of the court.

Without looking at the stranger the king raised his hands. His voice carried easily across the square.

'We live in a time of trial. Invaders threaten our borders; our vassal towns say that a poor harvest means that the coming winter will be lean, and now, those wise in the ways of the heavens tell us that in three days the sun will be assailed by darkness. This is a time for caution, for prudence. But it is not a time for fear. Dark times have come before, and will come again. Naralakt will survive.'

After a respectful pause Requarn spoke. Older, more querulous, his voice did not carry so well. 'During this most inauspicious time the risk to our ruler must be commuted. Until the immediate danger has passed, another will assume the role of king, and so take on the danger of ill luck. In earlier times the choice of the surrogate was made by drawing lots amongst the high-born, but our lord Arzachel has chosen to permit the return of the royal exile.'

The crowd stirred as the rumours were confirmed. Though his mother had been a commoner this man was the son of the old king and the only living relative of the current one. But not his most loyal subject. Arzachel had only summoned him because Requarn had insisted that the king needed a substitute as close to him as possible for the upcoming time of darkness.

Ignoring the crowd's reaction, Requarn stepped up and took the stranger's hand, leading him up to the impassive figure of King Arzachel. 'This man, Tashvar, comes to us now as a newborn, without past, without guilt. The hand of Fate moves in ways we cannot understand. The stars have shown the path we must take and we have no choice but to obey.'

Iralae saw Tashvar glance at his half-brother's masked face. Two attendants stepped forward to unclasp the king's black robe and take its weight. Another raised the golden crown from the king's head. Arzachel himself undid his copper mask. Beneath his finery, he wore the same plain white robe as the man who was to assume his role for the next three days.

The king turned to face his surrogate and spoke, 'Take now from me the weight of responsibility.' The attendants, trying to maintain decorum without hurrying or letting the robe drag, laid the robe of state on Tashvar's shoulders. 'Take also the glory of divinity.' Another attendant placed the crown on the surrogate's head. The king handed the mask over. 'In the eyes of our people, take on all that I am.'

Once Tashvar had fastened the mask over his face, Arzachel turned away and walked down the steps without a backward glance. The crowd shrank back, fearful of contact with this king-but-not-king, a man in limbo.

Iralae watched her husband make his way through the square. Arzachel had been so busy with the preparations for the ritual that their leave-taking had been hurried, and she followed him with her eyes until the crowd closed behind him. She did not realise she had stepped forward to stand beside his substitute until Requarn joined them at the balustrade.

Once the boat had cast off, the crowd looked back up to the terrace. Requarn waited until he had their full attention then, indicating Tashvar with a claw-like hand, shouted, 'Behold your king.'

When the crowds had dispersed, Iralae visited the king's apartments. Arzachel had said little about how she should conduct herself with the substitute and she was curious to talk to this stranger who had known both terrible poverty and the dangers of the wild lands.

The guards admitted her and she walked through to stand at the threshold of the dining room. Within, Tashvar ate like a man who did not know where his next meal might come from. He would have spent several days fasting on the tiny island where, even now, her husband would be tying up his boat.

Iralae waited, confused by the combination of the familiar and the strange, until Tashvar glanced at her over the rim of a jeweled goblet. He smiled, looking abashed. 'My lady, I am sorry, I did not see you there.' His voice was harsher than his brother's, his frame leaner, all softness burnt away by the years of privation.

'Please,' she said, 'do not be embarrassed. May I come in?'

'Of course, my lady.'

As she perched on the high-backed chair opposite him she caught a whiff sweat and dirt, unfamiliar smells amongst the perfumes and unguents of the courtiers.

He gestured at the laden table, 'Will you eat? There is plenty here.'

'Oh, I have eaten already.' She resisted the temptation to add 'my lord'. He was not, after all, her lord. 'But I will sit with you for a while if I may.' After the initial shock she found his scent intriguing.

'Please do. I suspect this –' he gestured at the table laden with roast meats, bread, cheeses, pastries and baked fruits, '– may not be to your taste anyway'.

'Why, no.' She had no love of northern food, finding it bland and over-cooked. Last year Arzachel had arranged for a cook trained in the southern style to provide her meals, but they had been married for a month before he had noticed that she was not eating properly. For herself, Iralae had not been greatly bothered; stimulation for the mind mattered more than sustenance of the flesh for her, as for all Aisara. But she was disconcerted that this stranger should observe at once what it had taken her husband so long to notice.

'May I ask you something? Something which you may consider impertinent.' He stared at her directly as he spoke.

'Of course.'

'Do you miss your home?'

'Sometimes I miss the smell of salt on the wind, the warmth and the longer days. But we are a restless people, with little concept of nationhood or patriotism as other nations hold.'

'And the Naralakti accept you?'

'The common people see me as an outsider, though that will improve when I do my duty and produce children for the king. But I am accepted at court; perhaps the… mistakes of my predecessor made the choice of a foreigner as the new queen more acceptable.'

'You mean Magdil? I never met the late queen, though I heard rumours of her behaviour. I am surprised to hear you speak so openly of her. I understand she is never mentioned in court.'

Iralae was surprised at herself too, but this stranger seemed to invite her confidence. 'Ah, but you are not a member of the Naralakti court, if you will forgive me for reminding you.'

Tashvar smiled ruefully. 'Indeed I am not.' When he had emerged from the slums of the lower city to declare his lineage, and the Lord Stargazer and other diviners had discovered that he spoke the truth, Arzachel's response had been to settle money and land on Tashvar and send him to an outlying town. When charges of inciting rebellion had been laid against him, the king, unable to execute one of royal blood, had exiled his half-brother to the barren lands on the far side of the mountains.

Iralae knew these facts, but there was much she did not know. So she may as well ask. 'They say that you have lived the last ten years in a cave. Is this true?'

He laughed, and leaned back. 'Oh no. Only two years in a cave. Then I built myself a house…' He spoke of his life in the mountains, describing encounters with wild beasts and battles with bandits, the freezing winter nights and burning summer days. Iralae's conversations with her husband were filled with affairs of state or concerns for the welfare of his people. Even when they were alone he rarely ventured personal details. She was fascinated.

Finally he looked up and said, 'But I detain you, my lady. I believe we will both be very busy in the next few days.'

He was right. It was getting late. She took her leave and returned to her rooms. But her thoughts as she drifted into sleep were not of her husband.

By the time Arzachel has rowed himself out to the sacred island his shoulders ache and his hands are raw and blistered. He does not mind; such simple, common hurts compliment his exile. When they refer to it at all, the Naralakti call this island the empty rock. Every king that had subjected himself to surrogacy has waited out the time of ill omen here.

His half-brother's stay on the island for the three days leading up to the ceremony should have been spent in purification and fasting, though the scattering of small bones around a recent fire-pit implies otherwise.

The king is not expected to endure such conditions. His staff have left a torch burning on the shore to guide him, and piles of provisions to sustain him. He finds a small tent, a folding bed and more than sufficient food. And, as he has requested, his telescope and books.

At this time of misfortune the surrogate mixed with the people more than the king usually did, as though daring fate to strike, thus sparing the true king. Iralae found this invitation to disaster distasteful. The Naralakti viewed Aisara mind magics as primitive witchery, yet believed they could predict or even control their own destinies by observation and ritual.

So she and Tashvar burnt silks embroidered with the wishes of the people at the House of High Destiny, spun the wheels at the temple of Lady Fortuna, had lunch at the Clockmakers guild, watched the city guard drilled in the square, attended a presentation of awards at the College of Graces and finally stood with the Lord Stargazer on the roof of the palace, publicly watching the sun set over the mountains.

Iralae found the people accepted her more now, though she suspected she would never replace Queen Magdil in the hearts of the common citizens.

Tashvar played his part well, performing the required actions with only the barest prompt from the priests and officials. Though the king's guards watched his every move, he seemed to be enjoying himself, though the copper mask hid his expression.

Dinner was relatively informal, and as there were no commoners present, Tashvar removed his mask. Iralae found her pleasure at seeing his face – familiar, yet more alive, more open than Arzachel's – of greater interest than the food.

After the feast, Tashvar took her hand, kissed it, and bade her goodnight. The gesture, intimate yet formal, confused Iralae, and back in her own rooms she wondered if it was an invitation – and if so, whether she dared accept.

It had not occurred to her that she might want a man other than the one she had wed herself to; Arzachel was handsome, just and reasonable, and she loved him. But his brother had a warmth and humour the king lacked, and he gave her his full attention.

Unable to sleep, she put on a cloak against the night's chill and took the back steps down to the lake-shore. With no moon, the stars shone bright enough to cast shadows. She stood for a while on the palace's private beach, looking out. From here in daylight it was just possible to make out the distant smudge of the empty rock where her husband waited out his exile. She turned away from the lake and continued her walk.

Light flared overhead. From the position she thought it came from the Lord Stargazer's apartments. A moment later Requarn stepped onto his balcony. He stared out into the night, his gaze sweeping down the beach towards Iralae, outlined against the star-shimmered water. She formed in her mind the illusion that allowed a person in bad light to remain undetected. She must have reacted quickly enough, as a moment later he spoke, addressing someone back in the room. Iralae murmured a charm to sharpen her hearing, and heard the end of his comment '...can speak out here without being overheard.'

The light flared again and another figure strode onto the balcony. Iralae recognised Vuron, the captain of the king's bodyguard, a stolid, duty-bound warrior whose loyalty to his king was absolute.

'What is so urgent that I must neglect my duties to visit you at this late hour?' asked the soldier.

Requarn nodded. 'Ah, straight to the point. My divinations into the workings of Destiny have revealed something troubling.'

'Your dramatic phrases may impress the people, but I am a busy man.'

'It appears that our lord the king intends to revive the old tradition regarding the ceremony of surrogacy.'

'You refer to the killing of the scapegoat?'

111

Iralae's breath froze in her throat. Surely her husband would not sanction the murder of his own brother?

'Indeed I do. I had hoped our people had grown out of such barbaric practices, but these are ill-omened times: another failed harvest will see the kingdom starving; enemies bay at our borders, and there is as yet no royal heir. In such times the king feels such drastic measures are justified.'

'And what would you have me do about it, my lord?'

'You are the king's bodyguard, you are to guard his body.'

'Yes, the king's body. Not that of the surrogate. His life is already forfeit to our lord's wishes.'

'Then you would permit the king to commit murder?'

'Aye, for the sake of our nation, I would let the king commit murder.'

'Ah,' said Requarn, 'You think my own experience of the king's justice colours my judgment.'

'I could not say, my lord. I can only hope that your duty to your nation is stronger than any desire to stir up past... indiscretions.'

'So, you will do nothing?'

'The king will do as he sees fit. I will not intervene.'

The older man sighed. 'Once, I would have been angry, but I am too old for that now. I have done my duty. I have passed on the words of Destiny.' He moved away, and the light flared again.

Iralae waited until she was sure both men had gone back inside, then ran back towards the steps.

Few lights burned this late, and Iralae had no need to resort to sorcery until she reached the king's apartments. One of the guards was dozing at his post; the other she distracted with a simple illusion. Inside, the rooms were dark, but she had found her way through these chambers in the dark before, going to and from her husband's bed.

In the light of the shaded lamp beside the bed, Tashvar looked young, the years of worry and care slipping from him in the embrace of sleep. She called his name, then when he did not respond, reached forward and shook him awake.

He started, then focused on her.

'It's me. Iralae.'

When he sat up and the covers fell back she noticed that, unlike the king, he slept naked. 'Iralae? What is it?'

Along with the thrill of fear she also felt a less wholesome excitement. 'I have to warn you. You are in danger.'

'Warn me? What of?' He blinked sleepily.

'I overheard the Lord Stargazer and the captain of the king's bodyguard. I believe that Arzachel intends to have you killed as the darkness passes. Maybe even kill you himself.' She still could not imagine that possibility, though she knew there was little her husband would not do for the sake of his kingdom.

Tashvar looked serious, but not shocked or afraid. 'This news should not surprise me. Ever since I admitted my birthright, my brother has wanted me dead. This way he can kill me with the sanction of the people. I should never have come here.'

'Then you must leave!' She would not let this man die to appease Naralakti superstitions.

'That would be difficult, given how closely I am watched. Besides, I have some honour. In running from my duty I would confirm myself as the criminal my brother paints me as.'

'Then what will you do?'

'I am not sure. I have two nights and a day before your fears are confirmed. I hope you will not be insulted if I say that my initial thought is to hope that you are wrong. Though I am in your debt for warning me.'

Iralae said nothing. She had given him the news. Now she should leave. But she did not want to.

When Tashvar raised his hand to stroke her face she leaned into his touch. Such heat, such fire, almost as though this were the real man and her husband, distant and aloof, no more than his shadow.

She closed her eyes.

The skies remain clear, and Arzachel sets up his telescope on the beach and devotes the night to his observations.

Arzachel publicly defers to the Lord Stargazer in matters of Fate. But Requarn sometimes sees what he wants to in the stars, not what is truly there. Arzachel has been making his own observations for some time, and seen truths in the sky that Requarn has missed. Truths he hopes to confirm in the privacy of the empty isle. Because he is taking a terrible risk on the promise of Fate, and if he is wrong he may lose everything.

As dawn approached, Iralae eased herself from the crook of Tashvar's arm and dressed quietly. When he stirred she spun an illusion to convince him she remained beside him. She avoided glancing at her lover, lying on the bed she had shared with her husband.

Today's diversion was a hunt; yesterday, such a blatant ploy to tempt fate might have amused her, but now she found herself distressed at seeing Tashvar put into the path of danger.

The hunting party set off early, while the rest of the court made their way to the top of the steep-sided valley where the day's sport would culminate. For company she had Kasia, her body servant, and the source of much court gossip. Iralae normally enjoyed Kasia's observations, but today she half-feared that she would hear rumours of her own indiscretion from her servant's chattering lips.

The court took a light lunch on cushions under tasselled canopies, serenaded by musicians. Iralae tried not to watch the mouth of the valley where, once sufficient prey had been rounded up, the hunters would appear. She sat next to Requarn and as he twittered on she remembered something from the previous evening.

After the meal, while she and Kasia played tabula, she asked, 'What injustice might the king my husband have done to the Lord Stargazer?'

Kasia looked down at the game board and said, with uncharacteristic wariness, 'I am not sure what your highness refers to.'

'I overheard a comment to the effect that Requarn may have cause to resent the king. Is this true?'

Kasia looked around, then murmured, 'Requarn's youngest son was killed in an accident three years ago. The servants found him at the base of the staircase leading down to the beach. He must have fallen in the night. Some said it was no accident. That is all I know, my lady.'

Iralae let the subject drop and went back to the game.

A few minutes later a horn sounded and she jumped to her feet. A wild boar, followed by a small herd of deer, ran over the lip of the valley and hurtled down into the valley bottom. A few moments later the hunters rode into view, Tashvar at their head. His face wore an expression of fierce joy and his hair streamed in the wind.

Iralae's heart lifted at the sight of him, and she knew then what she had been trying to deny all day. She loved him.

At the evening feast the normally staid court seemed intoxicated, almost hysterical, perhaps due to the stimulating effects of a good hunt, or perhaps to the desire to forget the approaching climax of ill fortune.

Tashvar went unmasked, and few could fail to notice how he and the queen laughed together. But when the courtiers retired she returned to her own rooms.

The Aisara are not a passionate people, and she had never expected to be in this situation. Her response to Tashvar sprung from her love for Arzachel, from her yearning for such complete devotion from the man she loved first and last. She had not realised that yearning had existed until Tashvar had stepped in to fulfil it.

And now she would lose him. If Requarn was wrong, by tomorrow night Tashvar would have returned to his exile in the mountains. If he was right, Tashvar would be dead. Either way, she would have to choose between the two men she loved. She should spend the night meditating on her choice.

Instead she pulled the cloak of illusion round her, and went to the king's apartments.

Tashvar received her without a word and, perhaps sensing her unease, led her not to the bed she had shared so many times with her husband, but to a couch where they lay, without words, for some hours.

Later, as they lay entwined, she said, 'I will not let him kill you.'

'I do not wish to die. I have decided that I will run, though it is not the honourable choice, and I cannot see a way of escaping unnoticed. And I want you to come with me.'

She was tempted. But she could not leave her husband. Her love for Tashvar could easily blind her to sense, but the fire of that love was drawn from her love for Arzachel. Yet neither could she let her lover die. 'I cannot come with you, Tashvar. But I can help you get away safely. There is a way to allow the people to believe that the ritual has been concluded correctly, whilst allowing you to escape with your life.'

'How?'

'The same way I have come to you unseen. By use of illusion.'

He brushed a strand of hair from her face. 'You would do this for me?'

'I will do everything in my power to save you.'

When the final night falls on the empty isle, King Arzachel finds his thoughts returning to his young, beautiful, naïve queen. Her people are not like the Naralakti. Living on a bountiful yet remote coastline they have no great love of material things and only travel to explore, not to conquer. The constant fight to feed the people, to negotiate truces and maintain alliances with neighbours, to quell internal unrest, these are not part of the Aisara world. In that enviable state of statelessness they have grown comfortable with themselves and their Fate. But Iralae herself, though inheritor of that legacy, is very young, and knows little of the world. He adores her for her innocence, but it frightens him too. And, distracted as he often is by the needs of his kingdom, he knows he sometimes neglects her, a mistake he has sworn he would not make again.

The night is cloudy, and he retires early to his simple pallet, though sleep does not come for many hours.

The court was subdued the next day, in preparation for the coming darkness.

Iralae forced herself to attend the midday meal, then retired to her chamber to prepare herself for the casting of magics far beyond her people's usual playful illusions.

When the increasing hubbub from the square told her the time was near, she took her place on the grand terrace. The sun shone bright in a cloudless sky, as though defying the disaster due to

116

overtake it. Around her, courtiers stirred and murmured, then fell silent when the king's surrogate walked out among them to stand alone by the balustrade, his head bowed and his hands clasped in front of him.

The Lord Stargazer came forward, leading attendants who removed the surrogate's cloak and crown and mask to leave him naked to fate.

At first the lessening of the light was barely perceptible, like an illusion which can be blinked away. The less superstitious shaded their eyes and glanced up to see if they could see the darkness swallowing the sun, while the devout kept their eyes from the heavens. Then heads at the back of the crowd began to turn towards the lake. The king was coming.

King Arzachel walked slowly through his people, the crowd parting before him. Many averted their eyes or made gestures to ward off ill luck. The king had to be present to reclaim his power when the darkness passed, but if the surrogate's conspicuous attempts to divert misfortune had not been sufficient, he might still fall prey to it.

Iralae watched her husband approach. His white robe was stained at the hem, his beard and hair unkempt.

By the time he was halfway across the square twilight had fallen over the city, and with it, silence. With every step the king took up the steps to the balcony, the darkness increased.

When he mounted the final step the sun was reduced to a burning crescent. The king fixed his gaze on his half-brother. Iralae used precious power to sharpen her sight. Her eyes refocused: shadows washed out and faint outlines shone clear. In Arzachel's left hand, half hidden by his long sleeves, she glimpsed the glint of metal. She only spotted it because the hand that held it shook.

Iralae forced herself to breathe while she waited for the moment when the eye and mind were most easily fooled. As the last light drained from the sky every observer must see their king step forward to strike down the surrogate. The expectations of the watchers would fill in the details once the illusion had been set, but she must touch every mind here. At the same time, she must stay the hand of her husband, a man of uncommonly strong will, to give her

117

lover the chance to slip away unseen. If she succeeded, then all save Arzachel would believe that the rite had been enacted correctly, and Tashvar was dead. But once the illusion had passed and no body could be found, the truth would be known. She knew this, and had considered riding away with Tashvar as he had urged, but she would not run from her responsibility. Though it would lose her the love of both men, and perhaps condemn her to death, she must face the consequences of her actions.

With a final flash from the rim of the sun, darkness fell, sucking breath and hope from the watchers. The sun was transformed to a thin ring of flaming white around a heart of utter black.

The king advanced, dagger in hand. Iralae focused her mind and watched the ghostly vision of illusion break away from reality.

In the illusion Tashvar stood oblivious at the balustrade while his half-brother moved to stand behind him, awaiting the moment when the sun broke through to strike.

In reality Arzachel moved slowly, taking a tentative step towards the other man while shaking his head as though trying to clear it, giving his opponent time to escape.

But Tashvar did not run. Instead he turned to face the king.

Arzachel swayed, then lunged.

Tashvar turned, easily avoiding the befuddled king's blow. He reached out as Arzachel stumbled past, and grasped his wrist, then brought his other hand round to pry the knife from the king's fingers. Arzachel, off balance and confused by the illusion, flailed and twisted in his brother's grip.

She had thought her choice was to save the life of one of those she loved, at the cost of the love of the other, but it was starker than that: one would live and one would die. While her magic clouded Arzachel's perceptions it would be he who lost, he who died, while Tashvar would emerge from her illusion victor and – in the eyes of the watching crowd – king.

And she would be his queen, with power, possessions and a man who would love her as she should be loved.

A man who had lied to her. A man who had used her love to his own advantage. A man who would kill his brother not reluctantly, to ensure the stability of the kingdom, but for personal power.

She had been a fool, a naïve fool.

She dispelled her magic.

A gasp went up from those on the terrace. Tashvar had the knife. Arzachel had fallen and was scrabbling backwards, his eyes fixed on the blade.

Tashvar, never subject to the illusion, could not know that the spell was broken. He advanced on the prostrate king. He was so intent on his prey that he did not see the flash of silver, and by the time he looked up at the sound of a blade being drawn, Vuron's dagger had already embedded itself in his guts.

Tashvar staggered backwards, hands wrapped round the hilt of the dagger. Dazed but still upright, he backed up against the balustrade. From the corner of her eye Iralae saw more weapons being drawn.

Tashvar looked at the guards advancing on him. There was no way out. Before the first soldier reached him, he leaned backwards over the balustrade and fell into the square below.

The sun broke through and light flooded the world.

Guards rushed forward to help the king stand. Arzachel was still dazed. Captain Vuron was not. He ran to look over the balustrade, then shouted out to the crowd, 'This traitor would have killed your king. Destroy him!'

The crowd surged forward.

King Arzachel sits alone, watching the familiar constellations reflected in the lake.

His courtiers tell him that Requarn is ill and has taken to his bed. Arzachel knows what ails him – fear for his life. The old fool was too busy plotting his petty revenge to look up and see the truth in the sky, and too vain to believe that a mere king could also read the stars.

Requarn is a traitor, but is he an old, frightened traitor and now that Tashvar is gone, he has no allies. He is no threat, and punishing him now would only re-open old wounds. Arzachel will let him live.

His first formal action on reclaiming his throne was to make arrangements to have his half-brother's body interred in the royal vaults; whatever had been in the man's heart, royal blood had flowed in his veins. After this he retired to his room, where he bathed, and ate, and now sits thinking.

He wonders if the queen has eaten. She too remains alone in her rooms.

Queen Magdil would not have been so willing to face the consequences of her actions. Magdil, ambitious, passionate Magdil, had taken what she wanted without consideration or remorse. Arzachel still wonders how many others she seduced before taking up with Requarn's son, back before the king had learned to see painful truths in the sky. How many more there might have been, had he not found them together that night and, in a fit of jealousy, pushed her lover down the stairs.

From that impulsive act of violence came her admission that though her husband's seed was weak, her last lover's had not been. When he found she was with child he had briefly considered letting her carry the baby to term and claiming it as his own. But this last betrayal cut too deep, and he would not oversee the end of his own bloodline. So he had insisted she secretly rid herself of the child. He might never have given that order, had he read the stars better. Magdil had died at the hands of an old quack in the lower city.

Until today, Magdil's fate had been the greatest of his many regrets.

He had always known that he might have to kill his brother. Tashvar's ambition would never let him rest. That course was set from the start, and needed little prompting from the heavens. Perhaps Arzachel's treatment of his first queen was predestined too, a product of her nature. No, he had some responsibility for her infidelities. He never took the time to give her the attention she craved, a mistake he had repeated with Iralae. And however much he loved his new queen, he could not let himself get too close to her, not once he had realised that she would betray him too, when Fate demanded it.

Perhaps he can show more love, or at least consideration, to Iralae now. He has already forgiven her. He only hopes she can forgive him.

He stands up. He will not call her here, to the scene of her shame. Instead he will go to her. She will not refuse him, though it tears his heart to think that her motives owe as much to guilt as to love. He doubts she will ever confess to him the truth he already knows. He certainly will not tell her what he saw in the stars. But it will be easier on them both, if, when the long awaited child comes, Iralae believes that the royal seed that sired it was that of her husband.

Music means a lot to me. I need it in my daily life, I write listening to it, and I steal stuff from it (you say plagiarism, I say 'homage'). Combine this with a long-term amateur interest in astronomy, an ongoing obsession in the strange and sometimes illogical rituals we puny humans employ to give us the illusion of control over our fates, and a stubborn belief in the possibility of magical thinking (or possibly fate), and this story happened.

Twilight at the
Change House

Coming up to six o'clock and still no sign of the man.

Chao looked round the room for what felt like the fiftieth time. The dozen or so guests eating, chatting or lounging around the plastic tables and sagging armchairs didn't pay him any particular attention. From the ersatz alpine architecture Chao reckoned that Changers Hostel ('a warm welcome in the wilds') had been built a good fifty years ago, not long after the turn of the millennium. Amazing that it kept going in the post-tourist age.

He wondered why the contact wanted to meet here. Maybe because the sea-access from the loch made the location good for smuggling, though the score was meant to be pretty compact. Unless the whole set-up was Uncle Han's idea of a joke. Or a test.

All in all, if it weren't for the view, he'd probably be climbing the stripped-pine-and-stone-clad walls by now. He sighed and turned back to the picture window that ran the length of the ground floor. The bottom third of the window was filled with a wall of green from an untended flower bed, tendrils and spikes reaching up with the spurt of spring growth. Beyond that a rough lawn sloped down to the tree-edged loch. On the far side the heather-and-gorse-covered mountains had begun to fade from mauve and gold to shadowy purple as the light bled out of the infinite blue sky. It would make a fantastic picture. He remembered what Marie had said when he'd first showed her some of his paintings: 'You've got talent, love. But there's nothing to use it on in bloody Glasgow.'

And he'd said, jokingly, 'So if we went to live in a croft in the Highlands you reckon I could make a living with my art?'

She'd taken him seriously, and replied, 'I'd find it easier to live with a poor artist than a rich criminal.'

And he'd snapped back. 'How about a dead one?'

He winced now, remembering. She didn't understand how the Family worked. Because Marie was worth it, he had spent the next couple of weeks getting himself into Uncle Han's good books. When the time was right, he had mentioned the subject of buying himself out. After Uncle had stopped laughing he'd named a figure, ridiculously high. Almost as much as the stake for this job, Chao realised. That confirmed it. Being sent out here to the arse-end of nowhere was one of Uncle's 'life lessons'.

'Good evening.'

Chao jumped, and looked over to see a man sitting at the next table, facing the window. Chao hadn't heard him sit down. Trying not to act startled, Chao nodded and said, 'Evening.'

The description fitted – Caucasian, late twenties, slight build, black curly hair – and the shapeless green jumper looked just the sort of thing a smuggler might wear, but the man seemed engrossed in the view. Chao waited a while then said, 'I was meant to meet someone here an hour ago.'

The man, eyes still on the mountains, said non-committally, 'Oh, aye.'

Chao continued, 'Would that be you? Because if not I'll leave you in peace.' He began to get up.

'Oh stay, stay,' said the man, as though they were old friends and Chao had suggested leaving a party early. He looked over at Chao with eyes the same colour as the twilit foliage outside the window.

'You're Reef, then?' said Chao.

The man nodded eagerly, 'Yes, yes, as good a name as any. Come, sit down over here.'

Chao moved to sit opposite his contact. From the jerky movements and dreamy smile Chao suspected the man might have sampled his own merchandise. Carefully he said, 'I've got what you asked for. Three-fifty, as agreed.'

Reef made an expansive, dismissive gesture, 'Tush, it's not the money that interests me. It's you.'

Chao went cold, then hot. 'Now listen pal, no offence but I don't swing that way. I was told this is a simple cash deal, no extras, right?'

He wondered if Uncle Han had known the man was a ponce, if that was part of the lesson. If so then Uncle was about to find out where Chao's limits lay.

Reef looked confused for a moment, then laughed. 'Oh I *see*. No, it's not a tumble I want. I just want to know who it is I'm dealing with.'

Chao tried not to look too relieved. 'Well, I'm here on behalf of my Uncle.'

'I know that. But I can't help noticing that you're not entirely of oriental countenance.'

Chao found himself distracted by the odd way the man spoke. His accent wasn't quite the classic Highland lilt; maybe he had some Irish in him. Mixed race might give them common ground. 'My mam's white.'

'Scots?'

'Born here. Her mam was from south of the border originally.'

'And your mother's father?'

Chao had no idea why the man needed to know. Still, whatever it took to keep the deal sweet. 'Died before mam was born. Gran never mentioned him much.'

Reef sat back. 'Excellent.'

Chao wasn't sure whether he should be worried at the satisfaction in Reef's voice. 'Well, as long as you're happy to deal with me...' He let his voice trail away rather than actually say *can we get this over and done with?*

'Hmm, I am. Very.' Reef nodded eagerly. 'So, where would you like to try it?'

'Sorry, pal, you've lost me.'

Reef leaned forward again, dropping his voice to a conspiratorial whisper. 'You'll be wanting to try the 'merchandise' now I believe.'

Chao swallowed. Chao avoided drug deals where possible. Too many flakes and wasters. He only took this one because Uncle had said it was 'especially for him'. While trying before buying from a conventional source might be normal, out here, alone with this weirdo, it wasn't a smart move. Chao had stashed the sports bag full of used euros in his room, but if this stuff was any good, then Chao might find himself unable to stop Reef taking the key from him, going to his room and grabbing the cash. 'That's not necessary. Uncle trusts you.'

'Does he now?' Reef's raised eyebrow implied that he thought Uncle's judgment might be faulty. 'Well, gratified though I am, if you don't try it, the whole deal's off.'

Chao considered his options. If he accepted the offer then he risked the smuggler getting him wrecked and taking his stuff, in which case he'd be left with no money and no gear and might as well just throw himself in the loch. If he refused, then he'd still have the money but he'd have blown the score. The dishonour from that would be enough to ensure he spent the foreseeable future working for the Family, and never got the chance for a new life with Marie. He had to take the risk. 'All right,' he said.

'As it looks to be a fine evening coming on, I'd suggest we adjourn to the garden.' When Reef stood he was shorter than Chao had expected. He moved with a weird capering gait, stopping at the threshold of the back door to take a deep breath. He exhaled theatrically and threw his arms wide. 'Now isn't that wonderful?' he asked.

Chao had to agree. The crisp, pure air curled into his lungs, and the faint buzz of late-feeding bees on the overgrown border competed with the waves lapping the shore-line.

Reef led him over to a rust-encrusted bench where he sat down and produced a small leather pouch and a carved wooden pipe. He tapped a few grainy grey fragments from the bag into the bowl of the pipe.

'You smoke it then?' said Chao. Smokables were harder to cut than snortables.

'You can. If we conclude our business successfully then you can choose how you'd like to spread this around. You'll find it easy enough to deal with, despite appearances. Strong too: a little goes a long way in the right hands. And it won't be quite like anything you've tried before.'

An odd and slightly worrying sales pitch, but Chao decided to humour the man so he just said, 'Right then, let's give it a go.' The grey powder looked like it had already been burnt, but when Reef applied a match it lit easily. He drew on it then passed the pipe over. Chao took a moderate drag. The contents of the pipe-bowl flared and bittersweet smoke rushed down his throat.

The initial hit was gentle, just a slight uplifting feeling. Chao nodded appreciatively, 'Very mellow.'

'At first, yes,' said Reef.

Chao glanced up and found reality transforming around him. The already bright colours of the Highlands vibrated with life. Glancing from mountain to tree he felt a change of note, as though everything he saw sung a slightly different tune, an ever-growing symphony felt as much as heard. His nose twitched at the smells of nectar and growth and rot seeping up from the earth, the slow damp of decomposing leaves and the quick warm twitter of tiny flesh.

After an indeterminate time he remembered why he was here and looked over at Reef. The other man's face looked pointed and lively, filled with shadows, as though what Chao saw was not one face but a dozen, a hundred, all superimposed.

'It's great,' said Chao. His words struck echoes off nearby objects, travelling away, returning, fading.

'Oh yes,' said Reef. His voice sounded deep, musical and hypnotic, and it carried on and out, further than Chao's had. Chao thought suddenly of the loch, the deep, clear fathomless waters, and the world beneath, a world as real as the one above yet never seen. 'And it gets better,' continued his companion. 'Now close your eyes…'

Laura was lost.

Seven years ago she'd been travelling without a map or a plan. Back then, fresh out of art college and saddled with student debts, driving her battered old Mini up to Scotland had been a stretch on her finances, but she'd always wanted to visit the Highlands and she had decided she owed herself a holiday before settling down to worry about jobs and debts and finding her life-path. Except it hadn't quite worked out like that. A trip taken on impulse had changed her life and given her seven years of wonder.

Wonder now gone.

Today, richer, older, wiser, and in a world about to celebrate a new millennium, she had a map and a plan. But no luck. She'd driven up and down both sides of the loch twice, and she was sure this was the right road – she recognised the silhouette of the mountains, the way the land swept down from the road to the loch-shore – yet she couldn't find the damn place.

Though it was barely past four in the afternoon, darkness ate at the frosted grass and skeletal trees beside the road. No snow forecast, and the Range-Rover could cope with most conditions, but she should still head back down south to find a hotel soon. Perhaps she could try again tomorrow.

Addressing the night she said, 'Well? I've done my best.' Then she glanced down at the hessian bag in the foot-well. When she looked up again she saw a light ahead through the trees.

She slowed, and made out a whitewashed stone building, two storeys high, with a metal-framed sign. The sign had no picture, just the words, in plain script "The Old Exchange" lit by a feeble spot-light. A more welcoming reddish light glowed in a downstairs window. Laura didn't remember seeing the pub before, though it would be easy to miss. No sign of a car park so she pulled up on the verge outside. Though she could hardly ask for directions – 'Excuse me, can you tell me how to find the stretch of road where I met my lover?' – she might be able to get a cup of coffee and maybe even a bed for the night, though the place looked a bit small to do accommodation.

The front door opened onto a room lit by a low-burning fire and mismatched table-lamps. The flagstone floor was relieved by a motley covering of rugs, and the wooden furniture by a variety of brightly coloured cushions. Laura thought it looked like a place where old hippies went to die, but there was no sign of anyone, living or dead. She wandered up to the bar. Perhaps there was a bell.

'Evening, miss,'

She turned to see a man sitting in the pew beside the fire, elbows on the table in front of him. He had retro-rock star curls and a dark green T-shirt with a Celtic-style three-lobed pattern in red and gold. She put his age at mid-twenties, until she saw his eyes and revised it up by a decade. She wondered how she had missed seeing him when she came in.

'Good evening,' she said. 'I was wondering if they did bed and breakfast here.'

The stranger shook his head, 'Oh, I wouldn't want to spend the night here.'

Tired, stressed and taken aback by the man's rude familiarity, Laura said, 'Well, I thought I might ask the landlord anyway.'

'He's just stepped out for a moment. Left me in charge for a while.' He winked, a gesture Laura should have found lewd or at least disconcerting, but which, on him, seemed to draw her into a conspiracy. His eyes were the oddest shade of green.

'Fair enough. I suppose there's no chance of a cup of coffee then.'

'None at all,' said the man, standing up. 'But I'm sure there's passable whisky to be had.' He went over to the bar. At first Laura thought he had a limp, then she realised that it was just the way he walked, like a man trying hard not to dance.

'Oh, no, I'm driving.'

'A *wee dram* won't hurt,' he said, ducking behind the bar. He had affected a cod-Scottish accent, but he wasn't Scottish. More like Irish, or maybe Welsh.

'Just a small one then,'

'That's the way,' he said. He reached into the huddle of bottles lurking at the back of the bar, apparently chose one at random, and then poured two not-so-small-ones into heavy tumblers. When Laura reached for her bag he shook his head. 'This one's on the house.'

Though they were committing theft, Laura put her money away without a word. Something about this man reminded her of her dead lover. Not his appearance or his manner so much as the same feeling that this was not a person who fitted in with conventional ideas of normal behaviour and attitudes.

The man slid back behind the table and gestured for Laura to sit opposite him. He raised his glass, then stopped. 'It's not wise to drink with strangers,' he said gravely, but before Laura could say that it was all right, she trusted him, he grinned and said, 'So why don't you tell me your name?'

'I'm Laura,' she said, returning his smile.

'And I'm Ray. Slainte, Laura.' He clinked his glass against hers hard enough to jar her wrist then drank its contents down in one.

Laura sipped her drink more cautiously. The earth and fire of the malt flowed over her tongue like silk then ran down her throat like lava. She took a bigger sip. She hadn't realised how cold she was until the whisky started to warmth her.

'What happened to your hand?' asked Ray.

'Oh, I… it's from my carving. I studied sculpture at college, though these days it's more of a hobby.'

Ray nodded approvingly, then frowned. 'Well, no wonder you can't make a living of your art if you keep carving yourself up.'

Laura could feel the whisky burning through her, radiating out from her stomach, relaxing her. She realised, for the first time since *it* had happened, that she could talk about her pain without feeling it. 'I've lost someone recently and I was trying to work it out in wood. I know, sounds pretentious. Anyway, I couldn't concentrate and I ended up slicing my palm.'

'Ah, I see,' said Ray, sitting back. 'And would it be your loss that brings you out into the wilds all alone on this cold, bleak evening?'

'Yes, I suppose you could say that, though I'm not exactly alone. I'm here to keep a promise.'

'A fine reason. Whose promise do you keep?'

'My…' she hesitated, because the phrase she wanted to use seemed too sentimental, too absurd, for the cynical nineteen nineties. But if anyone would understand, this man would. 'My one true love,' she said defiantly.

Looking at the kerchief in his hand, James saw red spots against starched white. He gulped back another cough and tucked the kerchief back into his waistcoat, then murmured encouragement at the horse. He could feel how tired it was, every step an effort. He knew how it felt.

At least the heat had begun to relent as evening approached. So much for Scotland being cold and wet. If he did have to sleep outside tonight he wouldn't freeze, though the morning damp would play havoc with his chest, and his supplies were down to a rind of cheese and a single wrinkled apple.

He made out something white amid the trees ahead. Though it was only August the leaves had already begun to turn in the unseasonable summer, and the grass and heather at the side of the road looked withered and scrawny.

As he approached he made out a low whitewashed building with a rough thatch roof. An odd place for a croft, pinned between the mountains and the loch with nothing but scrappy woodland to make a living from. Then he saw the horses tethered in the small meadow out the back, two bays and a grey, all in far better condition than his tired old nag. This had to be a Change House, a combination public house and horse exchange more suited to the eighteenth century than the late nineteenth. Such places had become rare in the Highlands since the coming of the railways. He remembered reading Boswell's account of staying at the Change House at Loch Ness. He had referred to it as a 'wretched little hovel of earth' where the only fare available was goat stew. At this moment any shelter and hot food, even goat stew, would be most welcome.

From beyond the bare wood half-door he heard the murmur of conversation and a lilting, melancholy air played on a fiddle. He slid from the horse's back, tethered it to a hazel sapling, and went in. After the bright summer evening his eyes could make out very little of the dark interior, though he smelled wood-smoke and spilt beer and heard the voices – all speaking Gaelic – pause, then resume in murmurs as he crossed the threshold. As he took a step inside the fiddle stopped and a male voice said, 'Welcome, stranger.'

'Good evening,' said James, addressing the room's unseen occupants.

A man emerged from the shadows, wearing a lose shirt of indeterminate colour and a green leather cap over wild dark curls. 'And what brings you here on this fine summer evening?' said the man. His English was perfect, if heavily accented.

'Well,' said James, 'I would like food, a bed if available, and perhaps to change my horse.'

The amused murmurs from the room's recesses implied others here understood English and presumably viewed a well-dressed, demanding – and by implication rich – Englishman as a source of income and possibly sport. James felt the urge to back out. His life did not need further shortening by venturing into a den of avaricious peasants. But then, he had come to Scotland to try and connect with the stories, songs and traditions that his fellow Englishmen seemed determined to either sentimentalise or eradicate. People like these might have what he sought. He stood his ground.

The man took his elbow and steered him into the corner, 'Perhaps we should take things a step at a time. Food first, eh? And beer of course.'

James sat down at the wooden table across from his host. Someone – female, from the glimpse of cleavage – reached over and put a pair of pewter tankards down in front of them.

'Your good health,' he said gravely, and took a careful drink. In his recent travels he had sampled a variety of beverages, and discovered that whilst the Scots knew how to distil, brewing was not an art they excelled at. However this beer, despite its sour and spicy taste, he found quite palatable.

'Tis heather ale,' said the man across from him, though he hadn't asked.

'It's very good,' said James, resisting the urge to get out his kerchief to wipe his mouth.

His seat faced the only source of light, a small window that showed a square of sky fading from blue to lilac over the silhouette of the mountains across the loch. His position put the face of his companion in shadow, but James got the impression he was being watched. That was only to be expected, as such entertainments as a stranger provided would be rare in these parts. He continued, 'I'm James Murchison, by the way.' He considered offering his hand, then thought better of it. Such formality would be out of place, if not insulting, here.

'You can call me Robbie,' said the other laconically.

'Pleased to meet you, Robbie.' James saluted his companion with his drink and took another gulp. When he lowered the tankard he found a wooden bowl and pewter plate in front of him, and a candle on the table between the two of them. James was unsure how the table had suddenly come to be so full. Perhaps this heather ale was stronger than it looked. 'Ah, food, yes. Well, I hope you'll excuse me while I eat.'

Robbie gestured to show he had no objection.

For all he knew the stew might have been goat, but it tasted fine, and the platter held chunks of fresh bread plastered with butter and served with soft crumbly cheese. It was some time before James turned his attention back to the other man, by which time darkness had fallen. Though James had thought his companion to be in his twenties, looking though the candle-flame at him now, he thought him much older.

'That was excellent,' said James.

Robbie raised an eyebrow. 'And now you've had your repast perhaps you might answer my question.'

'Which question was that?' The food and beer and stuffy darkness had left him sleepily content and a little befuddled.

'The one I asked when you first came in. Why are you here?' The man's voice had an edge of one more used to giving than receiving commands, and James felt a sudden apprehension.

He tried to keep his tone placatory without being condescending. 'If you mean why am I in your beautiful country it is… a holiday, and a labour of love. I am a writer. I made my modest living writing the biographies of greater men than I, but I have always wanted to find and record stories of those who seem ordinary but are extraordinary. The people who preserve traditions whose origins are lost. I hope to perhaps find such people here.'

'A modest hope,' murmured Robbie, so quietly that James was not sure he had heard him. Then he continued, 'So then, you write of, and look to, the past.'

'Oh no. I am not one of those who believes the past to be some golden time of wonder untouched by care. I merely hate the idea that whatever was, for good or ill, may one day be lost. I would love to know the future too.'

'Ah then, a man for all times, but belonging to none. Just the ticket. Though when it comes to the future, I've generally found that if you wait long enough, the it'll arrive by itself.'

James considered carefully before replying. 'True enough for most. I, however, have very little future left to me. Eight or nine months, my doctor says. Hence my desire to spend what time remains fulfilling my dreams.'

People usually greeted news of his illness with degrees of sympathy and embarrassment, but Robbie made none of the usual responses. Instead he regarded James with renewed interest and said, 'And if you could have one wish before your time came, what would it be?'

In an attempt to deflect the other man's peculiar scrutiny, he said lightly, 'Oh, that my time might not come so soon.'

Robbie frowned, then laughed. 'You'd be a fool to ask otherwise. But leaving that aside, is there any one thing that you will leave this life wishing you had found or seen or done?'

James had planned to be the one asking the questions. He wasn't sure how things had switched about, but now he felt an absurd yet growing desire to impress his host. He began to formulate a reply touching on the success he had already had with his books and implying that he could have achieved more but for the undeserved imposition of his disease. Then he stopped. One thing about being doomed, he realised, was that one was free to say and do whatever one wanted. He cleared his throat. 'Well, though this might sound odd, my biggest regret is never having been truly in love. I have had infatuations aplenty, but never experienced the emotion the poets speak of.'

Robbie nodded with what James decided was approval then said, in a tone that reminded James of a huckster offering a never-to-be-repeated bargain, 'And what would you give for love, and enough life to enjoy it?' Robbie's eyes, which James' mother would have called 'witch-green' sparkled in the candle-light.

James' apprehension returned, though he could not say what it was that frightened him. 'I am not sure I get your meaning.'

Robbie leaned forwards, put his chin on his hands and said, 'I am offering you a trade. What would you give for the chance to increase your remaining time by ten, and in that time to find the person you are meant to find?'

Trying not to think of Faust, James forced a laugh, 'No disrespect intended, but I see no point in bargaining for something I cannot have.'

'You're a writer, a man of imagination.' said Robbie, sitting back in his chair with an expansive gesture. 'Could you not at least consider the possibility?'

James would love nothing more. And he had nothing to lose. Or perhaps he did. Forcing levity he said, 'I should warn you that I do not feel inclined to bargain away my soul.'

'Your body then? Once you have no further use for it, of course.'

Images of graveyard thefts replaced those of demonic pacts. James said, 'Sir, I am not sure what you want of me.'

'I want your trust, your belief. And in return I offer life, love and even a kind of immortality.' Before James could query the extravagant claims, Robbie continued, 'I can make this offer only once. And I would not make it were you not possessed of the rare quality of reaching into both past and future. Time needs men like you to keep it on its toes.'

Rather than try and fathom precisely what Robbie meant, he asked, 'And all I have to do to earn a little more time for myself is to agree to trust you?'

'To trust me, yes. And to return to this place when your time is up.'

'As it stands your offer seems very good. Perhaps too good to be true.'

'You reject it then?' Robbie sounded disappointed.

'No, no. I have less to lose than most.'

'And would you be willing to say goodbye to what little you have left? Because to get your reward you must leave behind all you walked into this room with save what lives in your head.'

James tried not to sound too cynical. 'So you want my money, my clothes, presumably my horse too, as part of this bargain of yours?'

'As a condition of it you must leave your old life behind, so yes, those things will not go with you.'

'I see.' James might be dying, and he knew he had occasionally been credulous when faced with wonder, but he was not an idiot. 'I

135

think not. Thank you for your kind offer to relieve me of the burden of my possessions, but I will hang on to them for now if it's all the same to you.'

Robbie leaned forward and said in a stage whisper. 'Do you not think that, if all we wanted was your worldly wealth, we could not simply take it?'

He nodded to indicate the room, and James glanced behind him. The place was a lot bigger and fuller than he remembered it. Though the tables nearby were still in darkness, way off he saw lights. The looked more like fireflies than candle flames, and they seemed to dance over the heads of the shadowed horde who thronged and milled beneath them. Though James could not make out anyone looking his way, he had the feeling that the half-seen figures were very much aware of what went on in this dark corner.

'What is this?' said James, suddenly afraid. 'Who are you?'

Robbie shrugged, all homely familiarity. 'Oh, we're nobody. A whole merry gang of nobodies. And we have no interest in the things you own. Just in your good self.'

James swallowed. He had been looking for lost folk traditions and legends, and he seemed to have found one. He considered his life, the little that remained to him, and his dreams, those few he had fulfilled, and came to decision.

'If I choose to enter into this bargain, what exactly would it entail?'

'I'll drink to that,' said Ray. Laura could have sworn his glass had been empty a moment ago. She finished her drink. It was an exceptional whisky. She would have had another if she hadn't been driving. 'So,' continued her companion, 'tell me about your one true love.'

Though she couldn't detect any mockery in his voice, Laura felt suddenly self-conscious. 'Well, we met here, seven years ago.'

'Here as in at this pub?'

'No, no, I didn't even know this place existed until tonight. We met on the road. I nearly ran him over, actually.'

'Careless.'

'Well, he was walking along the middle of the road. He was... confused. He had a rare form of amnesia, possibly the result of being attacked. He'd lost his clothes, his money, everything. I picked him up, took him to hospital. I know what you're thinking: the man's freezing cold and naked, he's not sure who he is, what kind of idiot would fall for someone like that? But I knew the first time I saw him that he was the one. Corny, eh? My friends reckoned it was because I felt responsible for him. But that wasn't the reason. It was love at first sight. We were together from that day on. Until he died.'

The tears came from nowhere. She let them. Ray sat silent while she cried. Every other time the grief had crept up on her in public – as it had a lot in the last three weeks – she had tried to suppress the tears and when she'd failed she had been filled with embarrassment on top of her sorrow. Crying in front of this stranger she felt no self-consciousness, only a sense of release, as though she needed him to witness her pain before she could start to get over it.

He made no move to hug her, but when the tears finally dried he offered a large white handkerchief. Though it had faint brown spots in one corner, Laura accepted it gratefully.

When she had fully recovered and returned the hanky he said softly, 'How did it happen?'

Laura found herself about to talk about James' death for the first time. 'He'd been preoccupied for weeks. He wouldn't say why. Anyway, we went for a walk in the woods and he collapsed. I phoned for an ambulance but he was dead before they arrived. He wasn't in pain, he just... ebbed away. The doctor said it was probably an aneurysm.'

'And the promise?'

'As he lay in my arms he kept repeating 'you have to take me back.' I asked where and he said he had to return to the stretch of road I found him, that he should have come back before his time was up – that's what he said: "before my time was up", like he knew when he was going to die. He wasn't delirious, he was completely lucid, he just kept insisting that I brought him back to the exact place we'd first met. So I promised him. Then he smiled and closed his eyes, and I felt the life just drain out of him.'

'It's a lot harder to keep a promise when you're dead,' said Ray with no hint of irony. In fact he sounded disapproving.

She didn't want this man's disapproval. In fact, she found she feared it. She stood up. 'No, I did what he asked. Wait here a moment.'

Outside, the darkness was complete, the air still and thick with cold. The warm fuzziness of the whisky had left her, and she felt determined, sure of what she had to do. She lifted the hessian bag out of the foot-well. Back inside, she put it on the table in front of Ray. 'The crematorium put him in a plastic canister thing, but this seemed more suitable. It's Victorian. He used to keep his papers in it.' She rolled down the bag to reveal a wooden box. 'I've kept his bargain for him, as best I could.'

Ray nodded slowly, then looked up at her with twinkling eyes. 'So you have,' he said.

'I'm probably going to think I'm mad in the morning.'

Ray nodded in agreement. 'Possibly. But morning's a long way off.'

'This *is* what he meant, isn't it? Coming here, and leaving... him... with you.'

'It is.'

Laura knew she was being selfish, but she had to say it. 'He came into my life with nothing, and now he's gone. I just wish I had something left of him.'

Ray leaned over the table and put his hand flat on her belly for a moment, then sat back and said, 'Actually my dear, you do.'

*

Chao opened his eyes.

Already the visions were fading, though he could still hear the echo of the music and laughter, still smell the food and flowers and incense, still feel the passing tingle of their graceful touch. Not that he recalled who they were now. He felt as though he had been transported for a while. Where, he had no idea. Somewhere like home, if home could be prised lose from memories of specific places and people and distilled into a feeling of belonging somewhere where everything was more wonderful than he could ever had imagined. And now he was back.

Darkness had fallen, though the after-effects of the drug allowed him to see clearly. Dilated pupils, he told himself, snatching for rational explanations. He was still outside the dilapidated hostel on the rusty bench. Above him the sky was alive with stars. As the dream faded and reality coalesced he felt deep regret for what he had lost. He spent a while trying to hold onto the feeling, but the more he tried to remember the details of the experience, the further they slipped out of reach.

'Don't chase it. Just let it become part of you.'

Though the voice was only a whisper, Chao jumped. He realised that Reef was still sitting next to him on the bench.

Chao had no idea what to say to him, so he said nothing. Instead he did what the other man had suggested, and absorbed the last of the dream. He began to see the world as he had always seen it. Almost. There was beauty here whether he was stoned or not. Beauty he had the skill to capture. One day he could make his living that way, creating art rather than colluding in destruction. And he wouldn't let Marie slip away. He remembered the one thing his gran had told him about his grandfather: that though he had died too soon, the love had never died. He would find the strength to hold onto his love, while becoming what he wanted to be.

'I take it you're satisfied,' said Reef.

'I... Yes. It's not like any other high I've had.'

'No, it wouldn't be,' said Reef. He sounded amused.

'I mean, I can't remember a thing, but I know it was amazing. And it's left me feeling sure of my path, if that doesn't sound too corny. How addictive is it?' Physically he felt fine, even if he would have given almost anything to return to the place the stuff had taken him.

'Ah, well there's good news and bad. It has no hold on you, but it'll never be as strong as the first time.'

Chao tried not to be disappointed. After all, he could have lived his whole life and never tasted the wonder. 'But it has changed me, hasn't it? Forever, I mean. Does that last, the feeling that the world's a better place?' He knew he sounded naïve, even dumb. He didn't care.

'For as long as you want to believe it, yes.'

'If enough people did believe it…' Chao tried to stop gushing, to make like a man closing a deal, then decided not to bother. 'You know, pal, this stuff could change the world.'

'Sometimes the world needs a kick up the arse,' said Reef laconically. He then added, 'So, do we have a deal?'

Chao had come here as a courier, closing a deal already made. But that was before he'd tried this stuff. Giving people something that made them re-evaluate reality and their place in it was not the same as just providing a means to escape from it. 'I reckon this'd be wasted on the people Uncle wants to sell it on to.'

'Then keep some back. A little will go a long way, but you'll still need to be careful who you give it to. Some need their eyes opened more than others.'

'That's quite a responsibility.'

'So it is, but you're the man for the job, assuming you're up to the task of putting a little magic back into the world.'

Was he? Didn't he have enough on his plate with Marie and the Family? Yes, but he knew he could live his life right now. And this was more important than any one life, because it could change hundreds of lives. 'All right. I accept.'

'Good man. The rest is on the seat next to you. Use it carefully, as you'll not find any more where that came from.'

Chao looked down and saw a square shape about the size of a shoe-box on the seat beside him. He lifted it carefully onto his lap, and was surprised to find that it was made of wood. He flicked the metal clasp and opened the lid. The powder inside sparkled in the starlight. He ran his hands through it, letting the rough grains flow between his fingers. It felt more like ash than dust. He turned to ask Reef what the stuff was called.

He was alone on the bench.

He closed the box and stood up. 'Hey, you still there?'

In reply he heard only the lapping of the water and the silence of the hills.

Then he remembered that the money was still in his room.

Reef must have gone back to his boat. Chao put the box back under the seat and ran down the lawn towards the loch. Even the action of running felt different, as though his body had somehow woken up. The cool night air on his face made him smile.

The lawn ended in a steep pebbly slope overhung with trees. There was no landing stage, no place to beach a boat. No one here at all. The surface of the loch was dark, speckled with the jewels of reflected stars, and utterly still.

A lot of stories come from the collision of two – sometimes disparate – ideas/inspirations. This story – which I feel still works well, even though it's a bit dated in places – was one such. I hadn't heard of 'change houses' until I visited the ruins of one on the shores of Loch Ness in 2005, but I immediately saw their potential to be liminal places where the normal rules of society, or even reality, might not apply. The other idea is an interest in stories that resonate across time, which probably came from reading Alan Garner's Red Shift at an impressionable age. Having a complicated relationship between future and past – even better one with a relationship in it – is always fun. And for the record, I wrote this before I came across Outlander.

Down at the Lake

Dawn already? Cold too: winter's on its way. As I stumble back up the slope to the cottage my feet break through a crust of frost; freezing mud squelches up between my toes, thick and chill and sticky.

There's no smoke coming from the chimney. *Damnit Papa, have you let the fire go out again?* A shadow passes over the sun and I shiver; before I can catch it the shiver becomes a shudder, something beyond a mere reaction to the cold.

Even as I wonder where this sensation comes from, it's gone and all that matters is getting inside, where I can be dry and warm.

The cottage is empty, but I should have expected that. Last night Papa was so pumped up with his great victory that he swept out without a word. He must still be over the far side of the lake, gloating. Ah dear, you poor, tragic birdies! Sorry, princess, looks like you got your hopes up for nothing. What a shame.

I just wish Papa would give me some credit for his triumph. I danced until my feet bled.

Or perhaps he's avoiding me because of what I found out yesterday, how spells work both ways: black needs white and night needs day. It's all about balance. Pay a price – and gain a reward.

There's a lot of crap talked about magic. To hear the villagers prattle on you'd think Papa could pull gold coins and fine linen from the very air. If only. You need to start with the right raw materials.

You can't just magic things away either. Which is why, between the fabric, beads, paint and knives Papa used to make me look the part, and the crusty plates, cobwebbed corners and unwashed laundry that built up while he was enchanting and I was practising, this particular sorcerer's cottage is a stinking hovel.

Jaine Fenn

I need clothes. Up in my room, I find and pull on a fairly clean kirtle, drab brown but warm and familiar on bare skin. While I fasten my dress I find myself looking at the shapeless frock hanging on the back of the bedroom door. Today, it's coarse black fabric sewn with cheap glass stones. Yesterday, I dazzled the courtiers in midnight satin and blood-red rubies, fitted to show every curve. I looked amazing. I *was* amazing. And Papa was so proud. But that was then; in daylight the romance and magic drains away.

Well, not entirely. If he'd given me the choice I would have kept the dress and lost the face. This insy winsy mouth would look better on a trout than a girl and these wide, trusting eyes make me look like a lost puppy. Shame magic sticks to flesh better than it does to cloth or glass. So I'm left with a peasant's costume and a princess's looks – at least while the sun's up. I imagine I'll get used to it.

May as well tidy up. Anything to stop him going into one of his strops when he gets home. I know him: after the party, the comedown. Despite the success of this latest scheme he'll be off again soon enough, pacing and muttering over injustices only he remembers, raging about vengeance for ancient slights.

If only I could stop thinking about Siggy. That wasn't a side-effect either of us foresaw. It's so dumb. *He's* so dumb. But the silly boy's also so very... cute. And he's a prince, of course. A real live, blue-blood, no-brain, pert-buttocked prince. When Papa gets back I'm going to ask when I can see him again. After all, Siggy loves me now: naturally he'll want to see me again. It can't end here. And if I do go back to the palace to see Siggy again, then that would make the revenge all the sweeter. That's what I'll say, soon as Papa gets back.

While I wait, I light the fire. I sweep the floor while the water's heating, then I put the plates in to soak, wash some socks and shirts and finally have a go at scraping Papa's work-table clean, though it'll take more than warm water to shift all this fat and dried blood.

When the sun starts to sink behind the trees and there's still no sign of Papa, I begin to fret. Remembering the odd feeling I had this morning – it's a wise sorcerer's daughter who listens to her intuition – I put on a cloak and shoes and go out.

I know where he'll be. I'm in such a hurry to get round the lake that it's a while before I notice how empty the water is. Not a swan in sight, even though it's still light. Something is wrong.

On the far side I come across footprints. Footprints made by delicate, girlie feet, the sort born to wear embroidered slippers and be carried across thresholds by adoring princes. Dozens of pairs, all running away from the lake. Which can mean only one thing. The birds have flown. Or rather, not being birds any more, run off.

My heart begins to patter. I call Papa's name, but get no answer. I won't panic. A sorcerer's daughter never panics.

Then I find him.

He's lying face-down in the reeds. I almost stumble over his body.

A noise, an ugly thoughtless squeal, breaks from my throat. Birds burst up from the willows at the sound. Then I'm crying, the tears rolling off my face like the first fat drops of a summer storm.

After a while I get control again and make myself look more closely. His right wing is broken and he's been shot through the heart with a crossbow bolt.

A crossbow bolt.

Siggy?

I never thought my silly, pretty prince had it in him. That's love for you. Not love for *me* though. I know that now. I might have turned his head when I danced for him in the glow of Papa's magic, but the one he really wanted was *her*, the leader of the cursed princesses. Her white innocence, her effortless grace; her pathetic need. He killed my Papa to free the stinking princess from Papa's enchantment. And it worked, too. Her and all the other girlies, back in human form all the time, no longer doomed – hah, doomed! – to be swans in the daylight.

I start crying again. This time the tears are all for me. I don't fight them.

When I came out of the lake this morning I had a father – not a good or loving father, but the only one I've known – and the love of a prince. Or so I thought. Turns out I don't have either. I rage at the trees, the sparrows, the reeds. I curse the world.

The world ignores me.

145

Finally I run out of anger and tears. I sniff, then drag Papa's body down to the shore. On his left side, he's got an arm, not a wing, and I wonder what this means. After all, if murdering him lifted the curse on the princess and her cronies, what will it do to me? They were normal girls once, back before Papa found them. I don't think I was ever a normal girl, not given the way Papa changed the subject whenever I mentioned mothers or birthdays. Now he's dead so the spell's broken and they're human all the time. What about me? Do I have to spend the rest of my life as this leggy, flightless girl-thing?

But when the last flashes of the sun disappear behind the mountains I feel the familiar tingle, soft as downy feathers and urgent as the need to pee. I hurry to get Papa into the water. As soon as he's free of the shore the lake pulls him out of my hands. He slips silently down into the dark, chill depths.

My skin is crawling now. I undo my cloak, pull my dress over my head and wade out further. Tiny buds of black are bursting out all over my body, unfurling into sleek feathers, a thousand pin-pricks becoming dark flowers. I raise my chin and my neck grows longer, filling my head with the sound of cracking bones. My knees twitch, then break cleanly and start to heal themselves, reversed.

It hurts. Every time, I forgot how goddamn much it hurts, until it happens again.

But it's a good pain. It's the pain that makes me what I am.

At the final moment I sweep my arms back, and now they're no longer arms, but wings. I plunge chest-first into the water.

When I come up, I'm a swan, black as a moonless night.

For a while I simply glide around, listening to the night-calls and the gurgles and the splashes; the life of the lake. It isn't that I *can't* think when I'm a swan. I just can't be bothered to.

I see light on the water, a sudden burst of gold, shockingly pretty. For a moment the sight foxes me. Then I realise it's a reflection and look up, just as a red flower explodes above the trees, its mirrored twin glittering in the surface of the lake. Fireworks. Fireworks to celebrate a royal wedding.

Well, they didn't waste much time. Fall in love one day, marry the next. Hell's curse on them both.

Then, suddenly, I know why they're – why *she's* – in such a hurry.

146

Another thing people don't know about magic is that there are some forces it can't stop. Like death. Or time. Oh, it can make people think nothing's changing, stick a nice comfortable illusion in front of reality. Magic can even put some things on hold for a while. But in the end, there's always a price to pay. I don't know how old I am but since I've started counting the years I've been through my fingers and toes once, and I'm back to fingers again. The white swans have been living on the far side of the lake for as long as I can remember, and Papa once told me that *she* was their leader because she's the oldest of them all.

Now father's dead and the spell's broken. Given I'm a swan again it would seem I've enough magic of my own to keep me going but as for her... any day now, time's going to start catching up with her. I bet she can feel it in her bones. She knows she doesn't have long. That's why she's so desperate to wed my Siggy at once.

It might be a week, a month, maybe even as much as a year, but one morning soon my poor, brave fool of a prince will wake up next to a woman older than his grandmother. Let's see true love survive that.

I can wait. It'll happen, sure as night follows day. And when it does I'll be here. After all, we swans mate for life.

At times like this, I almost wish I had a mouth to smile with.

Everyone loves a retold fairy tale (if not then they really should), though this is more a retold ballet tale. I love ballet and no character in the genre is more fascinating than Odette/Odile, two sides of the same being, danced by the same dancer. This is also one of my favourite stories to read aloud to an audience, as I get into this character far too easily.

The Sky Weeps,
The Earth Quakes

1ˢᵗ August 1541

Such irony: whilst most natives are simple rustics, and embrace the True Faith with childlike ease, it is those who once held high rank who show the greatest reluctance to accept the Word of God. The mission is increasingly forced to resort to the techniques of the Inquisition to save them, much to my unease.

Even so, some still resist. Their fortitude might be admirable were it not so misguided. Perhaps it stems from the assumption of power; if they believe their faith to be right, they can continue to believe themselves wronged. But their world is ours now, and their resistance only causes unnecessary pain – and, in the end, Damnation.

Luisa reaches out to the tiny bird. So intent is the jewelled creature on the scarlet bell-flower it sips from, it gives no sign of knowing she is there. She thinks to touch it. Then, as though called by a voice she cannot hear, it darts away, silent and smooth.

Is that how angels fly? She wonders, hand still outstretched. *Do the heathens of New Castile have such beings as angels in their twisted faith?* Her brother might know. But she has no intention of asking him.

3ʳᵈ August 1541

We have a new arrival.

He was brought to the garrison five days after my brethren left to take the message of salvation farther up the valley. The soldiers accompanying the prisoner were impatient to release their burden to me and be gone themselves, in their case to further plunder and pillage.

The man showed signs of harsh treatment: old bruises and brands and a dislocated shoulder – no doubt a result of an encounter with the strappado. He was perhaps two decades older than me and had, I think, already been thin before his current privations were visited upon him. Yet his gaze was not downcast. He regarded me only for a moment, as the letter authorising his transfer was handed over, then turned his eyes to the shining terraces that skirt the peaks around us.

When I looked for one of our interpreters the captain said, 'He speaks passable Spanish, Brother.' Then he added, 'He is quite the talker, when you get him going. Full of wisdom.' He spat to show what he thought of the natives' wisdom. 'My men dubbed him Solomon.'

'Why has he been brought back down the valley to me?' I asked. The prisoner's gaze was still raised, as though his rags and wounds and shackles meant nothing to him. It recalled the arrogant stance of my father.

The soldier nodded to the letter in my hand sealed, I now saw, with the crest of Father de la Cruz himself. 'These are your orders.' Then he appeared to remember himself. 'I am sorry, Brother, I meant these are the instructions from your fellow missionaries.'

I had the guards take the prisoner to a cell; we have several empty ones now. With the comparison to my earthly father and the guard captain's comments fresh in my mind, I chose one of the more odious of our windowless holes.

The letter stated my charge was a noble, named Apac Kunya in the heathen tongue, and that he knew of riches hidden to all but the highest and most privileged of his people. Attempts had been made to gain knowledge from him by 'all the usual methods' to no avail.

I heard the voice of my superior in the next phrase. 'He is happy enough to talk, but insists on picking the subject. It seemed appropriate to send him to one who prizes all knowledge indiscriminately.' The letter concluded, 'This man is of value: we give him to your care in the hope that your softer methods may succeed where firmer ones have failed. By the time we return to the garrison on our way back to Cuzco we hope that you will have gained the knowledge we require. Brother Ruiz, as you appear immune to the subtleties of politics and diplomacy, let me make the situation clear: this is your last chance to redeem yourself.'

'Is it true?'

The garrison commander does not look up when Luisa walks in. His shoulders twitch, then he puts down his quill slowly. Finally he meets her eyes. 'Is what true, señorita?' Captain Rodriguez does not much like her, but she does not much care, provided he shows her the respect due her gender and status. It was not as though she asked to come to this godforsaken place.

She steps closer to his desk. 'The rumours brought by those soldiers. About Señora de Salazar.'

'Those soldiers being the men escorting the prisoner?'

'Of course.' As though they have had any other visitors this week. 'I heard one of them telling Corporal Moreno that Commissar de Salazar's wife died in childbirth.'

The commander purses his lips. 'It is possible. I understand the poor lady has not been blessed with good fortune in such matters.'

Luisa schools her expression. She is sure the commander knows the truth, even if he would never say it to her face. 'No,' she says. 'She has not. So I take it you have had no official word regarding this unfortunate possibility?'

'I have not. And to be honest, Señorita Ruiz, news of such nature is unlikely to cross my desk.'

She smiles, though it is an effort. 'If it does, I would appreciate your letting me know. We receive so little news of interest here.'

'Such is the nature of living in recently conquered lands.' The commander's words are brusque, but his tone soft. 'I will endeavour to keep you informed, should I hear more.'

3rd August 1541 cnt'd

When Father de la Cruz oversaw interrogations, he insisted on having a guard present, even with prisoners barely capable of lifting their heads. Now that I alone enforce the will of God in the garrison, perhaps I should continue the tradition. Yet this new native was sent to me for my 'softer methods', so I chose to exclude the corporal from the cell, although he insisted on waiting outside in case the prisoner, shackled and quiescent though he was, tried to make trouble. In truth, I hold out little hope that I may succeed where others have failed; yet the final words of my superior's letter hang over me.

Away from the burning sun, in the rush-lit gloom, the prisoner finally looked up at me from his place on the floor. I found his gaze unnerving, and began to speak before I had fully gathered my thoughts. 'Are you Inca?'

He did not answer at once, so I opened my mouth to repeat my question, in case he had not understood.

'Not a ruler, no. My role was amautas.' His voice was hoarse, his pronunciation erratic.

I asked him to repeat that last word.

'Amautas.' He spoke slowly. 'In your tongue, is no match. Perhaps nearest is seeker of knowledge. Like you.'

'I am a priest, a servant of the One True God.'

He nodded, then winced as the motion set off some injury. 'And a seeker of knowledge. It is good to meet you, at the last.'

'You have heard of me?' This was not possible; no doubt his incomplete knowledge of our language had let him down.

'I knew I was to meet you.'

'I doubt that. But if it is true, then you know why you were sent here.'

'To tell you secrets I would not tell by torture.' His odd tone unnerved me; for a moment I thought I heard mockery in it.

'Quite so. Reason may persuade men where force fails, if they have the wit and intellect to appreciate it.'

'This is... flattery, yes?'

He *was* mocking me! I wished I had a guard after all, to strike him for his insolence. 'Not flattery, heathen: logic. Do you know the word?'

'I have heard it.'

'Then you also know that you are doomed, as things stand.'

'Such is true.' The thought did not appear to concern him.

'Yet you may save yourself, if you cooperate.'

'As my Emperor did, then?'

I cursed myself for giving him that opening. Here, in my private journal, I may confess that the elder Pizarro's treachery against the last free Inca ruler still disturbs me. But I could not admit that before this man. 'I am not here to discuss the past. Nor am I a soldier, who sees force as the only way.'

'Yet you serve the soldiers' cause, to take from us the tears of the Sun.'

'What I serve is a higher power, the highest power there is!' I was angry, yet shamed too. This was not the way things should go. 'We will continue our discussion later.'

With that I left, taking the light with me.

'So Father de la Cruz believes you will succeed where he failed?'

Luisa does not mean to sound disparaging, but Gabriel was never the most favoured member of the mission. And now he is stuck here, away from the action, sent down the valley from the frontier as she was sent up from Cuzco. Perhaps he is being punished too.

Her brother speaks tightly, looking up at the ridge of the Cordilleras, black and featureless now the sun has dipped behind them. 'Yes. Sometimes the head and heart may triumph over baser instincts.'

Luisa can't help herself: she snorts. But maybe it is time to speak of matters left unsaid too long, alone in the pure, fragrant evening. If God prompted them both to come out to the courtyard as evening fell – their first time alone outside the confessional in the two weeks since she arrived – then she should use the chance to mend things between them.

As she opens her mouth, a wisp of smoke drifts up from the ridge to the north. It thickens quickly, tarnishing the gold and turquoise sky. Luisa shivers, knowing what the smoke signifies.

Out of the corner of her eye she sees Gabriel's head turn. 'Luisa...' he begins, and she hears sympathy in his tone when, suddenly, she wants condemnation, something to fight.

'It's getting cold.' She turns to go, cutting across his words.

'Luisa, you should not be here.' His gentleness burns her.

As she hurries away one hand goes to her belly. No,' she mutters, 'I should not.'

4ᵗʰ August 1541

I should have heeded the warnings about this prisoner, and been less hasty. But, reviewing our first conversation as I arose this morning, I recalled his expression when the light was removed from his cell. Uncertainty crossed that haughty, swarthy face as darkness fell. Perhaps base bargaining might work after all. I left him alone, in the dark, for most of the day, only visiting his cell as evening approached.

Apac Kunya blinked when I opened the door, looking beyond me to the slender thread of golden daylight as though returning from some deep meditation. I ordered the corporal to wait outside once he had put the rush light on its shelf, and placed myself in front of the door. The cell was taking on that vile and familiar smell of occupation, a mixture of ordure and festering wounds.

For a while neither of us spoke. When I felt there had been enough silence, I asked, 'Can you conceive of any method by which we might extract from you the information we seek?'

I had given my opening sally much thought, and the prisoner now returned the favour. While I waited for his answer, I heard distant male laughter, and the cry of a bird overhead. Finally he said, 'I cannot.'

'Then I wonder why you are here.'

He lifted his hands, making his shackles clink. 'No other choice.'

I sighed, striving to keep the sound light and natural. 'Then it appears we have nothing to say to each other.' I reached for the light, and began to turn.

'Wait.' It did not sound like an entreaty, nor an order; more a suggestion.

I paused. 'So you think we may converse meaningfully?'

'All choice is yours. All power is yours. But yes, I think we may.'

I put the light back and turned to face him again. Then, on impulse, I squatted, with my back against the door, so I was no longer looking down on him. 'What should we discuss?'

'Instead of information, knowledge. If I see the difference right.'

'What do you believe it to be?'

'Information serves purposes, is a way to reach an end. Knowledge is its own value.'

I nodded. It was an accurate summation, however poorly phrased. 'And where does faith fit in?' I had questioned the servants about his claim to be an 'amautas' without getting a satisfactory answer, but the heathen religion is intertwined with their society to an alarming extent so perhaps he thought himself a priest.

'That is a hard question. Maybe not a good question, given our differences.'

He was right about that. But there was one question I wanted answered. 'True, but I would like to know why your people worship gold.'

'I may ask same of you.'

It took me a moment to realise what he meant. Then I was angry. 'How dare you! We worship God, not Mammon!'

'Yet your love of gold brings us to this.' He raised a manacled hand to indicate the dingy cell.

I could feel heat rising, a passion to defend my Faith. I took a breath before replying. 'I will not deny the avarice of those who first discovered your land, nor the brutality of some of their actions. But we – my brothers in Christ – see the hand of God in this, for our actions have allowed your people to receive His message.'

He nodded, as though I gave the answer he expected. This annoyed me, so I asked, 'What power do *you* see at work here? If your gods were so mighty, how come they are now thrown down?'

'It is… fate. The rightness of all.'

'You agree with what is happening to your land?'

'No. But it is as it was foretold.'

My heart sank. 'By your priests, presumably?' And so the Pagan justifies their defeat!

'Yes. You do not believe in foretelling?'

'In prophecy, you mean? Of course not.' But I spoke without thought, without the knowledge I pride myself on, for the Bible is full of prophecy. 'You still have not answered my question: if you do not worship gold, you do at least revere it.'

'We revere it, yes. That is the word.'

155

'Tell me more.'

I will not record our entire conversation, for it became esoteric. This native grasps concepts quickly, and understands distinctions only an educated man can. Our talk brought pleasure to me, a pleasure of the intellect which has been lacking since we came to this place. What the conversation did not do was bring me any closer to those secret hoards my countrymen are so set on finding.

My dearest E,

I do not know if this letter will reach you, for it relies on the promises of low men – and though those I entrust with it cannot read or write, it is still best we avoid names. Firstly, I forgive you. I understand why I could not stay in Cuzco and I know you were bowing to pressure from your superiors when you sent me away. But you know that, you said as much at our parting.

The reason I write now is that I have heard news of your wife, that she has passed away. Tell me please, is it true? She never gave you the son you craved. Nor did she love you as you deserve to be loved.

We sinned, may the Lord forgive us for that, but I can give you those children, many sons, healthy and strong.

You know that we should be together, you know this in your heart.

My fate is in your hands,

L

5th August 1541

Today's conversations with Apac Kunya followed on from yesterday's. He spoke freely of the learning of his people, which took on the learning of those tribes they conquered before they themselves fell our conquest. He also hinted at older wisdom. His people tell of a great flood, and while we know that this catastrophe was the will of the Lord and washed away iniquity, Apac Kunya says the deluge also washed away knowledge, knowledge he and others like him have worked hard to regain since.

Perhaps this talk should make me uneasy, yet we in the civilised world revere the knowledge of the Greeks and Romans, who were Heathen peoples.

We touched upon religion, and he expressed interest in the nature of the Trinity, how one God can be three entities, and how the Holy Virgin fits into our beliefs. I did my best to enlighten him. When I departed his cell this evening I left a fresh rush-light.

Still, I must be wary, and not let his words distract me from the task I have been set, for I find myself admiring this man. Not in the way I have confessed of elsewhere in this journal, not that. It is more that he reminds me of the kind of father I would wish to have.

It first occurs in the garrison chapel, as she is about to pray. For a moment Luisa thinks she is being struck down, punished for her sin. Her heart races and weakness shoots through her limbs. Then pain, like a kick in the guts. She reaches for the altar rail, gasping in the thin cold air. But her mind is turned to the divine, and in her head she remains calm, as her lips forms the words *Blessed Virgin, take pity on me*, repeating them over and over.

The pain abates. She is kneeling now, and her knuckles on the rail are white, but the spasm has passed. Already warmth flows back into her body.

Then, so gentle she is not sure at first, there is movement within, and she knows all will be well. She smiles, and changes her prayer, even as her baby kicks again. *Let my son be born healthy and strong, and into the house of his father.*

12th August 1541

I was right to cultivate this native's friendship!

For the last week we have talked of many matters: history, natural philosophy, medicine and the transmission of knowledge. I cannot remember such enjoyable discourse; sometimes I almost forget that this man is a proud and damned Heathen.

But in less than a month the mission is due to return, and Father de La Cruz will be unimpressed with treatises on the natives' learning.

Today we finally reached materially fruitful ground. We had been discussing faith, a subject I feel compelled to return to, for I truly wish to save Apac Kunya's soul: it grieves me that such an intellect remains impervious to the highest wisdom. I made what I thought to be a conclusive case for the current situation being God's will, but he shook his head – with less pain now, for I have procured medicine for him – and said again that we overthrew his people because it was foretold and, knowing it to be the will of their heathen gods, they acted against sense and welcomed the Pizarro brothers when they should have killed them. I was about to rebuff this argument when he said, 'Do you know of the Man of Gold?'

For a moment I forgot to breathe, then I mastered myself and said, 'It is a common legend.' In the glitter of his eyes I saw that he knew as well as I that this is the heart of the matter for those who hold power over us both.

'It is no legend.'

'It is not?' I was proud of how light I kept my tone.

'We have talked before of how my people take on the knowledge of others. One such was a priest fleeing the hot forests of the north. He knew the secret of making the king-who-sees.'

'The king-who-sees?' Another fascinating but damned piece of knowledge, I thought.

'It is a ritual, and gold is part of it.'

Or maybe not. 'You are saying there truly is a golden man? That El Dorado exists?'

'A man made gold, yes.'

Although the foreigner's grasp of Spanish grew daily, misunderstandings still occurred, and I feared this was one of them. I had to be sure. 'So you know how to make this man of gold?'

'I know the ritual. I would teach it you.'

'You would? Why?'

'Although fate makes us enemies, you are a man of learning, and learning must be saved. If I do not pass this on then it will be gone from the world.'

I admit I was flattered. 'So, in broad terms, what is involved in the ritual of El – of the king-who-sees?'

'Fasting and meditation, initially.'

Perhaps I had misunderstood after all. 'You did mention gold.' I was embarrassed to bring the subject up again.

'Gold dust yes. It is needed for the final part, to gain true sight.'

'But the ritual is not a way of procuring gold.' I spoke sternly, to remind him of how little he had to bargain with.

To my surprise, he smiled. Apac Kunya has a severe, though not cruel, face but it changes when he smiles. I wanted to smile back. He said, 'Not to make it fall from the sky, no. But to tell you where to find it. To become the king-who-sees is to know what is to come.'

Was he saying what I thought he was? 'Such as?'

'Anything the will is turned to.' His smile became wry. 'This power could be used, among other purposes, to locate hidden treasure. Or it could be used – was most commonly used, when we ruled – to see the future.'

At the time I dismissed his words, but since leaving him I have not been able to put them from my mind. The power of prediction would make moot the need for torture; it would be a benefit above gold!

I may be being deceived, for this would not be the first time I have fallen for the lies of others. I have prayed for guidance without cease from leaving the prisoner until I took up my pen tonight. But I so want this to be true!

Storms are common in the mountains, though they do not always bring rain. Last night's did, and this morning the world is fresh and new. Luisa's step is light as she crosses the courtyard. Although she only came here to escape past mistakes, on a day like this she feels some love for this bleak and unforgiving land.

Halfway across the square of beaten earth she pauses, knowing she is watched. A sideways glance shows Corporal Moreno, lounging under the eaves. He is smiling at her. She hurries on, before he can call out. She gave him coin to smuggle out the letter to her lover, but gold is plentiful here and she could tell he wanted a different payment. Even in heavy skirts the swelling of her belly is becoming obvious, and he thinks her already fallen. Were it not for the iron hand of the garrison commander, she would be fair game. Under her breath she murmurs, 'Holy Mother, protect me.'

Stepping into the relative safety of the kitchen block, she decides that all men are either self-serving bastards, like the soldiers, or weak fools, like her brother.

No, not all: she recalls the face of Eduardo de Salazar, and knows that one day they will be together again.

16th August 1541

The first steps, Apac Kunya claims, are simple. I must eat only certain foods, in limited quantities – a discipline I am used to already – and meditate. This latter skill I thought I had, but prayer, which we have already discussed at length, is not the same, he says: in prayer the mind is caught up in the words offered to Heaven, whilst in true meditation the mind is empty, and receptive. These last three days I have kept to the regime he suggests, and have tried to cultivate this un-minded meditation he recommends.

Is what I do a sin? This Heathen still refuses to accept Jesus as his saviour, for all he admires Our Lord's teachings. Yet nothing I do – to fast, to meditate – goes against God's word, and I have seen no sign from Above that I stray.

I have, I must confess, broken out the whip again, for the first time since Brother Pedro left. Such mortification fits with what Apac Kunya tells me of the rituals of an apprentice amautas, and I find it eases my soul even as it pains my body.

It is possible – nay, likely – that I am deluding myself, just as the prisoner's people deluded themselves. I may know the true heart of this Heathen people through my efforts, but I doubt it will bring me the power he claims to have.

With that in mind I asked him today if, given his foresight, he knows whether my efforts will be rewarded. He has already admitted that the future is rarely a clear and certain path. The only event he has spoken of as fixed is his own death, which, he says, will come soon. Whilst I fear he may be correct, under the circumstances such an assertion requires no special powers to make.

He counselled patience, saying that as I have the aptitude, we must try.

Impatience got the better of me and I said, 'This would be easier if I knew what I worked towards!' We have no firm timetable, and Apac Kunya gives no assurances, only suggestions.

He bowed his head. 'You wish a demonstration?'

'Yes!' Was he really offering to make a firm prediction, here and now?

For some moments, Apac Kunya sat very still, eyes downcast. He raised his gaze slowly, looking past me to the rush light. I tried to dismiss my unease at his blank gaze by remembering the tricks of gypsy charlatans back in the town fairs at home. But I do not believe this man is a charlatan. Or perhaps, I do not want to believe it.

Finally he spoke, as though making a casual observation, 'Do not be here this time tomorrow.'

'What do you mean?'

'At this hour,' he frowned, then said, 'no, a little earlier: halfway between noon and sunset. At that time, you should stand outside, in the courtyard, alone.'

I crossed my arms. 'Why, pray?' These were the words of a tinker who told fortunes, not a great scholar with unknown powers.

'That is all I can know, in here.' His gaze, clear again now, took in his cell.

'Is that so?' I said, getting up to go.

He nodded, not looking happy.

I fear I may have been fooled after all.

Luisa is surprised when her brother emerges from the cell block in the middle of the afternoon. These days he spends every hour of daylight with the savage. He starts when he sees her sitting by the well but she will not move. The soldiers are out on exercise, the day is fine but cool and she is at peace.

Gabriel hesitates under the portico, then comes towards her. His expression is odd; perhaps he wishes to talk.

She stands, and as she does so feels her son kick, hard enough to make her bend like a reed. Suddenly the earth kicks back, and she is falling. She reaches for support, but there is none. The air is still and silent but beneath her the ground bucks and heaves. She stumbles in panic, hearing Gabriel shout something about the well. She looks over her shoulder to see the stone she had been sitting on shift, tip and disappear. She can no longer stand, and drops to her knees, too numb with terror to form a prayer.

The shaking lessens, and she comes to her senses enough to cry out 'Jesu save us!'

Finally the jolts become tremors, and then cease.

Before she can find strength to move, her brother's arms are around her, supporting her.

'It's all right, Lui, everything will be all right.' Distant cries and crashes sound as the rest of the garrison feels the after-effects of the tremor.

He has not called her Lui in years, has not spoken like that since they left Spain. All at once she is back in the family home, and when Gabriel says 'Don't cry,' she hears his younger, softer voice, speaking in the darkness, after Father had come to her. With his wife dead, she is all he has, he says… she jerks upright, pushing her brother away.

'Lui?'

But the long-buried memory has awoken, and she cannot stand to be touched. She stands. 'Leave me alone! I cannot bear it…'

'Can't bear what, Lui? It's all right, really it is. That was an earthquake, but a miracle too, you won't believe what has happened! I was told of this, well not in so many words but told nonetheless…'

She looks at him through her tears. He is energised, excited: oblivious. Always, there is some piece of knowledge, some idea, that blinds him to the truth that stares him in the face! She cuts through his prattling flow: 'Why did you bring me here?'

He pauses, rocks back. 'I… I did not bring you to the valley, you were sent, from Cuzco, because…' He can't say it, but his eyes go to her swollen belly, and in that moment she hates him. She wants to know why he insisted she come with him to New Castile, whether it was to save her from their father, or punish her for her wayward ways, but all he can do is remind her of her more recent sin.

She finishes the sentence for him. 'Because I did what is natural to man and woman. Unlike you…'

His face falls. 'I never have…' he whispers.

'In your heart, you have, and God sees that. I know how twisted you are, for all your learning.'

'Please Luisa, don't say that.'

Finally, she is getting through to him, making him *feel*, not just *think*. 'I only speak the truth. You love the truth, do you not? Well, the truth is our father is a monster – you he only *beat* – and you are a pervert, and I will not be punished for following my heart, save by God alone.' She stalks off, unsteadily. He does not call out after her.

It is only later, alone in bed, that she considers that, had she not stood to greet her brother, she would have been sitting on the wall beside the well when the earthquake hit, on the very stone that fell. He saved her life. No, that was God's hand. Her foolish brother will not acknowledge his flaws, he could not save her from their monstrous sire and now he is oblivious even to the works of the God he professes to serve, preferring instead the words of a Heathen.

18th August 1541
'You knew! How did you know?'

I had not planned to greet my prisoner-turned-teacher with those words, not least because I knew the answer to the question, but even this morning wonder at his prediction brimmed over in me.

'Were many hurt?' he asked in return.

'In the quake? No, only minor injuries, from a fire in the kitchen.'

'Good. I saw... a possible loss.'

I thought of Luisa, and the well. A happy chance, I had thought at the time before correcting myself and thanking God for sparing my sister. Had Apac Kunya seen that with his unearthly sight? 'Did you know who could have been lost, or how that might have come about?' I asked carefully.

'No. This power, my friend, it is like grasping smoke. When you reach out, you disturb the patterns. The more precision you apply, the faster the truth will fly from you.'

'And can what you see be changed?' I was willing, at least, to entertain the truth of his claim, and my mind raced with the implications.

'It was forbidden to try, for that went against the gods. But we inherited tales from those we took the power from, of how what is seen will come to pass, even if the act of trying to avoid it makes it so. We could not change the future, but we could prepare for what it brought.'

'Can you show me more? Foretellings that reach farther afield perhaps?'

'I can try. But I will need to see the sun.'

Suspicion stung my breast, though only briefly: this man had neither means nor strength to effect an escape. But nor was he in a position to make demands. 'That is not possible.'

He shrugged, his maimed shoulder rising only fractionally. 'Then I cannot demonstrate what we work towards.'

'Explain!' I demanded.

'The power I hold is tied to two material anchors: gold dust to awaken it, and the sun's light to allow it to function.'

'Heathen claptrap,' I muttered. Yet his prediction, while cryptic and vague, had come true.

'I do not claim to know why this is. Some of my peers tried to unlock the links between the world of touch and the worlds of mind and spirit. But they are all dead now. I am the last Amautas.'

He had implied as much before, but hearing it said made me reconsider. 'Then I will indulge you. But,' I warned him sternly, 'if my indulgence gives no firm results then I will consider your first prediction to be mere fluke.'

I told the guards I wished them to check the integrity of the cell, although this building is converted from the old residences of the natives, and suffered little damage in the earthquake. The corporal gave me an odd look, but assigned a man to escort the prisoner outside.

There is one room beyond the cell, with an open doorway. As soon as Apac Kunya had clear sight of the bright courtyard beyond he tensed, like a hunting dog. When we stepped into the light he paused, and turned his face to heaven. The soldier who walked behind holding the prisoner's chains made to kick him, until I held up a hand.

Apac Kunya carried on, walking slowly now, like a man in a trance.

'Let the chain play out, and remain where you are,' I instructed the soldier, and began to walk alongside Apac Kunya. When the chain reached full stretch I murmured, 'You must stop now.'

Apac Kunya obeyed, though his face remained raised. His eyes were closed yet there was movement behind the lids, as when one dreams. His lips formed soundless words. I was reminded of the ecstasy of divine communion.

He sighed then muttered, 'Your people fight each other for the spoils of our land, brother against brother.'

Indeed they do, but he could have heard the guards outside his cell speaking of that. 'This is commonly known.'

He froze, then began murmuring again. I made out the words 'Your sister...'

'What of her?' I have not spoken to him of Luisa, but again, he could have heard her mentioned by the guards.

He whispered, 'She will find what she wants, soon... but in the end, she will get what she believes she deserves.'

Despite his vague words, to hear Luisa spoken of in this way filled me with cold dread, as though I looked down on events from a high mountain, unable to intervene as disaster unfolded. I fear he has spoken a painful truth, even if the details are not yet clear.

I was tempted to ask him further questions, but Corporal Moreno emerged from the cell block to inform me, in a voice somewhat lacking in respect, that there was nothing wrong with the prisoner's accommodation.

Back in the cell, speaking quietly to avoid curious ears, Apac Kunya told me of what I must do next if I am to become the king-who-sees.

I do not yet know if I dare.

E, my love,

I know why you did not reply to my last letter; I understand. But now I must tell you of a graver matter. I fear my brother has fallen under the spell of a Heathen warlock. A corporal in the garrison has told me of allowances being made, of overhearing strange conversations. I myself witnessed from the kitchen the Heathen being given temporary liberty, and falling into a trance in the courtyard.

I tell you this not only in the hopes it may convince you that I should not be in this place, but because it is my Christian duty. I have also sent a letter up the valley with a servant, to meet with the good Father who leads the mission, telling them to bring forward their return and root out this sorcery.

May the blessed Virgin protect and bless us both,

L

20ᵗʰ August 1541

As I write this two small but heavy sacks sit on my desk. I had to lie to Captain Rodriguez to borrow his keys, saying I wished to check the strong-room to ensure the share of the spoils belonging to my family was in order. He knows I have little interest in such things, but no doubt assumed my request was on Luisa's behalf.

It was strange to see so much gold in one place. Stranger still that it languishes in the dark. It stirred no greed or wonder in me, only unease at the price paid to get it.

I have no idea which soldier considers these two sacks to be his. They were easy enough to smuggle out in my robes.

As Apac Kunya instructed I have eaten a pinch of the gold dust, rolled in bread, washed down with wine in which a little more was sprinkled. I felt nothing at the time but now, two hours later, I am calm; I think I feel the change in me begin. Once I have made my record for the evening I will meditate, knowing I am one step closer to gaining the ultimate knowledge.

Luisa has stopped asking her brother to hear her confession. He is the only priest in the garrison, and so conducts mass and the other necessary offices. But he does so distractedly, as though his calling matters less than the Heathen prisoner who waits in the dark for him. Luisa shudders to think of what they get up to, what Gabriel will have to confess when his betters return.

Instead of talking to him, within or outside the confessional, she spends the time praying, alone.

She does not know whether her letter reached Father de la Cruz, but she prays that the might and order of the Church will return soon, to save them all.

22nd August 1541

Before dawn I will take the final step.

It is past midnight, and soon the guards will leave the cell block for the night. I have eaten my last meal of bread and gold. The remaining gold-dust I have transferred to a knapsack. In a few hours I will go to the cell-block for the last time, and release my mentor and friend.

We will use a pool farther up the mountain, part of the native's terrace cultivations. It is barely deep enough for me to immerse myself in, but all that matters is that I emerge from the water, washing off the gold the Amautas spread over me with the correct words and gestures, as the sun rises above the hills. I am sure now that Apac Kunya is right, and that when he completes the ritual I will become blessed with true foresight, as he has been. And I will use it for good, as he has tried to.

The time has come. We will only have one chance.

I must put down my pen now, and clear my mind in preparation.

Luisa once heard that the smell of human flesh burning is like roasting pork. Now she will find out if this is true.

Father de la Cruz is with the warlock, giving the Heathen a last chance to embrace the True Faith. From her place under the portico she sees the bound man shake his head. Father de la Cruz turns away from the stake in the centre of the courtyard, his face set. As soldiers come forward to stack the last faggots on the pyre the priest approaches her seat, his expression softening.

'You did the right thing, child.' It is the gentlest speech she has ever heard from this hardest of clerics.

She is touched, but her gaze still drifts to the far side of the square, where Gabriel stands between two guards, his head lowered.

Father de la Cruz says, 'Your brother is not the first to be so beguiled.'

'What will happen to him?' The priest's zeal when his party swept into the garrison while all – or almost all – slept had surprised and alarmed her; so eager were the priests they had ridden through the night. Had their family been of lower status, today's pyre might have been built for two.

'He will be sent back to Spain, to face a formal hearing by our order.'

'Will he be excommunicated?' Gabriel's soul can still be saved, she is sure.

'I pray not. But if he decides to remain part of the Church he will be stripped of all rank and assigned grave and lasting penance.'

Given that the alternative is to throw himself on the "mercy" of their father, Luisa knows what her brother will choose.

Captain Rodriguez approaches the pyre, a torch in his hand.

Luisa remembers Gabriel telling her how the Inca Emperor converted in his final moments. As well as saving his soul, he bought himself an easier death, garrotted before the fire took him.

The wood is dry, and the flames take quickly. The warlock stares straight ahead in silence as fire licks his robe.

'You do not have to watch this,' murmurs Father de la Cruz.

'I know,' she says, but if she looks away she will see only her brother, broken by his latest and most foolish, mistake. 'But I wish to see God's will done.'

The Heathen is wreathed in flame now. His hair flies up around his face, then catches fire. Still he makes no sound. A nearby soldier mutters, 'That's five you owe me,' to a comrade; no doubt the outcome of a bet.

Beyond the pyre she sees movement. Gabriel has raised his head to look at the man who entrapped him. Even from here Luisa can see that he is crying.

She looks away.

The dying warlock finally makes a sound. He strains at his bonds, moaning like an animal, the low moans barely audible over the fire's crackle. His skin is starting to blacken.

Luisa keeps her head up, but lets her gaze drop, focusing on a patch of dirt just in front of the pyre. She prays under her breath, though the words bring little comfort.

The wind changes and when the smell reaches her, she finds what she was told to be true. She presses a hand to her mouth, swallowing hard. But she will not disgrace herself, not in front of everyone. After a while the urge to vomit passes.

At a loud and splintering crack she looks up to see a dark form crash down into the pyre, sending up a shower of sparks into the darkening sky. The ropes binding the warlock to the stake have finally burnt through.

The falling body fans the flames briefly, then they die back. Luisa can watch again now there is nothing obviously human in the pyre, nothing still alive. In fact, she cannot look away.

Finally, with the first stars coming out in the east and the western sky fading to old gold, the observers begin to move off. As Luisa prepares to stand she sees Gabriel approaching, still under guard. The hurt and accusation in his eyes make her want to look away, but she must not. Instead she raises her chin and says, 'I will pray for you, my brother.'

He pauses – his guards let him – and shakes his head. 'You have no idea what you have done, Luisa. No idea. If you had only waited one more day…'

She is puzzled; Father de la Cruz said they found Gabriel awake in his rooms, apparently at prayer, when they arrived. It was odd for him to be up so late, but the good Father made no mention of anything else amiss. 'Why?' she asks, 'what will happen tomorrow?'

He laughs, a broken and mirthless sound. 'What will happen tomorrow? Why, dear sister, I have no idea. No idea at all. And now I never will.' He moves off, giggling under his breath.

Father de la Cruz regards her with kindly eyes. Looking for reassurance she asks, 'Do you know what he meant?'

'Not as yet, but we will.'

'I am not sure he will tell you.' There was madness in her brother's eyes.

'Worry not, child. We have his books.'

From: Commissar Eduardo de Salazar to Señor Gabriel Ruiz,
22ⁿᵈ November 1541:

Brother Ruiz,

I hope this brief note finds you before you embark for the motherland. News may not have reached you yet of the serious earthquake we recently suffered in Cuzco. Many lives were lost and it is with great sadness that I must inform you that your sister – my wife – and our baby son were among those now gone

169

to God. They were in the Cathedral of Our Lady at the time, in the new section, where the roof collapsed. I know that you, like me, will pray evermore for their souls.
Yours,
Eduardo de Salazar.

Another story that combined two sources of inspiration: Fortean matters (specifically hidden histories, as this was the brief here: stories supressed by the Catholic church) and the cultures of pre-Columbian America. By the time I wrote it I had been lucky enough to visit some of the old sites in Peru, though I didn't experience any earthquakes while I was there.

Liberty Bird

This is the moment. That first glimpse of space, coyly revealed by the widening doors. Kheo gives his instruments the attention they require, but his eye is drawn downwards, to the banded glory of Yssim, the cold and distant light of the stars beyond.

His exit is faultless. The Clan insisted he pre-program it, rather than take even the miniscule risk of their favoured son screwing up and dinging his yacht on the hangar doors. That would never do, not with the whole world watching.

Some impulse had made Kheo visit the engineering hangar three days before the race. He should either have been preparing himself mentally with relaxation and centring exercises – as his family would prefer – or drinking, gambling and womanising in the lowtown rings – as the media would expect – but he had a sudden desire to be alone with his yacht, without the tech crew fussing around.

The hangar was the largest open space on the liner and the ship's spin provided near-normal gravity here. After two months away from Homeworld, the echoey open space and illusion of full weight were disconcerting. In the low lighting *Liberty Bird* was a point of colour, although her red and blue hull was muted by the oily shadows.

Kheo reached up, tracing the fusion yacht's perfect lines, his hand passing just below the Clan crest emblazoned on her side. Someone had left the steps in place; it was only logical he use them to climb into the cockpit. He sighed as he sealed the canopy. *Liberty Bird* was the only birthright he wanted. Yet the race she had been built for might not be held for much longer, and if his family had their way this would the last time he would be permitted to compete. That made winning for a third time even more important.

He started at movement glimpsed out the corner of his eye. Someone out there, down on the hangar floor. A thief? A saboteur from a rival clan who had somehow got onto the Reuthani liner? His heart raced. The net was buzzing with stupid gossip: with no one to keep them in check any more, ancient clan rivalries were getting out of hand.

No, just Chief Mechanic Sovat. Kheo liked Sovat, respected him. Yes, that was what he felt: *respect*. Sovat often worked late, went above and beyond.

Except Sovat didn't appear to be working. More like waiting. Another of the tech team walked in, a younger man whose name only came to Kheo after a moment's thought. Greal: junior propulsion specialist, university educated, rather effete for the rough-diamond world of the yacht-techs. Why were this mismatched pair meeting here so late? Not for something nefarious, he hoped. They appeared to just be talking, standing close.

Oh. Had he really seen –? Did they really just –?

Sovat stepped back, then looked around. Kheo shrank down in the seat, holding his breath. The Chief Mechanic's gaze passed over him, and he turned back to his companion. More brief words, then the two men left, Greal following close to Sovat. Kheo had no doubt they were headed somewhere more private.

Kheo clears the great wheel of the hangar-deck at a pace the watching cameras will no doubt find pedestrian. Of course, speed is relative: the liner is in a high, fast orbit around the gas giant far below. The first thrust of acceleration as he brings the main engines online is deceptive; he actually needs to lose orbital velocity before the start of the race.

He rotates *Liberty Bird* and peels away from the Reuthani Clan liner; the huge blunt needle is strung with spoked rings, their sizes and positions determining their place in this microcosm of clan life: engineering, living suites, gardens, entertainments and accommodation for the few thousand citizens permitted to accompany their betters off-world for this annual jamboree. In a touching if tacky gesture, a block of portholes in the central midtown ring have been selectively lit to spell out the words *Good Luck Kheo.*

All around Yssim, other Pilots are leaving their liners. Most clans, including his own, only field one Pilot these days. Some clans no longer participate in the Flamestar Challenge. Other clans no longer exist.

The yachts head for the Royal Barge, a smaller vessel in a lower orbit around the gas giant. Though the Barge now lacks any royalty, tradition still dictates that the race starts from there. It will take several hours to reach it, and the formal start of the race. The approach is critical to a good start. In his five previous races, Kheo has tuned his coms into the razzmatazz that surrounds the biggest event in high society's calendar. All across the system, pundits are discussing the latest form reports released by the clans for their teams and mulling over the detailed ion-stream data. Every other year, Kheo has revelled in the sense of being at the heart of it all yet free, out in the vastness of space.

Not this time. He selects some roots-rock – not his usual sort of music, but it should blast his head clear – and stares out into the beauty of the void, urging his mind to remain blank.

Kheo was expected to show his face at the hangar the next day, both as a courtesy to the techs working on his behalf and to attend a briefing on the current configuration of the ion-streams. He had been looking forward to the tactical discussion of routes and fuel management, to sharing the respectful camaraderie of the men. Instead he was uneasy, almost nervous. He made himself chat to the usual people; act normal.

And everything *was* normal. In the daytime bustle, Kheo wondered if he had been mistaken; perhaps he even dreamt the encounter he had witnessed the previous evening. He spent enough time imagining such things.

Sovat was as brusquely efficient as ever when he took Kheo over the latest engine test results. There was no sign of Greal.

Sovat was the last to leave the briefing room, and he paused, as though waiting for Kheo to say something. When Kheo failed to speak, the Mechanic turned to follow his fellow techs out.

Jaine Fenn

Kheo took a different route back to the suite-decks, choosing rarely used corridors and secondary float-tubes, doing his best to avoid the crew, minor family and hangers-on with their ready smiles. He spent the journey trying to work out whether the look Mechanic Sovat had given him had been an invitation.

By the time he has the Royal Barge on visual, Yssim itself is too large for his mind to interpret as spherical. The gas giant is a sky-spanning backdrop of mauve and azure, lavender and turquoise. He is close enough to spot details in the roiling turbulence between the coloured bands. Thanks to the false-colour projections enhancing his view through the canopy, he can see the ion-streams: ethereal threads and skeins, twisting and curling out from the massive world, curved lines of force linking it to Estin, the pus-yellow moon constantly pummelled by Yssim's tidal forces.

Now comes the first test. The intricacies of orbital mechanics make an actual start line impossible. Instead Kheo, and every other Pilot, must interpret detailed positional readings then use them to apply delta-V, at the same time keeping track of the movements of the other yachts.

The exact moment the race starts is determined by the AI-enhanced stewards on the Barge, who are monitoring every one of the twenty-three yachts to determine when all of them are present in the prescribed volume of space. Just being in position isn't enough: you need to be on the right heading and, ideally, as near the front of the volume as possible.

Fifteen ships already lined up... another entering. And another.

He makes a tiny adjustment; raising his orbit slightly. He's in a good position but he can't afford to leave the start volume before the last yacht enters it. A false start not only annoys the watching billions, it means the culprit has to start in the secondary volume, behind everyone else.

The penultimate yacht enters the volume. Kheo's got less than five seconds before he leaves it...

The final yacht is in place.

His board lights green.

He keys the preset that maxes the drive. The gentle hand that has been pressing him into his seat becomes a grasping fist.

The Flamestar Challenge is on.

Two days before the race, Clan Reuthani held the pre-race banquet in the liner's Great Mess, a name which had made Kheo smile when he was growing up.

Kheo's first banquet had been seven year ago, shortly after his sixteenth birthday. Uncle Harrik had been First Pilot then, and Kheo had joined in with the drunken and enthusiastic chorus of the Reuthani Clan anthem which serenaded him to his rest. Harrik had won the Flamestar that year, a victory made more special because that had been the first time the race had been run since the Empress had been ousted; their Clan yacht had even been renamed in recognition of the coup. In all, his uncle had won twice in eight races. Impressive, but not as good as three out of six.

This year, as the diners picked over the second course of the third remove – sweet jellied consommé upon which floated spun sugar confections in the shape of fusion yachts – a lull in the quiet murmur allowed an overloud stray comment to surface.

'Liberation's become a dirty word!'

The speaker was Kheo's father, the Honourable Earl Reuthani. At his words silence fell across high table. Several people on nearby tables glanced at the chair between Kheo and his mother. Next to him, Prinbal sighed. His younger brother currently greeted most parental comment sighs but for once Kheo could have joined in.

'Surely you aren't suggesting we were better off under the Empress!' That was Harrik: no else would dare speak up, but the combination of being an ex-Pilot and having fought in the Liberation gave him the right to question the Earl.

'Course not, she wasn't even human.' His father was drunk, as usual. 'What I mean is, the commoners forget that most of us rose up when they did, an' fought beside 'em. And now they're angling for this 'New Liberation' – from us!'

At least Clan Reuthani still exists, thought Kheo grimly.

His brother was watching their father, absorbing the adult interactions even as he pretended to disdain them.

His Mother said, 'But I doubt the malcontents will get far. We need *some* continuity. Most people realise that. What we should be worrying about is all those other systems out there.'

'Surely contact could be to our advantage,' said Kheo, thinking of the new technologies he had heard about via the recently instituted 'beamed virtual' connection. After centuries of imposed isolation they were finally part of the universe at large.

A cousin chirped, 'Yes, who knows what outsider technology could mean for the Flamestar Challenge?'

Assuming it continued. Now the massive extravagance of moving everyone of note out from Homeworld to run a race around the largest body in the system was no longer maintained by the Empress's brutal taxes, the race was becoming unsustainable. Which just made it more important that he won it again this year. But as discussion returned to the upcoming race Kheo found his taste for the festivities dulled. He was glad when he was sung to his rest.

Alone in his room, his mood darkened further. He had spent much of his adult life being secretly grateful that he had been too young to fight in the War, that his elder sister had volunteered instead, although he doubted Father would have let an older son join the fight. Now, facing a life of responsibilities he never wanted and knew he was not up to – not to mention the frustration and hypocrisy – he almost envied his dead, heroic sister.

The first stretch is a long straight burn.

Kheo's initial gamble paid off: he has a solid starting position. But so have half a dozen others, including Umbrel Narven. She's one of two female Pilots, vanguard of the kind of changes the Earl hates; she has a reputation for recklessness and her clan has some of the best techs, inherited from now-defunct clans. With two close seconds and a third but no win to her name, Narven's the one to watch.

A couple of competitors are already lagging behind, possibly because their yachts aren't as well tuned as his, or possibly because their starts didn't give them the trajectory they wanted for their chosen path through the ion-streams. Everyone else is still a threat.

Thirty minutes in and the field is spreading out. Now the tactics start to show, as each Pilot plots the precise course they'll be taking through the near-invisible energy maze formed by the ion-streams. Kheo has assimilated all available data on the current disposition of the streams but now, close up, he can get more detailed readings and make final adjustments. It looks good: the provisional trajectory he agreed with his team won't need significant adjustment.

The projection of the streams overlays the view ahead, a shifting, sparkling curtain coloured every shade of the rainbow. The colours are a code imposed by his comp. He is heading for the golden-orange area, nearer Yssim than Estin. Running close to the gas giant has inherent risks, being liable to fluxes and gravitational effects that could affect his instruments and put stress on his yacht, but he has the skill to navigate it and *Liberty Bird* is up to the task. And the crowd will love it.

But he is not the only one risking a close skim. By the time they are fifty minutes into the race, his sensors show two other yachts lining up for similar courses. One of them is close enough that he thinks he can actually see the tiny black speck against the looming ion fields. His instruments ID it as the *Aurora Dream*. Clan Narven; he might have known.

The sense of emptiness lingered. He woke with a ridiculous urge to cry, but saw it off with a cold shower, along with all the other unwanted desires and unsafe emotions.

He was nervous at the prospect of going to the workshop but in the end, what else would he do the day before the race? His heart tripped when he saw Mechanic Sovat, and he looked away.

After the daily briefing he lingered, and was unsurprised when the Chief Mechanic did the same. Kheo searched for the right thing to say. Finally, as Sovat raised an eyebrow and turned to go, Kheo managed, 'Do you really think Clan Narven's directional thrust innovations pose a threat to us?'

If the mechanic had any idea that this wasn't what Kheo wanted to say he gave no sign. 'They might well, sirrah. You'd best take the lead from the start; they have the advantage in hi-gee manoeuvring.

Make Narven's yacht work hard to catch you, and stick the course. Just like I said.'

Which he had, in the meeting, only a few minutes earlier. 'Right. Yes.' Kheo looked at the man's hands, because they were safe. Except they weren't. They were fascinating.

'You're a good pilot, sirrah.'

Kheo tried not to be over-pleased by the praise. Before he could stop himself he looked up and said, 'I believe you worked late two days ago.'

Rather than answer immediately Sovat bent forward a little, leaning on his fists; those perfect, sinewy hands. Kheo got a heady whiff of oil and sweat. 'What makes you think that?' said Sovat quietly, then added, 'Sirrah.'

'Never mind my reasons, Mechanic,' Kheo was glad of the table, which was high enough his body's response to the encounter. 'Were you in the hangar the night before last?'

'I was.' Sovat's gaze never wavered.

Kheo found his own eyes drawn, once again, to those hands. 'And were you alone?'

'No, Sirrah. I had Apprentice Greal with me.'

Kheo must have imagined the small hesitation between 'Greal' and 'with'. 'And did anything happen?'

'Happen, sirrah?' Kheo would swear the man was *enjoying* this. 'What sort of thing were you thinking of, sirrah?'

'I... I could check the camera feeds, you know.'

'So you could, sirrah.' The mechanic smiled laconically. 'But I doubt you'd find anything to alarm you.'

Because Sovat had edited them. The Mechanic was careful, thorough: he must have lived with what he was for years. Kheo wanted to hate such forward planning, such contrivance, but found himself admiring it. This man could not only face the truth, but live with it. 'If,' he managed, 'I did see anything some people might find alarming...' he swallowed, half expecting an interruption, but the other man remained silent, 'I'm not sure I'd be alarmed, myself,' he finished in a rush. His face felt like it had caught fire.

Sovat's voice was soft. 'Perhaps you wouldn't, at that,' he said.

'And if, if I was not alarmed when, when most people would be. Normally, that is. Would that be... something of interest? To you.'

Sovat remained silent.

Kheo swallowed. 'I was asking you a question.'

'Were you now, sirrah?' Was that caution or knowing acceptance in Sovat's voice?

Acceptance, Kheo decided. They understood each other. No damning words, no absolute confirmation, but there was that connection, that shared experience. Except Kheo's experiences had been confined to fantasy, until now. 'What if I had been here, with you, instead of Apprentice Greal? Would something have happened? Something the cameras wouldn't see, and that no one,' he felt his breath growing short, 'no one ever needed to know about.'

Sovat paused before answering, then said, his voice regretful, 'No.'

'No? Why not?'

'A matter of taste, sirrah. Personal taste.'

'What are you saying? I'm not your *type*? But you're... and I'm...' *And no one else is. Except Greal, apparently.* 'I could report you, you know. What about that, eh?'

'You're free to do as you will, sirrah.' Sovat sounded calm; Kheo had no idea if he was concerned about the threat. 'Your word carries far more weight than mine.'

But with doctored cameras, it would just be his word. And he could never betray the only man he had ever spoken to in this way. Not even if that man rejected him. 'Well, just... remember that.'

'I always do, sirrah. Was there anything else?'

'No. Nothing else.'

After Sovat left Kheo sat alone in the briefing room. Then he locked himself in the nearest restroom alone, and privately explored the possibility that Sovat would walk in, and find Kheo was his type after all. Then he showered, thoroughly.

Having been both vindicated and rejected in one short conversation, he returned to the family suite, heading straight for his rooms. Here he checked the publically available information on Mechanic Sovat. The man's first name was Appis, and Kheo spent a few moments saying the name, *Appis Sovat*, before chiding himself and looking deeper.

There was nothing incriminating to be found. Had there been the technician would not be in the position he was in today. Kheo uncovered only one item of note, from before the War: when Sovat was twenty-six two of his male friends had been charged with gross indecency. One had opted for surgical readjustment; the other had not relented of his perversion and had been exiled 'at the Empress's service'. Further research revealed that the man had died two years later, at a mine in the bleak high plains of South Arnisland. The verdict was death by natural causes. It generally was, in the mines.

Kheo hisses in triumph as one of the two yachts peels away, slowing as it does. *Too rich for you, eh?* He has taken the shorter, riskier path twice before. The first time, he won. The second time overdriving the engines damaged his yacht, and ended his race. Who would have thought two other pilots were also willing to take the skim? Or rather, one now. Umbrel Narven is still in the race. And her yacht is going to enter the streams ahead of him. He'll be hard pressed to catch her.

No, that's defeatist talk: he is still the best Pilot, in the best ship.

Umbrel Narven no doubt thinks the same about her own skills and vessel.

'Ah, there you are!'

Kheo looked up from his desk and forced a smile for his mother. 'I thought I'd get an early night…' He waved the display clear.

'Very sensible. But first, I have news.'

Kheo knew that tone. 'You'd better come in.'

She swept into his room and perched on the more upright of the two chaises 'I didn't want to distract you until we were sure, not with the race coming up –'

'It's tomorrow, Ma, and I don't want to be distracted, you're so right.' Kheo ignored his mother's wince at being spoken back to.

'Ah, but this will give you something to race for.'

'Have you… finalised arrangements? You have, haven't you.' Making the right match was as much the duty of an oldest son as racing in the Flamestar Challenge. More, really: the Empress had dictated that Clan scions must prove themselves before marrying, but she was gone. Given the dangers of yacht-racing, many Clans, already depleted by the War, forbad their heirs from taking part. And whether or not the race endured, it was no activity for a family man, as his mother had reminded him on his last birthday.

'I have!'

'With Leilian Fermelai?'

'Well, you two used to play together so well when you were children. And the poor thing lost both her parents in all the nastiness.' Meaning: unlike Clan Reuthani, Clan Fermelai had not acted against the Empress. 'We'll announce the engagement en route back to Homeworld, and hold the formal party at the Manse.'

'This isn't what I want.' His voice sounded dead in his ears.

'Kheo, I know this is hard for you. It's hard for all of us. But you have to settle down. Leilian is technically the head of her clan but, she's only a woman, and with most of her family gone... this is better for everyone. She will be good wife.'

He wanted to protest further, to say he did not want a wife, good or otherwise, but it would be futile.

More gently his mother added, 'This marriage is a necessary thing. I hope you can find happiness in it, Kheo, I truly do. But if you cannot... provided you do your duty, a blind eye can be turned.'

Does she know? But he had done nothing to act on his feelings; on the contrary he had made every effort to live up to the image of the yacht-racing noble rake. 'What do you mean?' he asked as evenly as he could.

'The unsuitable women,' said his mother, in the verbal equivalent of scraping excrement from a shoe.

Ah yes, those women, the entertainers and hostesses; eager to please, and notorious enough that his rumoured liaisons with them maintained his reputation, yet low enough that his failures and foibles would never reach the wrong ears. He had been careful in his choices. He wouldn't miss the embarrassment and guilty revulsion; nor the fear that they saw him for what he really was.

'You won't have to worry about them,' he said.

'Good.' His mother's smile told him that she, like everyone else, believed the carefully cultivated image. 'That's settled then.'

The *Aurora Dream* is pulling ahead, Narven's lead opening up second by second.

So, no win. No glory. No final chance to shine before subsiding under the weight of duty and acceptable behaviour. The best he can hope for is second place.

Why can't I just be happy with the privileged life I was born into? He knows the answer: because he can't be himself.

Am I being selfish? Perhaps; there were choices, plenty of them. He could have fought in the War, despite being young. He could admit what he really wants in a lover, although where would he find that in the world he lives in, where such things are never spoken of, even if they are no longer punished with more than a fine? He could stand up to his father, although the old man is quite capable of disinheriting him; an unthinkable prospect.

Plenty of choices there. Shame he has been too much of a coward to take them.

He blinks away stupid self-pitying tears and focuses on *Liberty Bird*'s instrument panel. Here is the one thing that is good and simple and right about his life, directly in front of him. And he is about to come in second, in his final race. It's all downhill from here. Winning isn't just desirable any more: it's the only option, whatever the cost.

There isn't much time: he scans his readouts, their meaning as comforting and familiar as the drapes above his bed, or the face of his childhood nurse. It would be a minor adjustment to his trajectory.

He makes the change.

An alarm sounds.

He ignores it.

Kheo never slept well the night before a race. He doubted any Pilot did. He ended up resorting to the chemical remedies offered by the Clan doctor.

Perhaps that was why, when he was escorted through the halls and corridors of the liner the next morning amid cheers and thrown petals, he felt as though he was watching the festivities from afar, rather than being the reason for them.

Sovat – Appis – was in the hangar, amongst the honour guard of techs who stood respectfully silent while their Pilot crossed the floor to his yacht. Kheo gave him no more regard than was normal, including him in the faint nod of gratitude to his crew as he passed.

Only when he took his seat in *Liberty Bird* did he fully wake up. He performed the usual pre-flight checks with a combination of the utmost care and little conscious thought. By the time the hoist had inched him into the hangar's massive airlock, he was as ready for his fate as he had ever been.

The trajectory alteration is subtle; a matter of a few degrees in one plane. The difference between passing through a volume of space with no appreciable matter in it, and the lower path, where the number of molecules in the vacuum might constitute the start of an atmosphere. Enough of an atmosphere to cause drag and test *Liberty Bird*'s engines, certainly. But the ultimate shortcut – if it works.

He is deep in the ion-streams now, their flickering representations dancing around his yacht. Every other racer is above him; some still appear to be ahead, but they have further to go. It is too early yet to know if his crazy ploy will bring victory.

His com flashes: the support team requesting emergency contact. No mean feat given the ionic interference; they must be juicing up the signal with everything they've got. If he answers, will it be Appis Sovat on the com? He is Chief Tech, after all. The prospect of hearing Sovat's voice again makes Kheo hesitate. Then he catches himself and turns his attention to his console. The drive readout is already edging out of the safe zone, and there's a constellation of amber warnings. Suddenly one of them spikes red: a jolt thrums through his yacht. What was that? Ah, navigational thrusters. Even this is too much atmosphere for them. Well, he's stuck on this course now. As for what happens once he's on the far side, whether they'll blow clear... first make it to the far side, then worry about that.

The ship feels wrong. It's a subtle sensation, a faint vibration, but if he carries on, it's only a matter of time before structural integrity begins to fail.

His life is so complicated. The tension of duty and desire. His inability to be himself. And always he has taken what seemed like the easiest path, only to find complications besetting him. Not now though. Now everything truly is simple. He will either win this race, or die trying.

Another red light: radiation warning. There is only so much energy his suit and canopy can protect him from. The view outside is more spectacular than ever, like a great forest of energy, the psychedelic ion-streams like twisted trunks of impossible trees.

This in itself is the easy way out, of course. Yes, even as he defies death, he's still a coward.

The vibration becomes a shudder. Suddenly Kheo is scared. At least his body is: racing heart, dry mouth, dizzy head.

What am I doing? This insane stunt isn't bravery: it's avoidance, the ultimate avoidance.

The ship begins to shake. The drive readout spikes into the red. He reaches for the console but everything's moving, wild forces pulling at him. And even if he could get his hands on the controls, what could he do? The course is set. Too late to change it now.

I'm a fool. A coward and a fool.

A great concussion hits, throwing him in every direction at once. He is going to die, here, now. Die without facing himself.

Massive constriction – *but I was expecting an explosion!* – and he is wrapped in chilly gel. As the sedatives kick in he realises two things: he has lost the race and he is still alive. When, seconds later, the drugs ease his stressed system into therapeutic unconsciousness, his last thought is that the former doesn't matter, only the latter.

The media love it. Kheo Reuthani's miraculous escape after his death-or-glory bid for victory eclipses Umbrel Narven's win. Kheo feels sorry for her.

The rescue clipper barely arrived in time to stop *Liberty Bird* drifting into the nearest ion-stream, an experience he would not have survived even encased in crash-gel. By the time his yacht was hauled in, he had received enough radiation to increase his risk of long-term health problems – and to destroy any chance of him giving Clan Reuthani an heir.

Mother visits him in hospital. 'I've seen your results.'

She could be talking about an exam he failed. 'I guess the wedding's off then.' He tries not to sound triumphant. He feels sorry for Leilian Fermelai too. He does not, for once, feel sorry for himself.

'Not necessarily. There may be a medical work-around to the, ah, fertility issue. Perhaps even some advance from out-of-system.'

'Ah, so you'd accept outsider medicine to solve the Clan's problems, then?'

'One must adapt.'

A shame, then, that she had not pressed his father to adapt to the proactive approach many Clans had instituted after the Liberation, of taking sperm or egg samples from their Pilots in case of such accidents. 'Yes, one must. I'm sorry Mother. I won't marry that poor girl just to save face. Let Prinbal have his chance. He wants to lead the clan more than I do anyway.'

He is treated to the rare spectacle of his mother lost for words.

The general consensus is that he had a lucky escape. If his drive had not cut out when it did, *Liberty Bird* would either have shaken itself to bits, blown up or been crushed by Yssim's atmosphere. Kheo keeps his opinion on the matter to himself.

He is still welcome in the hangar, where work is underway to ensure that *Liberty Bird* will race again. He might even be the one to fly her, when and if his father forgives him for declaring Prinbal the Reuthani heir. Assuming the Flamestar is still going then.

It is only natural that Sovat leads the repair work. And it is only natural that Kheo and he should take the chance to talk about the state of *Liberty Bird*.

Their conversation, held in the meeting room while the techs work outside, begins with an assessment of the damage, and what is being done to fix it. Kheo looks at Appis Sovat's hands twice, and his face once. He realises that the Chief Mechanic loves the yacht as much as he himself does, perhaps more.

'She was lucky, wasn't she?' asks Kheo. 'Well, we both were. *Liberty Bird*, and me. Losing power at exactly the right moment to bounce us off Yssim's atmosphere.' He hopes his words don't sound too disingenuous.

'So they say.'

Kheo seizes his chance. 'You don't think it was luck then?'

'It was *fortunate* the engine shut down soon as the rads and outside density reached critical. But not luck, sirrah, no.'

'Ah.' There had been a move, immediately after the Liberation, to install overrides to stop Pilots overdriving their engines but it had been deemed unnecessary, and insulting to the Pilots. 'I... see.' Kheo picks his next words carefully. 'Having such a *fortunate* shutdown wouldn't be hard to arrange for someone with the right skills.'

'I imagine not, sirrah.' The tech's tone is careful.

Kheo ploughs on. 'But one would have to ask why anyone might arrange for such a thing.'

'I've seen it before, sirrah.' Sovat is looking at him directly now; he can feel it. 'More than once.'

'Seen what?' says Kheo slowly. He manages to raise his gaze as high as the tech's chest.

'The boys who can't live with themselves.'

'Wait, you think I made the choices I did just because I... because you... You know nothing about me, Technician!' Except the one thing Kheo wished the man didn't know. His embarrassed anger lets Kheo meet Sovat's eyes.

'True enough, sirrah.' The tech's voice and gaze are gentle. 'And I'm not saying there's just the one cause. But that's part of it: us being what we are. It's not worth dying for, you know.'

'It's pretty damn hard to live with.'

'Hard for others to live with, yes.'

'What do you mean?'

'Just that, sirrah: we're what we are. It's those around us that make it a problem.'

'Unless we get caught.'

The tech shrugs, though it is a considered gesture. 'That's still true, for now. But not every change is for the worst.'

'No, it isn't. Listen, I know I'm not, er, your type… but if I did want some advice about, well, safe places, where people like me, like us…?'

'I'd be happy to give it.'

'Thank you.' Kheo hesitates. 'And thank you for knowing what I needed even if I didn't. Had anyone found out what you did –'

'I'm better at my job than that, sirrah.'

'Even so, you risked your career for me.'

'A career don't matter a s – spit compared to a life, sirrah.'

Kheo nods. 'Quite so. Good night, Engineer Sovat.'

Alone in the briefing room, Kheo exhales. He calls up the plans for his yacht. The thought that he might never pilot *Liberty Bird* again is hard to face, but face it he will. Who knows, perhaps when contact with the rest of the universe strengthens he might fly something more amazing, perhaps even travel between the stars? Now that is a good dream to hold onto.

After a while he shuts down the display and goes to find his mother. There is something he needs to tell her.

This started with a holiday to the Lake District. To be precise, a trip on Coniston Water in a steam gondola (yes, that is as cool as it sounds). Along with the wildlife commentary we got the lowdown on Donald Campbell's final, lethally unsuccessful attempt to break the water speed record, passing the various points which marked out the events of, as they say, that fateful day. The mystery of it intrigued me: no one would ever know why he did what he did, because he didn't live to tell the tale. I wanted to explore that, though in a rather different environment, because I like space yachts.

The other half of the story – that of forbidden love – felt quite dated to write about because, y'know, most sensible cultures aren't saddled with that kind of bigotry (at least, not in the worlds I like to imagine), but this is a story set in the aftermath of a repressive regime, specifically the rulership of the Sidhe Protectorate – see my Hidden Empire series for more on that.

I was stunned (in a good way) when this story won the BSFA short fiction award.

A Dormitory Haunting

It is sometimes said – most often by men – that there is no more chaotic mental space than the mind of a girl on the cusp of womanhood. But whilst I have had to deal with my share of confusion, disruption and pigheadedness amongst my charges, the commotion which roused me that late October night was not of the usual kind.

The moon was half-full, hidden intermittently by racing clouds, and the first chill of winter had blown across the hockey fields during the afternoon's match with St Hilda's. We had lost, again: perhaps I should encourage Miss Simpson to take her well-earned retirement, but she is popular with the girls, and I pride myself that Rosewood Academy is a place which values pleasure in education above prowess in sport.

Lights had been out for a while, and I was dozing over some paperwork when a faint yet chilling shriek came from above. More cries followed, and I picked up the lamp and left my office, breathing a little hard. The dormitory is on the top floor and I was breathing harder still when I reached it; however, as the other teachers had all retired to bed, I was first upon the scene.

The room was in a state of borderline hysteria. The lower school girls were shadowy shapes sitting up in their beds, some with covers drawn to chins; a couple were standing, but leapt back onto their beds when I entered. They had been looking down the length of the great attic room, towards the curtained alcoves where the fifteen senior boarders slept.

'Back to bed and back to sleep, girls. It appears you must set an example for your older schoolmates.' For indeed, the upper school boarders all appeared to be out of bed, congregating in the centre of their dorm in a storm of over-loud whispers and gasps. As I strode forward and raised my lamp, white faces turned to stare. 'What is going on here?' I demanded.

No one rushed to answer. Behind me, I heard a step on the boards, and caught a whiff of lilac eau de toilette; our French mistress, if I was not mistaken. I glanced behind to check and, supposition confirmed, called back, 'Miss Fournier, please ensure that the younger girls settle without further fuss.' I turned back to the seniors. 'Well?'

'Please Miss Hunter,' Jenny Miller put her hand up, presumably in response to the unexpected invasion of the girls' intimate space by the highest authority in the school; I tried not to be amused to see such a gesture from a girl in a nightshirt, 'there's a ghost.'

I raised my lamp higher. 'An invisible ghost, presumably? How novel.'

'Not in here,' said Jenny, 'out there.'

She pointed to the arched window at the far end. Through it I saw a faint glow, as of the cloud-covered moon. Girls were slinking back towards their beds, and silence had returned to the dormitory. If left to their own devices, after a stern warning everyone would no doubt calm from this latest fancy. However, the shriek had been imbued with genuine terror. 'Well, I had best see it off then.'

I admit that my steps as I approached the window might not have been as firm as those when I entered, but I believe the girls did not apprehend any hesitation on my part. I have no love of attic spaces, and kept my eyes upon the window, seeing only that faint silvery glow. The girl in one of the two alcoves nearest the window had not been amongst the gossipy huddle which had greeted me. Rather she sat on her bed, hunched over something in her lap. Mary Fraser. No doubt the scream had been hers. For a moment I considered asking her to put down her rosary and hold the lamp – to face the fear which, by her rocking motions and murmured prayers, patently gripped her – but I relented, and handed the lamp to Jenny, part of the cluster of girls one step behind me.

I eased open the catch on the window, drawing a gasp from the girls and a whimper from Mary. It loosened all at once, and I had to grab for the handle to stop the wind slamming the window back into the wall. I stuck my head out as the moon broke free of the clouds, flooding the world with silver. My heart, I admit, did beat a little quickly, but I saw nothing more unsettling than the shadows of the trees upon the lawn. Certainly no ghost. I pulled the window to and fastened it shut then turned to my escort and held out my hand for the lamp. 'Thank you Jenny. There is, you will be glad to hear, nothing untoward outside the window. Now, if you will all make your way back to your beds, no more will be said.'

I did not have to tell them twice.

Turning back to Mary, I found her looking up at me. 'There was no ghost,' I said gently.

'There was no ghost,' she parroted back. Since moving up to the seniors she had taken to agreeing with the words of her elders, regardless of her own opinion. Whilst it made her pliant in class, it was not a healthy trait. I sighed, tempted to leave it at that. But she was a troubled young lady, and trouble untended only increases. I sat down on the end of her bed. 'Mary, what did you see?'

Mary stared at the beads in her hands. 'Nothing.'

'All right. What do you *think* you saw?'

'A ghost.' She flicked her chin up in brief defiance before dropping her gaze again.

'Not... some other kind of apparition?' When she first came to my school two years ago Mary had claimed to see the face of the Madonna in a stain which appeared on the refectory wall after some particularly damp weather. She had been teased for it, and at assembly the next week I had delivered a lecture on respecting the religious views of all those who hold to the Christian faith, in whatever variation.

Mary shook her head, then in a low voice said, 'It was a ghost, one of the unquiet dead, and it was white like bone and it flapped and beckoned to me and I was sure it was going to come through the wall and take my soul.' She dropped her head, hugging her knees tighter.

I had an urge to touch the poor girl's hand, to comfort her. But that would not have been appropriate.

I would have liked more details, if not from poor Mary then from the other girls, on what they thought had happened here, but asking questions would give credence to what was most likely no more than the moon emerging from the clouds, or some piece of pale debris blown past the window. Instead I asked Mary, 'Would you like to move?'

'Move, Miss?'

'Yes, to another alcove.' When Mary became a senior at the start of term I had decided to put her in the end alcove because she was an asthmatic: being near the window would help her breathing when the weather allowed it to be open, and not being surrounded on all sides by other girls would make her unfortunate tendency to snore less disruptive.

'No Miss. I don't want to be any trouble Miss.' Amongst her other challenging traits, young Mary Fraser can be very stubborn.

'I think Miss Hunter has a point.'

'Thank you Mr Connor.' I managed to hide my surprise at this unexpected support. The Walsall Historical Association enjoy sharing knowledge, but the suggestion that those industrial techniques which are, as Chairman Stevens had put it during tonight's presentation, 'over-running traditional craftsmanship' might themselves be of interest to historians in a hundred years' time is not one he favours. Suspecting this, I had waited until after the meeting to put it to him. My new ally continued, 'I believe Miss Hunter's own establishment was once a brewery?'

'A malt-house,' I corrected, then regretted speaking out. Mr Connor had done nothing to deserve my ire. Chairman Stevens, however, was beginning to annoy me. But I bit my tongue. Even so, the esteemed leader of the Association gave his characteristic *harrumph*, and excused himself with a curt, 'Good Evening, then'.

I turned to Mr Connor. 'You came back.' He had arrived unannounced at last month's meeting for the first time; late, greeted with frowns and stares and forced to claim the one empty seat next to mine. At the time I had ignored him save basic pleasantries, but I had noted his fine bearing, strong features and thick head of auburn hair, a shade not dissimilar to my own. This month he had arrived early and chosen to sit next to me, having asked permission and introduced himself first.

'I did.' His voice had a faint burr, perhaps Irish. 'And you would probably consider it forward of me to say this, but I came back partly in the hope that you might be here.'

'I could consider that forward, yes. In fact I probably should.' I glanced at his hand and saw no ring, but whilst the estimable Mr Holmes would no doubt deduce the potential existence of a wife, any offspring and the family income at a glance, all I could say with certainty was that this charming gentleman was well turned-out.

'So to state that it would be a shame to wait a whole month to see you again would be downright scandalous?'

He was keeping his voice low, but over his shoulder I saw the looks we got from the knots of townsfolk making their leisurely way out of the hall. As a person of status in the community I would be expected to disengage from such shameless open attention at the first socially acceptable opportunity. 'It would,' I said curtly, but somehow failed to step away.

'But not so scandalous that you have discounted it.'

I do, of course, have my reputation to think of. And that of the school. Yet sometimes I find myself wishing to do what is not expected and required, within acceptable boundaries. 'It appears I have not.'

'Then would the possibility of meeting me at The Singing Kettle this Saturday afternoon be one you would entertain?'

'I do believe I would, Mr Connor.' People would gossip anyway. I might as well give them something to talk about.

Four days after the panic in the dormitory, and three days after I accepted Mr Connor's offer to meet for tea, there was another incident. The girls were at study in the library when, according to Miss Grainger the mathematics mistress, who was with them at the time, several textbooks 'leapt off the shelf'. Miss Grainger is not prone to exaggeration, but without being present myself I cannot say whether the books leapt, fell or were simply pulled down when Miss Grainger's back was turned. I can say that Mary Fraser was in the room at the time.

'A widower, you say?'

Mr Connor picked up the teapot. 'As of six months ago. My dear Anna contracted a fever. She passed quickly, and in many ways she is still with me.'

'My sympathies. Yes please, I will have more tea. And was she also, ahem, Irish?'

'Irish? Oh, the accent. I left Ireland when I was a boy, as so many of my countrymen do. I lived most of my life in America, where I met Anna and made business connections in the mining industry which have, whatever else, left me in a favourable financial position.'

A man looking to turn a woman's head might make such a statement; but would such a man, a few breaths earlier, also imply he has not fully accepted the death of his wife? But Mr Connor was nothing if not direct, and I decided to follow suit. 'Strange then, that you should leave the United States, and chose to settle in a quiet town in the Midlands. Assuming, that is, you plan to stay in Walsall?'

'I've taken rental of a modest house on Ablewell Street. As to why: half my family went to the United States, the other half to work on the railways here. Those who came to England did well, and some still live in the area. With no wife or children in this world, I thought to try and reconnect with them. How long I will stay, I am not yet sure.'

I took a sip of tea. 'Ablewell Street is near St Matthews. I myself attend St Matthews for evensong most weeks, yet I have not seen you there.'

'I worship at a different church.'

I had thought as much. 'Ah, your Irish roots perhaps?'

'I was raised a Catholic, but have drifted away from the faith of my fathers.'

He had not, I noted, admitted which church he attended – if any; I would not put it past this unusual man to be an Atheist. But his upbringing could provide knowledge relevant to the other matter on my mind. 'Your familiarity with Catholicism still outstrips mine. May I ask a question?'

'Related to the Catholic Faith? If you wish.' He took a sip of tea.

'Where does Catholicism stand on the matter of ghosts? I had thought the Church of Rome's view not dissimilar to the Protestant one, but would welcome contradiction in this matter.'

'Ghosts?' He put down his cup and cleared his throat. 'In essence both branches of Christianity state the same view: ghosts are manifestations of the spirits of the dead.'

'A view which, as we enter the twentieth century, is hard to credit.'

'Many do, Miss Hunter.'

A suspicion was forming. 'Including yourself, Mr Connor?'

He inclined his head.

'Then I am guessing,' I said, 'that Sunday may find you on Caldmore Road.'

'You guess correctly. I am a Spiritualist.'

'Ah.'

'Does knowing this preclude our meeting again?' He sounded regretful.

My heart softened. 'I think we may agree to differ on certain subjects.'

He smiled. 'I will take that to mean that tea next week remains a possibility.'

'It does.' Something about Mr Connor's company made me inclined to take risks.

Three days later the 'ghost' made another appearance in the dormitory. Miss Langham dealt with the crisis this time, as I was sound asleep, having taken a draught to combat a minor chill. All the staff who live at the school had been made aware of the previous incident, and my judgement that it was youthful hysteria, so she did not wake me. But breakfast was a strained affair, and Miss Langham approached me for a private word. When I asked whether Mary had been the one to raise the alarm, she replied, 'Why yes, Miss Hunter. The poor girl was terrified out of her wits.'

The tense atmosphere persisted into the morning, with pupils and teachers alike on edge. I summoned Mary to my office after supper and told her that I was moving her to the alcove at the far end of the dormitory, next to the lower school girls. She responded with a curt, 'Yes, Miss.'

'Mary, is there anything else you can tell me?'

'I'm not sure what you mean Miss.'

'Were you asleep when you saw this apparition?' Some girls had nightmares, and to confirm this was all in Mary's imagination would calm the situation.

'It wasn't a dream, Miss! Jenny and Jane and Sarah saw it too.'

Mary herself would give no further detail beyond insisting again that she had seen 'an unquiet spirit'. I spoke to the other three alleged witnesses. Whatever they saw had been directly outside the window, white in colour and had moved unnaturally. Only Sarah, the girl in the alcove next to Mary's, had caught more than a glimpse, claiming to have seen the ghost 'flying off, up and away'.

There was, of course, a potential expert close at hand. But whilst I found myself content, even perversely pleased, to endure a degree of gossip regarding my dealings with the town's newest resident, the idea of inviting a Spiritualist gentleman to carry on investigations at my school was unthinkable.

There was, however, another place to go for advice in matters this far outside my experience.

My dear Mr Holmes,

I greatly enjoy reading of your exploits as recounted by Dr Watson and am writing to you now in the hopes of some assistance. You may recall our brief acquaintance, some years ago, as immortalised by the good doctor. I suspect you remember every detail but in case you do not it concerned my brief sojourn as a governess at The Copper Beeches, a somewhat unwholesome house in Hampshire, and the deception perpetrated there of which I was an unwitting part.

I have since found my place in the world as headmistress of a modest school for girls of the upper middle classes. Most of my pupils are local, but we do have some boarders, and one of these has, on two occasions now, claimed to see a ghost outside the dormitory window, an experience which has left her greatly disturbed. Whilst she is unwilling to speak freely I do not doubt that she believes she has seen something out of the ordinary, and knowing the girl in question I do not think this is behaviour designed to draw attention: on the contrary, she endeavours not to attract notice to herself. Whatever the case, the incident is causing considerable unrest at the school.

I know you for a rational man, and like myself you will seek for an earthly explanation for these incidents, yet the girl in question's refusal to cooperate and the lack of reliable corroboration have brought me to an impasse.

Given your many commitments, and the unlikelihood of any criminal connection, I would not expect you to travel up to the Midlands, and my own position will not permit me to attend you in London. However, any advice or guidance you can give which might permit me to quietly resolve this mystery would be greatly appreciated.

Yours etc.,
Miss Violet Hunter.

The letter was sent on Friday afternoon. On Saturday I again took tea with Mr Connor. I confess I was looking forward to the meeting. This man caused feelings in me which I had thought myself long past.

We spoke of many things: of the seasonal changes in nature, of the differences between American and British culture, of the life of the town and of possible walks to be had in the vicinity, although Mr Connor joked these would be tame compared to those he had experienced in the Rocky Mountains, where a walk might soon become a scramble or climb. I found myself picturing this rugged man on a rugged slope, and had to take a mouthful of tea to bring myself back to the room. We did not mention our differing beliefs and I said nothing of the trouble at the school, relishing the chance to talk about matters outside my everyday responsibilities.

I had no problem promising to meet him again the next week. From our discussion I suspected he might ask for a less public meeting soon, perhaps a walk along the canal, or even a meal taken tête-à-tête, and though this would set tongues wagging further, had he asked, I might have accepted.

Out of his presence, however, sense returned. Even if, as my heart insisted, I should make room for this man in my life, what would that do to my world? Even if, as my heart hoped, his intentions were what they appeared to be, what would happen to the school if – and here my heart skipped foolishly – I were finally to be married?

A telegram from Mr Holmes arrived on Monday morning, It read:

Currently tied up in Sussex. Two pieces of advice. Look to past history for matters of note, most especially that of the girl in question, and examine the scene with utmost care.

His first suggestion sent a pang through me, for a hidden past had been the key to my own small mystery, nearly a decade ago now. The second was, now he mentioned it, obvious, though care would have to be taken, given the private space in question.

I started by interviewing Mary again. This time I took a different tack, asking her who she thought the ghost might be, given the school had only been converted to its current use thirty years ago and so lacked any such folkloric tales. She paled and shook her head, which I took to mean she had a good idea. After some coaxing she murmured that she feared it was her little brother.

'Did he pass away recently then?' I asked gently.

Again she shook her head. Normally such slovenly manners would earn a reprimand, but I could tell this girl was fighting inner turmoil.

'As a young boy, then?'

She nodded.

'I am sorry to ask this but was his death... particularly unfortunate?'

She looked at her hands.

'You have no other siblings, I believe?'

Mary shook her head.

As far as I knew, the poor girl's only living relative was her mother, a thin flighty woman with an unsteady gaze who I had met only a few times. Fees for Mary's education came direct from a small trust fund, administered by a lawyer in Birmingham. If I recalled rightly, at the beginning of this term Mary had been accompanied to the school only by a household servant. 'So, it is just your mother and you. Your father is dead?'

Mary started, as though burned, then said in a harsh whisper, 'We do not speak of that.'

A sad ending, then. Yet not one which Mary believed had resulted in this 'ghost'. But I had distressed the poor girl enough; I let her go.

Another matter I had not considered before Mr Holmes' missive was the relative proximity of Mrs Fraser's home to the school. She only lived in Blakenall Heath, close enough that she could have sent Mary to Rosewood Academy as a day girl.

This proximity provided my next avenue of investigation. Given Mary's attitudes and behaviour I surmised she had been born into her faith, and hence the family births, marriages and deaths would be recorded at their nearest Catholic Church, rather than an establishment overseen by the Church of England.

Whilst my work is never done, I pride myself on the efficiency of my school and so, should I wish to take a quiet Tuesday morning off and travel to a nearby town, I might do so. As I climbed into the cab I wondered if my fellow teachers thought this uncharacteristic behaviour related to the gentlemen I had been seen taking tea with. I would correct their misapprehension when and if it became important.

When I located the Catholic Church in Blakenall Heath I found it in the process of renovation, with men working on the roof. The young priest in attendance was taken aback at a lone, veiled female visitor but soon recovered his composure. When I asked whether I might see records of his parishioners to resolve 'a personal matter' he asked whether I was myself a Catholic. I considered lying to encourage cooperation, then chided myself. 'No,' I said, 'but the individual whose welfare I am concerned about is.'

'Most of our papers were removed for safekeeping when the restoration began. I would have to send for them.'

'Ah, I see. I am putting you to some trouble.'

'No, I mean yes but… you must understand, I have to consider the welfare of my flock.'

Though I am no expert on the moods of men, especially the clergy, I believe he found me intriguing. I smiled behind my veil, then said, 'It is the welfare of one of them that concerns me.'

'Ah. May I ask whom?'

A reasonable request and as it appeared I would be forced to return at a later date, I needed to be certain my errand was not futile. 'A young lady called Mary Fraser,' I said, watching his face.

He knew the name, though he regained control of his emotions quickly. 'The Fraser family are of this parish, yes.'

'So Mrs Fraser worships here?'

'When her health permits.'

'She is unwell? Do you know what ails her?'

'My foremost concern is with the spiritual wellbeing of those under my care, although I pray for all their health.'

His taught expression implied I would get no more from him on that. I tried another tack. 'And Mr Fraser, he is buried here?'

The priest started. 'Buried?'

'Yes. He has passed away, I assume.'

'No. Mr Fraser still lives.' The priest's lips thinned.

'Ah. But he does not worship here?'

'I can have the records here by tomorrow afternoon. Other than that...'

'... you cannot help me?' I try not to over-use the combination of steel and disappointment which has served me well with girls and parents alike, but it is second nature by now.

'I should not say anything.' He forced his gaze back to me. 'But whatever you find, or hear, please remember this: divorce is a Sin. Now, if you will forgive me, I must prepare for Mass.'

'Of course. Thank you for your assistance.' I made sure he saw the donation I put in the box by the door before I left.

A chance to put Mr Holmes' other suggestion into practice came the next day, while the girls were on the sports field. I resisted the temptation to borrow a magnifying glass from the biology mistress, and took only myself and – in accordance with Mr Holmes' practice – an open mind up to the dormitory.

The window opened easily, as it had on that first night. I examined the hinge, and found it well oiled, although whether this signified more than diligence by the housekeeping staff I could not say. There was no wind, but I secured the window with care anyway.

The view was pleasing: across the busy playing fields, out beyond the town, and towards the higher land to the west.

I leaned over the sill and looked down. This side of the school has an impressive growth of wisteria but the branches were all but bare now, just a few yellow leaves clinging to them. I looked up, then cursed myself for a fool.

Above me, underneath the overhanging gable, was a hook. It was a great solid metal construction, left over from the days when the school had been a malt-house, when it must have been used to haul sacks of barley up into the drying loft. And there was something odd about the hook.

I dragged a chair over and stood on it, then peered upwards, into the shadow of the overhanging gable.

The chair rocked. I grabbed for the sill.

I allowed myself a moment to catch my breath then looked out again. There was something on the hook.

Without letting go of the sill I craned my neck up. My thighs pressed against the window frame. I hoped the lower fifth were too busy with their hockey practice to notice their headmistress in such a precarious and undignified position.

Yes, there was something pale caught on the hook. I leaned harder. The chair creaked, but held. I reached a hand up and snatched at the hook. My fingers found fabric, and I pulled it free. The chair rocked back, and I teetered for a moment, before steadying myself on the window-frame. I climbed down with as much aplomb as I could manage.

Once safely on the scrubbed planks I opened my hand to find that I held a torn scrap of boiled cotton sheet, bunched up and tied with a light but coarse rope.

I was in two minds about returning to Blakenall Heath. After all, I now knew that poor Mary had nothing to fear: the 'ghost' was a trick, most likely a bed-sheet bunched up and tied to a rope threaded through the old hook. The sheet was a match for those in the dormitory; the rope, such as was used by many saddle manufactories locally. Both nights the 'ghost' had appeared the wind had been strong enough to agitate such a prop, and Sarah had spoken of it disappearing upwards, as it would were someone below to pull on the rope, whisking the fabric up through the hook, and away into the night – or not, when it became caught. The explanation for the ghost was as mundane as I had thought.

But my curiosity over Mary's wider circumstances had been piqued. Therefore I returned to the Catholic Church the next afternoon.

The priest was as good as his word, and even pointed out which pages in the great ledger might be relevant to the Fraser family, 'Although,' he added, 'these things only tell part of the story.' I took this to mean that my enquiries still intrigued him.

I soon located records of Eileen Fraser's marriage, the birth of her daughter eight months later, then two years after that, of a son. The son's death was also recorded here, four years ago, shortly before Mary came to my school. There was no other issue listed.

I found the priest tidying the votive candles outside the vestry and said, 'I am afraid you were right.'

'About what, madam?'

I did not correct his assumption about my marital status. 'The records show only bare facts. I am not sure how helpful these will be to poor Mary.'

He looked down at the candle in his hand, and frowned. But he did not make his apologies or move away, so I prompted, 'Though divorce may be a sin, separation is sometimes for the best, is it not?'

He looked up, and placed the candle on the table. 'I would not want to repeat hearsay. Gossip never does the Lord's work.'

'In that we are agreed. I wish only for confirmation of the facts. Mr Fraser does not live with Mrs Fraser, is that correct?'

'He does not, no.'

'But he has not moved away?'

'It might be better if he had.'

'Ah. So his continued influence is not a wholesome one. I am sorry, that takes us into the realm of gossip and opinion.'

'No, it is a reasonable supposition. Mr Fraser was never a likeable man, and by all accounts excess money and a lack of human contact have caused him to twist in on himself.'

I suspected that the weight of confession, formal and otherwise, lay behind this young priest's willingness to open up to a stranger. His soft heart was a credit to his calling. 'I imagine that knowing her husband is in such a dark place does nothing to help poor Mrs Fraser's health.'

'Indeed not. Though they have little contact, thank the Lord.'

'And she lost her youngest, I see.'

'Ah yes. A tragic accident.'

'May I ask how it happened?'

'I should not say more.' I understood his reticence, given the mother of the dead child was still one of his flock; I would exercise the same tact with my girls. But then he continued, 'There has been an interesting recent development in the family which I can share, though I am not sure it is of relevance to young Mary's situation.'

'Oh?'

'It concerns another family member, one who has slipped far from the faith.'

I had a sudden, unpleasant, suspicion. 'Please,' I said, my throat tight, 'do go on.'

'Will you not sit down, Miss Hunter?'

'No, Mr Connor, I will not.' I would rather not have had this conversation in public, but nor did I wish to be alone with Mr Connor. Any townsfolk who chose to visit The Singing Kettle today in the hopes of seeing a something of interest would not be disappointed.

'Please, what is wrong?'

'Why did you not tell me you were related to one of my pupils?' Though I kept my voice low I would not speak names where they might be overheard.

'One of… oh, you mean my cousin's girl?'

'Yes, your cousin who was Eileen Connor before her marriage.' When I had read Mary's mother's maiden name in the church register I had thought nothing of it, but then the priest told me of the cousin newly returned from America and it had all fallen into place. I had the *how* of the matter in that scrap of white fabric; the *why*, I admit, was still to come; but here, surely was the *who*: a member of that ill-fated family, with some knowledge of my school, quite capable of scaling a wall covered in a knotty growth of a wisteria to hang a rope from that hook.

'I did not think it relevant. I was under the impression that the last thing you wanted to talk about with me was the school which takes up so much of your life.'

Perhaps he had a point, but I would not be deflected. This man took an active interest in the so-called supernatural. Quite how faking a haunting at my school would further his cause I could not yet say, but he had to be involved, somehow. 'Mr Connor, I am no more inclined to believe in coincidence than I am in ghosts.'

'I'm sorry, but I am not sure what –'

'That is enough. I do not want to hear another word.' As I turned on my heel every eye was upon me. But I did not look back.

When I took Mary aside and explained the matter of the ghostly hoax she listened in silence. When I asked who she thought might perpetrate such an unpleasant prank she shrugged. I saw relief in her, but uncertainty too. I hoped the truth would soothe her but she was such a fragile thing, and I did not want to press the point.

Perhaps, in a few weeks, I might be able to objectively analyse Mr Connor's part in the affair, to work out what he sought to gain or achieve. For now, I determined not to think of him at all.

I interviewed Mary's senior dorm-mates individually, a process carried out with some delicacy, as I wished both to reassure them and to find out whether they had any more to add to this not-quite mystery. They did not.

Similar tact had to be employed with the servants. It would not do to act without evidence.

On Tuesday evening, to my surprise, Mary came to see me.

I showed her into my office, and waited for her to speak. She sniffed, blinked and said, 'Please Miss Hunter, don't send me away.'

'Why would I do that, Miss Fraser?'

'Because of the trouble I've been.'

Aside from a complaint about her snoring, which could hardly be helped, Mary had been no trouble at all since moving beds. 'The past is the past, Mary. And as I explained, there was no ghost. All is well.'

'So I can stay?'

'Of course you can. What makes you think otherwise?'

'The letter from Father.'

'What letter? When did he write to you?' I looked over all mail before distributing it to the girls. I had seen no letter.

'Yesterday, Miss.'

'Would you be willing to tell me what the letter said?'

'I... yes Miss. He said that seeing as how things were not working out here at the school, and how Mama's health is getting worse, I should come home to him.'

'You live with your mother outside of term-time, yes? She is your legal guardian.'

'Yes but... she is not well, and she's getting worse. Her nerves... When Peter died it was horrible, and she never got over it.'

I quashed my unsatisfied curiosity at the circumstances of her little brother's death. What mattered was the family's current pain. 'But you would still prefer to remain with her when you are not here, and not spend time with your Father?'

'Miss, I would rather sleep in a ditch than enter that man's house!'

I tried not to let my surprise at her passionate words show. 'I can assure you it will not come to that.' But her desperate if incomplete account put a new light on the hoax which had disturbed my school.

I called the suspect to my office the next morning, having slept on the matter to ensure I had, as Homes would say 'all the data'. My suspect was Elizabeth Munton, a lanky girl from a populous local family who had worked at the school for two years, reporting to the housekeeper. I had spoken briefly to her, along with all the other servants, when making my initial enquiries. At the time she had claimed to 'not know anything about no ghostly prank' but had refused to meet my eyes, and the way she said 'ghostly prank' implied she knew more than she was saying.

This time I tried a different tack. Having asked her to shut the door and sit down I asked, 'Munton, what are your usual duties?'

'Cleaning, laundry and whatever jobs Mrs Clews requires, Miss Hunter.'

'Including, on occasion, the distribution of the post to the girls, I believe.'

Munton squirmed in her chair.

'Did you insinuate a letter which did not arrive by the usual means into Monday's post?'

'I...' the girl's eyes darted round my office, looking for escape.

'Did you, Munton?'

Her hands fluttered up from her lap, and she sobbed, once. 'It wasn't my idea, Miss!'

'Then whose was it?'

'It came from the same man, I think, though Ma didn't say, she just gave me the letter to bring into work, told me to get it to the Catholic girl, the nervy one.'

'What 'same man' Munton?'

'I don't know his name, Miss. He first called on Ma last month, and they spoke in the kitchen. I didn't mean to overhear...'

'What did this man say?' Mr Connor had arrived in the vicinity last month.

'Something about a prank at the school, and how he needed help with it.'

'And why would your mother acquiesce to such a request? Did she know this man?'

'I don't know, ma'am.' The girl's face reddened. 'But Ma needs money, what with Pa gone and another baby on the way...'

'And this man offered to pay if you carried out this "prank"?'

'Ma never said but... yes, he must've. We've had meat on the table twice a week since.'

'What precisely did you do, besides deliver the letter?'

'I got the sheet, and Jeb – my middle brother – he got the rope. I strung it up the night before the storms, while I was in there cleaning. Later on, he sneaked in below and tugged on the rope.'

'Twice?'

'Aye, ma'am. Twice.' From her face she knew how much trouble she was in. Why do people never consider the consequences of their actions?

'Did you also disrupt a study session in the library?'

'What study session, Miss?'

'Never mind. The man who came to your house, did he speak to you?'

'No, just to Ma.'

'But you heard him speak? Did he have an accent, perhaps an Irish one?'

'No Miss, he was local, by his speech.'

'And his appearance: what colour was his hair?'

'His hair? Dark, though thin on top, Ma had me take his hat when he arrived. Please, what'll happen to me?'

'I think you know what must happen to you now, Munton. I cannot have untrustworthy staff at my school.'

'Yes, Miss Hunter.' Though there were tears in her voice, I saw acceptance too.

'Kindly pack your things. I will not require you to work out your notice.'

Her shoulders sagged and she whispered, 'As you will, Miss Hunter.'

'I would advise against telling any of the other staff why you must leave the school's service.' Not that I minded if she did: knowing the mechanism behind the disruptive incidents might help restore calm. 'Come back and see me before you leave.'

When she was gone I sat back, then leaned forward and reached for my pen. I had two letters to write.

The first would be references for Munton, along with a bankers' draft for a week's wages. Foolish though the girl had been, she had been obeying her still-more-foolish mother. Up until this incident she had been a competent housemaid, and although she could not stay here, I would not sabotage her future.

The second letter was harder. No one enjoys admitting they are in the wrong.

'You came, then?' I tried not to sound too relieved, but the maiden aunts who so enjoy my meetings with Mr Connor were not even pretending to address themselves to their Darjeeling today. After last week's show they watched us raptly, straining to hear the latest development in this low opera of emotions.

'I did. Please, Miss Hunter, sit down.'

I did so, feeling a sigh escape as I did.

'I will come straight out and say this, Mr Connor. I am heartily sorry for the way I treated you last week.'

'I accept your apology. You were applying that fine mind of yours to a problem without being in possession of the full facts.'

'Quite so, to my chagrin. It would seem coincidences are more common than I care to admit. Certainly they are more common than conspiracies.' I left it unsaid that I had wanted to think the worst of him, rather than face the changes he might bring into my life.

Mr Connor nodded; graciously, I thought. I could imagine myself spending more time with this man. 'And how is my cousin's girl doing?'

'She is nervous and scared, but that is, sadly, normal for her. I am not sure she will ever find happiness and ease, but for my part I will do all I can to help her.'

'And for mine, I will ensure that her wretched brute of a father does not cause any more trouble.'

'He strikes me as a man who will go to great lengths to get what he wants.'

'Only if unchecked.' Mr Connor smiled. 'I have a purpose here now: to watch over what remains of my family.'

'I am delighted to hear that.'

'It is not a purpose which will take all of my time, Miss Hunter. I might hope, when spring comes, to explore the byways of the local countryside, with a suitable guide.'

'That sounds like a pleasant diversion.'

'More pleasant than chasing ghosts.' I had given Mr Connor the gist of the affair in my letter.

'Now, you know there was no ghost, Mr Connor.'

'Indeed not. But that is not the same as saying there are *no* ghosts, is it? "There are more things in Heaven and Earth than are dreamt of in your philosophies..." as the Bard puts it.'

'Perhaps.' Having been both right and wrong in recent weeks, I could concede that much.

Mary fell ill the next week. A bout of brain-fever was not unexpected after her recent traumas. She took to her bed, now out of sight of the fateful window, her rest aided by strong medication prescribed by our matron.

I had yet to replace Munton, so when autumn rain gave way, in the space of an hour, to winter's still and bitter cold, I took a spare blanket up to Mary myself. I found her dozing, rosary entwined in her fingers. As I unfolded the blanket over her she opened her eyes.

'Don't worry, Mary,' I murmured, 'just rest.'

'I dreamt Father came for me.'

'I can assure you that will not happen.'

Her gaze was febrile and bright. 'Are you sure? After Peter died, he said such terrible things.'

'All untrue, I'm sure. Peter was your brother, wasn't he?'

'Yes.' She looked past me, as though at something unseen. 'He fell.'

Whilst I did not want to cause the girl further pain, curiosity still pricked me. 'An accident, yes?'

'Yes.' Her gaze focused on me. 'He fell from the attic window.'

No wonder she had connected the flapping sheet outside with her dead brother! 'Oh Mary. It must have been awful.' I shivered; the cold had taken hold up here.

'It was.' Her face twisted into an odd, feverish smile. 'But it's all right. No one saw.'

As I opened my mouth to ask what she meant a sharp bang resounded through the dormitory. I jumped to my feet, heart pounding. The noise had come from the far end of the room. I looked to the source of the sound then, suspicions confirmed, hurried up the room.

The window was wide open. Before fear could get the better of me I leant out and grabbed the latch. My glimpse of the world outside was pure normality: a bright winter's afternoon, girls on the sports fields below, rooks in the elm trees.

When I tugged the window closed I half expected the catch to be broken, but it was not. Whoever last opened it must have failed to fasten it properly, leaving it to be caught by a stray gust of wind.

I walked back to Mary's alcove to find her sound asleep, that same peculiar smile still on her face.

I've never really explored the ghost story genre, as I feel I wouldn't have anything to say that hasn't already been said by others. Also, is this really a ghost story? I'm not entirely sure myself. What it is, is my tiny addition to the huge canon of Sherlock Holmes stories, a fun commission which gave me the excuse to re-read the collected works of Arthur Conan Doyle.

Sin of Omission

It should never happen like this. They must always be strangers to us. There are rules, and we have those rules for a reason. It goes against the will of the Empress. How could those sacred mechanisms fail?

How can I be standing here in this darkened bedchamber, staring down at the slack face of the stranger who fathered me, waiting for him to die?

His current wife is with us. I say 'current wife', I think she's only his second. Maybe third. There is a young man somewhere in the house too: I heard shouting as I was being shown upstairs; from the sound of it he's at the age when everything warrants shouting. My half-brother I guess, probably complaining about being excluded from his father's final moments.

The only other person here is the priest, and he's hamming up the litany as if auditioning for the stage and not just doing his job. I find myself struggling to stay still and calm and act like I'm just doing mine. My instinct is to walk away from this, but the old man hasn't got long: too late to get a substitute. And now the shock is subsiding, and curiosity is seeping in.

The figure slides through the shadows towards the townhouse, utilising gaps between the pools of relative brightness cast by the streetlights, its movements stealthy enough that the eye glides over it, but not so stealthy as to appear unnatural. Anyone looking this way will see a heavily-built man of moderate age and average appearance, possibly up to something mildly nefarious. Seeing this, a respectable citizen might look away, or even cross the street. Which would be for the best, for all concerned.

*

I steal a glance at the wife: her expression tends more towards grief than relief. She obviously has no idea who I am.

The priest finishes the litany and I look back at the client (in that moment, that is how I think of him, because I am a professional). Yes, he is about to go. There's that awkward pause, which doesn't go on too long, thank the Empress. Then he expels his final breath. I lift the corpse-cake from the now-still chest. And hesitate. I don't want to know after all. But I have no choice.

The wife is already walking over to the bedroom window, ready to throw the shutters open, to release her husband's newly-cleansed soul to its eternal reward.

I stuff the small round cake into my mouth, biting down hard.

It is a matter of personal and professional pride that I can recall at least something about every one of the seventy-eight souls I have shriven. I would have written details down were that not forbidden. Every client was a unique individual who had led their own life, generally a full one (children are both the easiest and hardest, because there is so little to take on). Every client was different, in matters of memory, sensation, emotion, and intangible aspects of self. Taking on their sins to shrive their souls was a powerful, all-consuming experience.

But this, this is like being hit by a speeding tram.

The figure pauses. Within its head is a map of the city, all the additional information it needs to fulfil its mission and a range of senses unavailable to most people. It has no name, and only basic self-awareness; it is a creature of low-brow legend, night-time scare-stories.

Most people don't think golems are real, though some argue that if this ultimate avenger enacts the Empress's justice on you, you'll be left in no state to give an eye-witness account. Those who take an interest in such things claim golems are hulking monsters, as befits a semi-mindless tool of divine vengeance. However, looking just like everyone else makes it a lot easier to operate without attracting attention.

I go and see Yavi, as soon as I have enough of myself back to risk it. I fugue in the street at least twice on the way, but nothing unusual there. The intensity, though, that's hard. The final time, a shopkeeper, seeing the robed and half-masked figure writhing on the pavement, came out with water and salt for me, Empress bless him.

Yavi takes a while to answer the door and asks me to wait on the step. My suspicion that he has another of his women inside is confirmed when he shows me to the parlour, not the bedroom. I briefly consider being polite, asking if I should come back later. Fuck that. I listen to the sound of fulsome farewells from upstairs and try not to sigh. No doubt she thinks the gifts she brings him reward his love, rather than purchasing it. A few minutes later, Yavi enters the parlour.

I smile. He smiles back.

We fuck like beasts on the parlour rug.

When we roll apart it's getting dark. Yavi gets up to switch on a lamp then lies back down beside me. With the vital oblivion of sexual pleasure receding, the memories are back. I'm briefly lost in an inherited memory of a not dissimilar moment from my father's life. Mercifully briefly, but enough to bring bile to my throat.

Yavi rolls over onto his elbow and places a hand in the sweat-slicked hollow between my breasts. On some men it might be a possessive gesture, but with Yavi it's like he's grounding me, helping me refocus on the here and now. Pushing away those flashes of paternal memory.

'Difficult client?' he murmurs.

I don't love Yavi. I've never loved anyone except my mother. But I love having him in my life. He is considerate, skilled in what he does, untroubled by what others think, and gloriously shallow. Not stupid, but in possession of a butterfly mind that lives in the moment, and often shifts without logic or agenda. Probably a necessary asset in his line of work. Just what I need in a lover, to help me deal with mine.

I sigh. I could leave it at that: Yavi has a child-like curiosity, but he accepts being told to drop a subject without question. How much to say? Not the fact that I just took on the sins of my actual, long-absent, heart-breaking bastard of a father. But there is stuff I need to share, and he is the closest I have to a friend.

'Do you ever find out things you wish you hadn't, from your clients?'

He doesn't hesitate. 'Frequently. And then I forget them. Just like you have to.'

Indeed. Sin-eaters and whores have a lot in common.

I plough on. 'Do you think heretics can be saved?'

He does that half-giggle which makes him sound more of a fool than he is. 'You'd be better qualified to answer that than me. By heretic you mean someone who keeps breaking the Strictures, yes?'

'Not exactly.' My father was smarter than that. He kept up appearances. But he thought the unthinkable. And that sin was constantly with him: I didn't receive the knowledge of it in a fugue or a flash, I simply know it now, for a fact. And unlike the more transient sins whose imagery and sensations will plague me for the next few days before fading into the hidden mass of dead lives I carry, this is not something I can ever unknow. 'What if you don't believe that after you die you become one with the Empress?'

'Well...' I hear rare uneasiness in my lover's voice. Of course, he's thinking of my situation. Because I, willingly burdened by the sins of others, can never reach that heavenly reward. Instead I have the sacred privilege of ensuring others do.

'I'm not talking about sin-eaters.' I make it sound light-hearted, but experience a stab of doubt, there then gone. I swallow. 'Just an ordinary person.'

'I'm assuming this is about your last client so... you took on the sin of their unbelief when they died. And that allowed them to pass into the Empress's grace.'

'Except it's not a sin like lying or hurting others, it only affected himself. It was part of who he was.'

'And now, thanks to you, he has no sins, and he is with the Empress.'

Another sigh escapes me. 'You make it sound so simple.'

Perhaps it is. My judgement is hardly at its best right now.

The golem is walking along a late-night backstreet when it receives an update: the original mission has been invalidated by the target's natural and correctly shriven death.

Anyone viewing it would have seen it hesitate mid-step, then a few moments of uncanny stillness, then a change in direction. It feels nothing, because it is incapable of feelings.

Further updates are pending. In the meantime it must remain in the vicinity, but unseen. It selects a nearby warehouse to wait in, standing motionless amongst stacked sacks of rice and maize from the farmlands.

It does not have to wait long.

I was still getting flashes after I left Yavi's, triggered by random things – the sight of a half-eaten apple in the gutter, the smell of burnt sugar, the shriek of a petulant child. More intense than for any other client I've shriven, but following the usual pattern. It was still a relief to get off the sultry streets to the boarding-house, and the familiarity of my room. Knowing I had a client, the landlady has left the lights on for me.

I am not looking forward to falling asleep.

When a sin-eater turns off their own consciousness in sleep, the client's memories flood their mind. We re-live their lives. Or rather, we re-live the bad bits, the bits they're ashamed off. It's never good, but it has to happen. Once absorbed, the sins must play themselves out.

My father's sins are not terrible. He never killed anyone. He lied and cheated and on occasion stole, but he tended to regret his misdemeanours afterwards. He was no monster, just a weak and ordinary man. A lot of the memories associated with his invisible sin, that of unbelief, feature a man of a similar age, though better dressed. They met indoors, most often in a study with an impressive collection of books. It is, as memories of sin go, not that traumatic. But vivid. All of this is way too vivid. Way too close.

I don't know if the problem is that we were related by blood. Or it could just be that my mind is grasping at what it should be releasing because some of the people in his recollections are known to me. Or, in some of cases, are me. Every glimpse, every thought of

215

the girl he knew before he abandoned her mother is a heart-stopping jolt. When we get to the memory of the day he hit her, and she told him to stay away for good this time, it jolts me awake. My heart is beating fit to burst and I can't breathe. I sit up with a gasp.

The room is dark, but there is a hint of grey under the curtains. I've been leaving the window open in the humid weather, and I hear early movement on the river below, a barge puttering upstream.

I lie back down because I will, at some point, need to let my mind work through everything I have taken on, no matter how personal, no matter how painful, and the sooner I do so the sooner I'll be free of him. I wonder if receiving this unexpected burden was the will of the Empress, some sort of test or tempering process, part of some grand plan incomprehensible to mere mortals. It takes me a while to work that possibility, and discard it as unlikely, and that banishes any chance of further sleep. When the grey behind the curtains becomes more than a hint, and the sounds of the city start to impinge, I give up, and get up. The early light picks out a small pale square on the floor across the room. I pad across the rug and pick it up. A piece of folded paper, presumably pushed under the door some time overnight.

The paper contains an address. Nothing else, just an address.

It's written in a distinctive, curlicued hand. I recognise that writing. It's my father's.

Amended orders: new target. The golem walks out of the warehouse. Outside, dawn is breaking, the city waking up. A baker making an early-morning delivery passes by on her peddle-cart as the golem is leaving. She gives the figure a passing curious glance, before deciding to pretend she didn't see anything.

I spend the next day in denial. Or rather, just as I would any other post-shrivening day: braced for more of a dead person's memories while indulging in the pleasures that make life worth living.

I start with a breakfast of buttercream pancakes, cured bacon and honey syrup, all foods I enjoy which my late father had no strong feelings about – or no associated sinful memories, at least. Then to the bank to check that payment for my services is in (it is of course);

withdraw some of it to buy that gold-shot silk scarf I'd seen in the window of the clothiers on Willow Lane, which feels wonderful and looks good, though I'm not sure when I'd wear it; also some sweetmeats and whortleberry liqueur. During a lull in the shopping I wonder about contacting the guild to ask how I ended up having to take on my father's sins, but decide it'll cause more problems than it solves: either it was a genuine mistake (I guess they can happen) or someone with more power than me did this for reasons no one is likely to tell me. And I can't quite discard my absurd notion that this is the will of the Empress, not a human mistake, and as such I need to go with the flow.

I consider another visit to Yavi – I left my mask in his parlour and I'll need that before I take on my next client – but decide not to. That's a pleasure for tomorrow, when I'm clear of the last few flashbacks.

I sit down to a dinner of prime steak accompanied by a full-bodied red from the Brightstone vineyards. Father's favourite vintage, which he apparently drank to excess, though I won't hold that against it.

When I reach for my wallet to pay, feeling a little tipsy, I pull out an unexpected piece of paper.

The piece of paper has an address written on it. Oh my, I'd forgotten all about that.

No, I hadn't.

I sigh and ask the restaurant to call a rickshaw.

When the golem attempted to fulfil its new orders, matters did not go as planned. An unfortunate incident ensued. And the objective was not attained.

However, it did acquire a considerable amount of new information, albeit in a cumbersome format. Next step: look over the written matter and send back a digest of what it contains, then be prepared to follow up if appropriate.

As it is now full daylight, it must exercise caution, and find somewhere safe read the acquired papers. It consults its inner map, finding a waste-water processing plant nearby. The facility is automated, the realm of mundane yet divinely maintained machines – and hence forbidden to citizens. The perfect place to hole up.

This is an upmarket district. Too good for the likes of my late father, even after he made his somewhat dubious fortune. But he visited here, more than once: I get vague flashes of déjà vu as the rickshaw passes various vistas. The frequency of memory intrusions is falling off, as is the intensity – same as for any other client – but what I remember stays with me in a way I've never experienced before. Thanks, I assume, to my link to the man, I will always have access to his memories.

The house itself is as grand as any on either side, four storeys high, almost every window lit. But, as the rickshaw drops me off, I sense something amiss. There's no single thing that tells me this: sin-eater's intuition I guess.

I did consider stopping off at my rooms to put on my robes for the protection they give out on the streets, before remembering the misplaced mask. I now wish I had, even without the mask. I also wish I was a bit more sober. And maybe that I'd come up with an actual plan, rather than rushing over here before I had a chance to think better of it.

But here I am, standing before a solid wooden door with a cast metal bell-pull. Which I pull.

The young woman who opens the door wears a servant's smock and a stricken expression. 'Can I help you?' she says with a mixture of anxiety and subservience.

'I hope so.' I offer a smile, not exactly anxiety-free myself. 'I'm a friend of Adresh Telver.'

The woman looks confused.

'Who is it, Dena?' The voice from deeper in the house is tremulous, and female.

The servant – presumably Dena – opens her mouth, probably to ask my name, but the other speaker continues, 'Are the constables back?'

'A visitor,' Dena swallows before calling back more loudly, 'she is enquiring about Mister Telver'

'Is she now?' A woman appears from a side door as though propelled from a trap. She is well-dressed, middle-aged and distraught, but more nuanced assessment has to wait as she strides up the corridor, her face flushed, her expression twisted. I take half a step back.

Dena presses herself against the wall as the woman comes to a fuming halt just inside the door. 'Who are you? What do you want?' The words tumble out, more upset than angry.

'I…' What in the Void's name am I doing? Suddenly sober I get a perspective on the situation: this woman is rich and powerful, something bad has happened here and I have no idea what her relationship to my father was, assuming there even was one.

While I stutter, her eyes narrow. 'Are you her?' she hisses. 'His daughter? The sin-eater?'

I nod, not sure whether to be relieved or worried.

The woman appears to deflate, the passion draining out of her. 'Then you'd better come in.' Her voice is a whisper.

I do as she says, following her past a not-quite-closed door to which violence has been recently done, to and through the next, open door. Dena trails her, waiting on the threshold of the room until her mistress waves her away. The servant closes the door, leaving the two of us alone in a sumptuous day-room. There are more lamps in here, including an actual chandelier of cut crystal, and I get a better look at her face, specifically at the familiar puffy redness around the eyes. I know the signs of grief very well.

'Do you know who I am?' The tone of the question isn't haughty, or irritated; more exasperated, a little despairing.

'I'm sorry, no.' Though a suspicion is forming.

She sinks into a padded chair. I remain standing.

When she doesn't say anything further, but instead puts her head into her hands, I say, 'My late father sent this address to me.' I keep my tone neutral: she might well be one of his women, in mourning for the unfaithful old bastard.

She barks a bitter laugh without raising her head. 'My name is Amoria Estry. Sister of Councillor Olander Estry. My brother had that note sent after your father died.'

I digest this. Councillor Estry. One of the most powerful people in the city. And, my subconscious suggests with a brief image of a man in a red-lit room, no stranger to my father.

'I never approved of their friendship.' I blink at this almost prescient statement, but Madam Estry continues, oblivious. 'They met in an establishment that caters to men who... never mind. None of that matters now.' She looks up, though she doesn't see me. 'He died un-shriven, you know. One more irony.'

I got this all wrong: she's not father's lover at all but the sister of the well-dressed man from my father's memories. 'Your brother. He's... Oh. He's dead too, isn't he?'

'My brother...' She focuses on me, drawing free of her all-absorbing grief for a moment, '...was murdered in the early hours of this morning. It appears that someone broke into our house, searching for something they expected to find in his study. Perhaps they found it: the constables tell me a number of papers were taken. Olander must have heard them. He went down to investigate. He had a candlestick in his hand when the servants found him, he must have tried to attack the intruder. But he was no fighter. There was some sort of struggle, he fell, hit his head on the corner of his desk... such an absurd way to go.'

'I'm sorry.'

'Are you though?' Now I have her attention I find it somewhat disconcerting. 'You never met him. From what little I know you weren't close to your father.' Resolve is growing in her voice. 'Olander suspected something bad might be about to happen, though of course he never told me what. Looks as if he was right...' Her tone strengthens 'So he made arrangements.' She springs to her feet. I manage not to recoil but she isn't coming at me; rather she turns on her heel and strides over to a bookshelf against the back wall. I have some questions – to put it mildly – but I'm pretty sure she isn't going to answer them, even if she can, so I bite my tongue.

She runs her hands along the books and pulls one out; opens it and flicks through the pages. She pulls something out then puts the book back on the shelf and comes back over to me. She holds out a piece of folded paper: a letter. 'Take it!'

I do. She waves a hand, slicing the air. 'I have no idea what this contains. I do not want to know. And – with all respect, as due to one in your profession – I hope never to see you again.'

I can take a hint. I let myself out.

The papers do not contain definitive answers. They do, however, provide some leads. The golem decides to start with a recent entry in a ledger; one of the late councillor's last acts was to arrange the sending of a note to a certain address.

It is late evening now, an ideal hour for acts of stealth. Gaining access to the relevant room in the boarding house is a little complicated: the other residents must be avoided but after the unfortunate incident with the late Councillor subtlety is required. Fortunately sin-eaters benefit from the respect of those in their community: this one has only a simple lock on her door, easy enough to fool into opening.

Except, it is already unlocked.

The golem turns the handle with slow care. The door swings open.

A young man looks up, startled. He is standing by the bed, straightening after placing something on it. 'Who are you?' More surprised than hostile.

The golem's thought-processes are lightning-fast and unencumbered by physical distractions like fear. This person is not known to it. However, they are presumably known to the sin-eater. The golem's current plan is to capture the sin-eater, alive and in a state where she can be questioned: the Councillor's death removed one source of useful information; it must be more careful here. This person may know something, but even if not, he can be used to get access to the sin-eater. This will, however, require interpersonal skills, and this is not the golem's strong point. It orders its face into a smile and says, 'Good evening. I am trying to find Mora Telver. Can you help me with this?'

The young man's face goes through a number of subtle expression changes, which the golem finds hard to follow. Finally he says, in an oddly flat voice, 'If you want a sin-eater you'd best contact the guild.'

221

The golem considers and discards a number of responses to this and settles on. 'I really need to speak to this particular sin-eater.'

The boy's face takes on a more fixed expression. 'Who did you say you were again?'

That is not a question the golem can easily answer. It discards the conversational approach in favour of a new plan: capture and incapacitate the youth, in the hopes he may be of use later. The golem is faster and stronger than any citizen, and has comprehensive tactical knowledge.

It is, however, not great at predicting human responses.

Even as the golem initiates its leap across the room to attack the boy, he has made a jump of his own, onto the bed. The golem is momentarily thrown by this unexpected move. By the time it has recalculated its options the boy has completed his move, grabbing the sill of the open window by the bed and vaulting out of it.

The golem lands on the bed anyway, and looks out of the window in time to see the splash as the boy dives into the river two storeys below. It gives the option of following only cursory consideration: there are practical difficulties (though as it does not need to breath drowning is not a concern, neither can it swim) and the value of the boy was unknown. It waits for approximately a minute in case the boy resurfaces within sight.

When he does not, it sets to searching the room.

It has not got very far when it hears a commotion on the stairs.

I resist the temptation to tear the letter open as soon as I take my seat in the rickshaw. Even if I could read it by the light of the lantern swinging above my head, I am, effectively, still out in the street. This needs privacy.

And I need to think. My father was friends with a Councillor. I cast back for the memory that flashed up while I was talking to Lady Estry. That red-lit room… not just a single room, and my mind recoils from some of my father's memories of the place. A high-class brothel both he and the Councillor frequented. And from their chance meeting there, outside of normal society, an odd friendship grew. Part business: the morally flexible Councillor was happy to take advantage of my father's more dubious contacts, and my father's schemes benefited from having a contact at Council level. But also a meeting of minds. Both of them doubted truths most citizens never question. But they were careful in their heresy. Nothing incriminating written down. So when they die, their little conspiracy dies with them.

Except it hasn't, has it?

It was no administrative error that put me at my father's deathbed. Nor was the Empress testing my faith by allowing such an unthinkable thing to happen. A canny Councillor has contacts everywhere – even in the sin-eaters guild. My father wanted me to have his memories and he used his Councillor friend to ensure I got them.

It would be a comfort to think he did this out of love, that having abandoned me in life, he was giving me part of himself in death. Of course not. But whatever else he was or wasn't, my father was clever. He wanted his little conspiracy to live on. And who better to pass it on to than someone who knew him – albeit briefly – and who is already excluded from their eternal reward at the Empress's side by what the Strictures call 'the sin-eater's blessed taint'.

But whilst my father's death was natural, a slow decline with an inevitable end – and plenty of time to plan – Councillor Estry's was not. He had feared death was coming for him, and it did.

I remember another, pithier, verse from the Strictures: 'Curiosity is a trap.'

I should step away from this: burn the letter unopened and apply a combination of meditative techniques and extreme intoxication to purge my father's memories from my head. I should forget this ever happened.

The rickshaw stops. We're at my boarding house already.

Inside, I hear raised voices. The landlady arguing with her prideful lummox of a son. She's saying he and his dubious friends should stay out of this; he says he's dealing with it, no need to call the constables. I open the door on the two of them standing in the hall; they shut up the instant they see me. I give them my most enigmatic sin-eater's smile.

She says, 'You've had visitors.' The boy is already slinking off.

223

I raise an eyebrow.

'Your man friend, first of all. I let him into your room – I hope that was all right.'

'Of course. You said visitors, more than one.'

She clears her throat. 'Someone else must have got in. I'm not sure how. Pedren heard noises: he knew you were out, and didn't realise I'd let your friend in. When he went up he found a stranger in your room! Pedren says he was turning over your things, looking for valuables. When Pedren challenged him he attacked my poor boy. The rascal knocked him over, then ran off!'

'Where's Yavi?'

'Yavi? Oh, your friend. I... don't know. Sorry.'

'When was this?'

'Oh, no more than a quarter hour ago, I was about to call the constables when –'

'Don't call them yet!' I push past her and take the stairs two at a time.

My room looks like a whirlwind has passed through it. But there on the bed: my mask. Yes, Yavi was here. But where is he now? Is he all right? If someone hurt him because of me... but who was the other man? And what was he looking for?

So many questions. And I don't have answers. Or perhaps I do.

I sit down heavily on the bed, not looking at the chaos of my rifled possessions, and tear open the letter.

It is typeset, not handwritten, which throws me for a moment; but of course a Councillor would have legal access to printing technology. It starts 'My dear Mora, if you are reading this, you will have some knowledge of what myself and the Councillor have discovered...'

I look up, as stupid tears blur my vision. Could you not, Father, in your final message to me, your first attempt at communication in nearly two decades, show *some* sign of affection beyond the word 'dear'; maybe even, I don't know, apologise for the damage you did to our family?

Apparently not. *Fuck's sakes, just deal with it, Mora.*

I read on.

The letter is long, and detailed, and it puts my personal issues into perspective.

Once I know what the letter says, I'm tempted to burn it after all. Not because I'm going to ignore it: this is too big to ignore and – yes, those personal issues again – I have to know Yavi isn't involved in any way, that he's safe. But possession of this letter is enough to damn me.

Except of course, I'm already damned.

Making me the perfect person to pass this on to.

I stash the letter in the inner pocket of my robes, then put them on, along with my mask.

I'm going to need all the protection I can get.

The golem computes a high likelihood of having reached a dead end: whilst it did not have time to complete its search, all indications are that the sin-eater, like the Councillor, did not commit anything incriminating to paper. And it is no closer to finding the true object of its search. However, it is programmed not to give up until it has definitively exhausted all avenues of investigation.

Keeping watch over the boarding house is more of a holding pattern than a plan, but then it sees the sin-eater emerge. It steps forward, preparing to emerge from the shadows of the alleyway.

'Oi! You!'

The golem turns to see a heavy-set young man standing behind it; the same one it briefly incapacitated earlier. There is no reason to believe it cannot do the same again, although perhaps this time a more permanent solution may be called for, despite its directive to minimise the unnecessary loss of life.

The golem steps forward. The youth stands his ground and grins.

This unexpected response momentarily confuses the golem. Thus distracted, it fails to sense the youth's equally burly friend stepping up behind it, until a large lump of wood connects with the back of its neck.

Below the various shocking revelations and accusations in my father's letter, there are some mundane instructions:

Go to the place I used to take you for a sweet treat. Choose a quiet time and make sure you are not seen.

The directions would, of course, mean nothing to anyone else, but I know exactly where he means: a small square with a few benches and trees in the centre, and off at one side, the 'jelly-toe shop' as I apparently called it once, when I was too young to pronounce 'gelato' properly. It was two streets from the apartment where I grew up, and where my mother lived out the rest of her life, until bitterness and booze did for her.

As for timing, we're pretty much in 'middle of the night' territory. And whilst wearing my robes would make me stand out in a crowd, it also confers the anonymity of my calling and, more importantly, at a time of night when decent folk are meant to be asleep, a sin-eater apparently out on formal business won't be bothered by the constables. Now is the perfect time. The only time, before I lose my nerve.

I consider going via Yavi's to check he's all right then refer myself back to the 'before I lose my nerve' thought, adding a garnish of guilt that I'm not doing anything about my lover possibly being in trouble.

The square is five streets from my current lodgings, on the far side compared to my childhood home. I've crossed it a few times in my adult life – there's a tram line along one side – but never on foot. Walking into it now in the dark, at the opposite corner to the one father and I used to enter from, is momentarily disorienting. I realise I'm braced for another flash of father-memory and hear my own relieved sigh when there isn't one: none of my father's transgressions involve this place. It was simply somewhere nice he took his daughter on those rare moments when he had the time and inclination to show he cared for her. Turns out I don't need his memories to disconcert and rile me. Just my own.

I walk across the square without looking to either side, following the next part of the instructions: *stand outside the shop.*

It's closed, of course, and equally predictably looks smaller and scruffier than in my childhood memories.

Look left: you'll see a narrow alleyway.

I do, and I do. The sign at its mouth says it's a dead end and I've never had cause to enter it.

Go down the alleyway.

Well, I'm here now. The alley is short and ends in a blank wall. There are three doors along its walls: the two on the left are back entrances to apartment blocks, with a row of colour-coded boxes between them containing the inhabitants' assorted waste for reprocessing. The door on the right-hand side is larger, set into the wall and has no obvious lock of handle, just an inset panel beside it. The kind of door every citizen ignores, because they will never go through it.

Slide aside the cover on the door panel.

Of course he means the forbidden door. I reach out, then pause to clench and unclench my fingers. There, hardly shaking at all now.

The cover slides open to reveal a keypad, numbers one to nine arranged three by three. I find this oddly reassuring: keypads are rare but not actually blasphemous. And I'm pretty sure there's no verse in the Strictures that explicitly states Thou Shalt Not Slide the Cover off a Maintenance Keypad.

The next line of the letter is a string of six numbers. Now we are moving beyond the permitted. Good job I'm already damned.

I stab the code in with my index finger, half hoping it's wrong. It isn't. The door slides open as smoothly and noiselessly as the panel did. Beyond it, darkness.

I hesitate. If I go inside I'm pretty sure the door will shut automatically. Will I be able to open it again? Is this some sort of elaborate trap or test?

Of course it isn't. I shake my head at myself. But then I check out the bins, specifically the dark green one, and – perfect – find a broken table leg, pleasingly chunky. I place it lengthways in the corner of the open doorway, and step into the darkness.

Lights come on to reveal a large open space of incomprehensible function. Directly in front of me is a heavy fence of metal links, its top higher than I can reach. Beyond it the room is crammed with skeletal metallic trees arranged in clumps, and between them chest-high boxes studded with fins and wire coils. The air hums with power. And that's not just my overactive imagination reacting to being in a forbidden place: I mean actual power, stirring the hairs on my scalp. The closest I've felt to it was when, as a girl, I attended an open-air performance by a speed-rhythm band in Reunion Square and, in an attempt to impress the boy I'd gone with, pushed to the front and stuck my head in a bass speaker. That headache lasted the rest of the evening.

Another chance to turn back. Which I don't take. I step into the room. The door does indeed slide shut behind me, until it catches on the table leg.

Take the stairs up to the gantry.

The gantry? Oh yes, on the right-hand side. The stairs and railing look like metal but have a slight give to them, more like hard rubber, with a walkway of the same material running along the wall, a waist-high railing on the open side. There's a gate near the far end, with a ladder down into the enclosure of humming metallic structures. The wall up here is covered in... stuff. Levers, buttons, sliders, dials and panels of dark glass. Those panels... a suspicion is forming.

The Strictures give us three allowable media for remote communication: the spoken word (recorded, broadcast, transmitted on permitted devices); the written word (by hand, printed on permitted devices, transmitted by telegram) and visual – this passage in the Strictures goes into a lot of detail, covering, amongst other things, 'purely physical dials or readouts, as required for commerce or comfort', but that's not what those currently-dark panes of glass look like.

I get out the letter again, this time scanning back to the relevant section, so shocking the first time I read it.

A technomancer came a cropper: they are not demi-gods, just fallible humans.

My initial thought in reading the phrase – so typical of my father – 'came a cropper' was to brace for the memory of how he might have been involved in the downfall of one of the Empress's most blessed. But there was nothing. Whatever happened to the 'mancer, it wasn't his doing.

That individual is lost. But one of their devices was found.

My attitude to technomancers is probably no different to any other citizen's. Being a sin-eater doesn't give me any special insight into the rarely-seen servants of the Empress who live beyond the walls of the world. I live in the world, and will die in the world, and never leave it. They enter it only to do the Empress's will, to touch the untouchable, find the unfindable, fix the unfixable. On the handful of occasions I've seen a technomancer in their odd dark blue one-piece with all those pouches and pockets I've looked away, just as any other citizen would.

I scan down the letter, looking for the last part of the directions. *The device is on top of the tool cabinet at the far end.*

At the far end of the walkway a large metal cupboard is attached to the wall. I lift the catch and yes, it is full of what I would describe as 'tools' though I have no idea what any them are for. I close it again. Then I stand on tip-toe and run my hand along the top. Just cold metal, with a light covering of dust.

Then, at the far end, my fingers brush something. I stop, step back. It isn't visible from the front. Well hidden.

I reach up again, flailing a bit to bring whatever-it-is to the front, then hooking a finger under it. It slides free and I grab for it and there it is, in my hands.

The *device* is rectangular, about eight by six inches, but slender, no thicker than my finger. The back and sides are made of something not unlike the stairs here: tough but with some give in it. The front is black glass. I turn it over in my hands: the back isn't flat like the glass front (like the *screen:* call it what it is). There are indentations and something not unlike the clip on a clipboard. When I am not instantly burned to a crisp by the remote wrath of the Empress, I refer back to the letter.

It may need power: use the cradle here.

Here being... oh yes, on the far wall, a power-cradle, the first familiar object in this place of uneasy wonders. Something tells me this cradle is used to juice up more than just pocket flashlights or walkabout wirelesses. I place the technomancer's device in it.

Nothing happens, but father expected this.

Press the button below the clip to wake it up.

I do. Still nothing. No wait: the screen is facing downwards. With one finger, I flip the thing over.

The following words are displayed, in a commonly-used font, black on white: 'Take this item to the nearest temple at once! Do this, and no sin will have been committed.'

Seeing those words, my heart thuds and I take a quick breath. I get control again, and consider doing what they say. But only briefly. Apparently some servants of the Empress use forbidden technology. This should probably shock and surprise me more than it does.

And now the final instructions: *To access its functions draw two fingers down the front slowly, from top to bottom. To activate a function, touch the words displayed.*

I place two fingers as instructed. Still no thunderbolt. I drag my fingers down, and the message dissolves away, like ink in water. Four new phrases appear on the, the *screen: Message centre; Schedule; Technical Manuals; System Access.*

Whoever knew heresy could be so mundane?

Another unfortunate casualty: whilst one of the thug-like youths escaped their foolish encounter with a broken arm and the return of his earlier concussion, the one with the plank was the unlucky recipient of the golem's pre-programmed fight response, much faster and stronger than any human. He ended up with a broken neck.

However, the first blow in that brief but brutal fight did something unexpected: it caused damage. Not enough to incapacitate but enough that, after the golem dealt with the two youths and moved away from the site of the conflict, it was forced to run a diagnostic. This determines a level of impairment that requires immediate action; self-repair routines are initiated.

They are partially complete when new input is received. Somewhere not far from here, someone has broken into a forbidden building.

Where to start?

Not the 'message centre'. Any messages here are not intended for me: similarly I'm hardly going to try sending any messages.

Let's try the 'schedule' function.

Numbers and letters, initially incomprehensible, but wait, there's a reference to Lantern Row; and another two street names. If I read this right, this is a list of places where maintenance is required, the exact nature of which is beyond me but basically it's all stuff to be fixed, as though technomancers are just plumbers or engineers... which they are, of course. That's exactly what they are. They fix the stuff we mere citizens are not allowed to touch.

Which means the manuals probably just tell them *how* to fix the stuff. Mundane indeed. But still forbidden. I open a random one and catch my breath to see images, diagrams and photographs, displayed *on screen*. When I come across a picture that *moves* I slide my finger up to remove the blasphemous vision. Too much, even for me; maybe I'll come back to this unholy sight later. But what about 'system access'? That sounds like it might be interesting –

What's that noise?

The golem pauses outside the door. It has picked up a faint signal from within. There are no technomancers active in the locale which, combined with the fact that this door has been jammed open with some broken furniture, implies its mission may be reaching a conclusion.

The mechanism has glitched, so it needs to heave the door open, which it does with a unique combination of stealth and strength. Inside, the signal is stronger, coming from above – from the access catwalk. It races up the stairs in silent, speedy steps.

At the far end of the catwalk, the sin-eater looks up from the screen.

What the fuck?

Well, I left the door open; I guess someone might have wandered in...?

No, that's not it. The big man takes two purposeful steps towards me and says, in an oddly flat voice, 'Give me the device.'

My first instinct is to say 'what device?' and hide the screen behind my back. Must still be channelling my father. While I search for a more useful response the stranger takes another step towards me. As if words will stop his progress I blurt, 'That would be heresy.

For you to handle it, I mean.' Apparently the effort of not panicking has stolen my ability to apply logic.

He says again, 'Give me the device.'

There must be some way out of this. I just need to think. A quick glance around reveals that I still have walls behind and to my left, and a nasty drop to the dangerous-looking metal forest beyond the fence to my right, and straight ahead... No, there isn't any way out of this. And he's taking another step.

I hold out my empty hand, 'I'm already damned!'

Somewhat surprisingly, this gives him pause. Only for a moment, but enough for suspicion to stir. This is no ordinary citizen. He advances and says, yet again, 'Give me the device.'

He's going to take it whatever happens. And it's not my immortal soul that's at stake here, it's my actual life, in the world, right now. Sin-eater or not, I've broken too many Strictures tonight to see the next dawn.

Even so I half hold the device out, as though giving it willingly will make some difference to my survive chances.

He steps forward –

Then pauses.

Movement beyond him.

He turns, fast but oddly clumsy.

A piece of wood appears, sweeps round, and connects with his neck. He reels.

Suddenly there are two figures there, grappling each other, the big man and a smaller one... Yavi!

They turn on an invisible axis, Yavi raising his impromptu weapon again – that's the table leg I used on the door – his opponent drawing his own arm back then stabbing forward. They whirl slow, then fast, and Yavi pushes back to ease free, then kicks out, high and hard. It's a streetfighter's move, and it surprises me, but not as much as it surprises his opponent, who stumbles back against the railing – except it's not the railing, it's the gate, which pops open under his weight. He topples backwards off the gantry. He doesn't scream so I clearly hear the sound of his landing: a meaty thud then a weird sizzle-snap. The lights dim, then come back up.

Yavi is sliding down the cabinet, leaving a red smear on the metal. I rush over as he lands in a heap, confirming with a passing glance that his opponent is out of the fight.

Yavi's gaze focuses on me, at once intense and distant. His hand is pressed to his side, but does little to stop the blood soaking through his shirt, which is already damp, for some reason.

'I had to follow you...' his voice is hoarse and low, '...I thought you were in trouble.' Oh that smile, that lovely smile. 'But I'm the one in trouble, aren't I?' He looks down. His shirt is sopping red now, blood pooling under him.

'Yavi...' I breathe. I can't save him, but I have to shrive him. I pat the pocket which would have a corpse-cake in, if only I'd remembered to bring one. No! I can't just let him die like this!

'Silly me...' his whisper fades and then he's gone, just like that.

An unexpected wave of grief rushes in, and I stand abruptly before it drowns me.

I steady myself on the rail next to the broken gate, and look down. Yavi's killer is impaled on one of the metal trees. There is no blood, just a whitish fluid; where one of the bits of metal has ripped into his side the innards look wrong, pale and lumpy. The smell is a memorable mixture of fried flesh and burnt plastic. Oh yes, that was a golem.

I stride back up the catwalk and scoop up the screen, which I dropped when I ran to Yavi. I half raise my hand to hurl it across the room.

Which would what achieve exactly? I lower my arm.

I need to be smart. My father and his co-conspirator knew they were in danger, and now they're dead. But not before putting me in danger.

Am I, though? No one knows what happened here tonight, no one knows the fate of the forbidden device. Not even the Empress herself.

If I leave the screen here then when the technomancers come to fix the damage they'll find it, and find poor, dead Yavi and conclude he was the one who... No. No way. Yavi died trying to save me. And he died unshriven, outside the Empress's grace.

The Empress, who sent that *thing* down there to fetch her property, lost foolishly by another not-so-divine servant of hers. This holy instrument of Her will led to at least two unnecessary deaths, all for a lump of glass and whatever-else-it's-made-from.

The Empress, whose grace I'm already excluded from by my calling. The Empress, who we all worship as a god. Though my father suspected otherwise.

I pause at that thought *just in case*, even now, at the last, this is all some test, and she can somehow hear me and will strike me down. Nothing happens, other than my pounding heart slowing just a little.

I have, objectively speaking, come out of this pretty well. And I can come out of it even better if I lose the screen. Discard this proof of the Empress's fallibility, this key to her hidden world. Maybe I can even forget the knowledge foisted on me, in time.

Last chance. Leave the damn thing behind, pretend none of this ever happened. Walk away and get on with my life.

As I pass Yavi's body I slip the screen into my robes.

I don't fucking think so.

Some writers found the pandemic productive. Not me. I turned in a contracted novel in May 2020 (although, for reasons beyond my control, it will never appear) then stopped writing fiction. I had the time, I knew I needed to write but I just couldn't. The block (and I didn't believe writers' block was a thing before this) lasted nearly 18 months, although I was still writing video-games (that being my day job), plus a journal which helped keep my head straight – just not my own stories. Then an odd phrase turned up in my head while I was out walking, and I realised I had a new story to tell. I'm not going to tell you the phrase (sorry) because that story is actually a novel, and I'm still writing it (recovery is slow). But this is a short story set in that world, to be going on with.

Acknowledgements

My thanks to Ian Whates for giving me the chance to collect two decades of stories in one volume (even if he wouldn't let me call it *Quantum Toast*), and for the various stories of mine he's published in various places. Thanks also – though they'll probably never read this – to the magazine and anthology editors who originally accepted, and in some cases commissioned, the reprinted stories here for their publications. Last but not least, thanks to my lovely patrons for their continued support, especially: Pete Randall, Cathy Holroyd, Jim Anderson, Nina Merewood, Razvan-Gabriel Popa, Liz Burak and Chris Banks.

About the Author

At the age of 12 it became apparent she wasn't going to be a ballerina after all, so Jaine Fenn decided she would be a writer. She decided to focus on short stories as much as novels, because a lot of ideas work best as short tales and because it takes a lot less time to write a short story than a novel.

She made her first professional short story sale in 2001. After impressing her future editor with her hangover at the 2007 Eastercon, she secured a three-book deal from Gollancz. Further novels followed, but she never lost her love of the short form, a love that was rewarded in 2016 with a BSFA award.

Also in 2016 she finally achieved the dream of becoming a full-time writer, although she has to use her video-games writing day-job to fund her fiction-writing habit.

ALSO FROM NEWCON PRESS

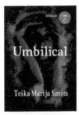

Polestars 2: Umbilical – Teika Marija Smits
Debut collection from one of the finest short story writers to emerge on the genre scene in recent years. Her storytelling relies on keen observation of the world and people around her interpreted through the lens of her imagination, dancing between science fiction, realism, and horror.

Polestars 3: The Glasshouse – Emma Coleman
Contemporary tales of rural horror from one of genre fiction's best kept secrets. An avid haunter of libraries, Emma's fiction is steeped in local colour and rooted deep in her native Northamptonshire, drawing on her love of nature, her passion for literature, and her keen eye for detail. Her fiction is atmospheric, mesmeric, and frequently disturbing.

The She – Terry Grimwood
A devil's dozen of outstanding stories from one of the UK's most consistent writers of short fiction. Witness the fall of Adam and the rise of Lillith; discover what really happened to band leader Glen Miller's plane; meet the third man on the moon, whose name will never be remembered; and see who the true survivors are in a post-apocalyptic world…

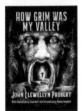

How Grim Was My Valley – John Llewellyn Probert
After waking up on the Welsh side of the Severn Bridge with no memory of who he is, a man embarks on an odyssey through Wales, bearing witness to the stories both the people and the land itself feel moved to tell him, all the while getting closer to the truth about himself.

Best of British Science Fiction 2022 – Donna Scott
Editor Donna Scott has scoured magazines, anthologies, webzines and obscure genre corners to discover the very best science fiction stories by British and British-based authors published during 2022. A thrilling blend of cutting-edge and traditional, showcasing all that makes science fiction the most entertaining genre around